TIME'S TIDE

TARINA ANTHOLOGIES

© 2022 Tarina Anthologies

ISBN 978-64923-068-3

CONTENTS

DREAM ABOUT DAYS LONG AGO
BY REBECCA HENELY-WEISS

A DEMON'S SCORN
KATE SEGER

THE SOLSTICE LEGACY
LORE NICOLE

AS MANY TIMES AS YOU WISH
THOMAS VAN BOENING

ON A DISTANT BATTLEFIELD
C.J. FERRELL

NEVER A NO
LINDA MARIE PANKOW

LET ME GROW YOU A GARDEN
AMANDA FAYE

DREAM ABOUT DAYS LONG AGO

BY REBECCA HENELY-WEISS

It's December 18, 2022 and Naomi Tabor is looking forward to an un-Happy Hanukkah. Her marriage to her husband of six years is fraying, and while he'll be taking their 4-year-old twins to celebrate Christmas with his family, Naomi will be spending the holiday week alone in a near-empty Jersey Shore apartment, finishing up a job that's set to end after the new year. When she realizes on the first night of Hanukkah she doesn't even have a menorah, she rushes out to a small Orthodox shop and buys the first menorah she can find ... one that sends her back to December 22, 1989.

Is it a miracle, magic or madness? Naomi can't be sure, but every time she lights a new candle, she re-lives a previous night of Hanukkah. What's the purpose of these mysterious trips to the past, and can they lead her to a happier future?

CHAPTER
ONE

SUNDAY, DECEMBER 18, 2022 — BEFORE THE
FIRST NIGHT OF HANUKKAH

G o fast but don't fall ... Go fast but don't fall ...
Naomi Tabor chanted those words to herself as she ran down the slick streets of the unfamiliar New Jersey town. Her eyes darted quickly between the names of the stores, the map on her phone, and her short, black boots with the belt across the ankles that she'd loved when she'd bought them at Kohl's back in November but hated more and more with every passing day. They'd seemed so cute and stylish while also being flat and sensible, very suitable for her job hauling boxes at a mid-sized law firm. But on a December day like this — cold but nowhere near cold enough for the wished-for holiday snow — the damp air cut through the thin pleather to chill her ankles, and the tread-less soles seemed a millimeter from slipping on the pavement and knocking her flat on her back.

Go fast but don't fall ... Go fast but don't fall ...

The listing on Google Maps said she only had 20 minutes until this store that she'd never heard of before would close. In this particular moment, in this particular week, in this particular year, that prospect seemed unimaginably devastating. Naomi's blue dot nearly approached the red location marker on the app, but she still couldn't see any sign reading the correct name. She could feel the panic she'd been trying to keep down suddenly spike in her chest. Did she have the correct address? Did the store even exist anymore? Honestly, maybe she was foolish to expect a store like this would exist after the pandemic but —

Naomi's eyes caught the letter "D" on the half-glass paned door a few feet ahead and she skidded as she tried to stop, her arms flailing in circles so she wouldn't lose her balance. Behind the window and the words "Dreyfus's Judaica Antiques" written in gold on it in both English and Hebrew — well, it could have been Yiddish, she supposed, but Naomi wasn't good at reading either language — a man with a long white beard and visible *payot* curling on either side of his head stared back at her, a ring of keys in his hand and a shocked expression on his face.

Shit, Naomi thought as she forced her mouth into the most painfully cheerful smile she could muster. "Hey! Wet day, huh? Do you work here?"

The man shook his head and opened the door. As he closed it, he found a particular key and put it in the knob.

"Wait! I thought the store doesn't close for at least 18 minutes!" Naomi protested.

The man looked back at her with a raised eyebrow. "You know what day it is, *nu*?"

"Well, of course," Naomi clasped her hands together. "I actually really want a menorah. Do you have one?"

The way the man looked back at her after that question — bugged-out eyes, mouth curled down, both eyebrows now raised — made her feel like the world's biggest idiot. And she probably was, deciding to come here on the first night of Hanukkah, so close to when the store closed, to a community largely made up of people who wouldn't consider her really Jewish ...

"We have a few ..." the man said slowly.

"Please," Naomi shook her clasped hands, which made her feel like some sort of 15th-century peasant beggar. "I'll choose quickly and can pay cash if that's easier. I'll even give exact change."

The man sighed and opened the door. "Please be quick," he said as he entered the store and gestured for her to follow. "We have over an hour before sunset, but I do have to drive home."

"I understand. Thank you."

As the man led Naomi inside, she tried, even through her single-minded drive, to take in the store. It was dimly lit and small — just four aisles that ran out from the width of the cashier booth and couldn't have been longer than five feet each. Yet each aisle was crammed with religious objects and other keepsakes of varying ages and quality. Shiny new *shabbat* candlesticks overlapped with sets coated in a thick film of dust. *Shofars* of varying sizes — small enough to hold in one's hand or large enough to span the length of Naomi's outstretched arms — lay in a heap on a bottom shelf. Seder plates were propped up on a diagonal so more could fit on a top shelf. There were piles of tangled *tefillin* and intricate *havdalah* sets and some silver containers that Naomi didn't recognize, but they were shaped like apples and pomegranates, so she assumed they had something to do with Rosh Hashanah.

I should come back here one day, she thought to herself. *I could buy so much nice stuff.*

But then the next thought came and knocked all of the awe out of her. *For whom?*

The menorahs were displayed on one shelf out of four mounted on a wall in the back of the store. When Naomi first saw them, her heart sank. Technically, what most people thought of as a menorah — and what Naomi would probably continue to think of as a menorah — was actually a "hanukkiah." A regular menorah was only seven branches, three on each side with one in the center, and while Naomi had never seen them used in a religious service — only displayed on the logos of Jewish or Israel-affiliated organizations — it seemed at first that this was all the store had.

When she looked a little closer, though, there were three 9-branch menorahs left. She stepped forward and crouched down slightly to assess them.

"These three all use candles, right?" Naomi asked. "Nothing that uses actual oil?"

The man laughed. "Yes, all candles, and we sell those if you need them. We do have one that uses oil but it's displayed behind the counter. Dates from the 19th century. Goes for about $3,000.00. I don't expect you to pay cash for that."

Naomi winced. "No, thank you."

The first 9-branch menorah was probably Naomi's platonic ideal of one. It was a slightly varnished brass, with the elevated *shamash* — the center candle that would be used to light the others. The menorah didn't have much decoration beyond the little circular bulbs running from the sconces down to where the branches started to bend toward the center.

A little simple, Naomi thought, *But it's better than something I'd pick up at CVS and that's why I'm here.*

The second was arrestingly beautiful at first glance. It was made of crystal, white with blue accents. On each side, the eight branches of the menorah melded together into two lions whose paws held up an emblem on the *shamash* with the Star of David.

It's kind of gaudy, though, isn't it?

The third was gold and had seen better days. If the brass menorah had a small bit of varnish near the bulbs, this one needed a shine all over. The branches were thick and flat, and on each branch, a Hebrew letter was carved out and inlaid with silver. At first, Naomi wondered if it was spelling something, but she quickly realized that if read right to left, the letters just ran from *alef* to *chet* in the Hebrew alphabet.

One through eight? Naomi wondered.

She'd never seen a design like that before. But what really surprised her was the center decoration on the *shamash*. It was a silver *hamsa* — a traditional symbol of a hand with the pinky and thumb fanning out at equal lengths that was meant to protect against the evil eye. Like many of these designs, there was an eye in the palm of the hand, but along the blue iris, a Hebrew word was written there. Naomi crouched closer to the menorah and tried to read the word. It looked so familiar — maybe she'd seen it during her *bat mitzvah* classes — but she couldn't quite place it.

"*Zachor.*"

The man's voice was quiet, but Naomi still jumped. When she turned to look at him, his arms were crossed and he had a frown on his face.

"The word in the center is '*zachor*.' It means 'remember,'" the man said. "Common instruction in the Torah."

Naomi took a deep breath. It was hard not to feel like she was being condescended to, hard not to launch into the indignant — *I don't care if I'm not wearing a wig and ate a cheeseburger for lunch. I am just as Jewish as you and if you think otherwise, you can take it up with my ancestors, you son of a bitch* — rant that on some level she always felt on the tip of her tongue in an Orthodox community.

And yet, that wasn't the vibe that she was getting from this guy. There was frustration in his manner but something else, too. Awe? Disbelief?

Naomi grasped the menorah around its stem, her thumb moving to rub the eye in the center as she did so. "I'll take this one. Will $200 cover it?"

The man shrugged. "If that's what you're willing to pay, sure."

Naomi sighed with relief as she followed him to the register. Honestly, she had the money to go up to $300, but hoped to pay $200 or less. She handed him the money in a stack of $20s fresh from a local ATM that would be charging a fee that she hoped her bank would still refund, making sure she held it out to him so he wouldn't have to touch her hand.

"You're married," the man said as he took the money.

It wasn't a question but an observation. Naomi realized he said it because he'd noticed the rings on her left hand. Naomi bit her lip. Had it really been seven years since Anthony put that engagement ring on her finger? She still thought it was a beautiful ring — a large princess cut in the center, circled by smaller diamonds that looked white at first glance but had visible blue and pink tints if you looked at them more closely. Back in ... she supposed it was 2015 now, the year of their engagement ... she would be flush with joy whenever someone noticed it. Now it was like an ice pick through her heart.

"Yes, I'm married," Naomi said because, at the moment, that was the easiest explanation.

"Do you have any children?" The man asked.

She wondered if this question would be opening her up to some sort of specifically Orthodox judgment, but she decided to answer it truthfully. "Just two. A set of twins — boy and girl. They're four now."

The man nodded, and Naomi could see the standoffishness in his manner melt away. "Ah, good. Good. Are you planning any more?"

Naomi was still unsure if he was judging her worth as a good Jewish woman ready to birth more children into the tribe or if he was just trying to relate to her as a parent, but she decided to answer this question truthfully as well.

"No," she said. "I have my boy and my girl. No reason to try for a third." In more secular company she would have added something along the lines of *unless I wanted to go for the nonbinary lottery,* but she suspected the concept might go over his head.

"Well, I understand," the man said. "My Esther and I had six blessings, but fewer can be good. I love them, but after the third child, they start to feel like a horde."

Naomi laughed. "Well, since I have twins, I already feel like I have a tiny horde."

"I suppose," the man said. He finally picked up the box from beneath the counter, wrapped the menorah in white tissue paper to keep it safely packed. "I think I would have missed something, though. A baby becomes a toddler and then a child. It's such a relief when they grow. They do more for themselves, become their own person. And yet, you miss the baby they leave behind. Another new sibling gives you the chance to go back to that time. I think it would be hard, never re-living those times again, knowing when your babies grow up that you'll never have babies again."

Naomi took a deep breath. She couldn't really say anything at times like these — it usually ended in screaming or crying — so she just watched the man tape up the box.

"But," the man continued. "My youngest is seven at this point, so that time is over for me, too. And I am glad, but sometimes I miss it."

Naomi took the box. "Thank you so much for keeping your store open."

The man let out a loud breath. "Of course. I ... I don't know if I should tell you this. But you just lost me $50."

Naomi's eyes opened wide. "Excuse me?"

"This is my brother's shop. I help him every couple of weekends," the man said. "We first gained possession of that menorah five years ago.

One of a few nice things we found at an estate sale in July. That November, a man who was ... well, let's say he was not from the community."

Naomi wondered if the man had a ruder word for his former customer, maybe *apikoros* or some other Yiddish insult for a heretic that she'd never heard of, but she didn't say anything.

"This man comes into the store. My brother was the one who saw him, but he said he was a good-looking man. Dressed in a suit. No beard but wore a *kippot*. He buys the menorah, says his father just died and a sister he didn't particularly like very much got to keep the family menorah even though he was the one taking care of their father ... but anyway, he needs a new one. Despite that, he brings it back right at the end of Hanukkah. Says he doesn't need it anymore. We tell him that we can't give him any money so soon after the holiday, but he says he doesn't care. Just that it needs to go somewhere else.

"Well, we put it back on the shelves — who knows, sometimes gentiles buy them as Christmas gifts for their Jewish friends — they don't care if Hanukkah has already happened. But Christmas comes and goes, and nobody buys it until December of the next year. Another man comes into our store. He is not so good-looking. He's wearing a stained coat and jeans, hasn't shaved, smells a bit — I smelled him. Definitely not from the community. He asks for the menorah, says his friend is giving him a place to stay and he wants to celebrate the holiday.

"In January, he gives it back, says he doesn't need it anymore. We also tell him that we can't give him any money so soon after the holiday, but he says he doesn't care. Seems strange, he doesn't seem so rich and it's still in good condition. Can't even see any wax on it.

"Next year, a young woman comes into the store in early November and buys the menorah, says it's for her mother in hospice. She got the–," the man sighs. "–the COVID-19 earlier in the year and wasn't doing so well. We don't see the young woman again until May — we actually forgot about the menorah for a bit — but she says her mother is dead, and that before she died, they both agreed the menorah needed to go somewhere else.

"Then last year, also in November — Hanukkah started in November last year, if you remember — a young man comes into the store. He is a very, uh … a very slight, feminine man. Handsome, but … I think he is a homosexual. He doesn't seem very happy."

What the hell have I gotten myself into? Naomi thought.

"He buys the menorah, says he needs it for a new apartment," the man continued. "And then, once again, it's back to us in February of this year. The man didn't even come into the store. He just left it in a box on our stoop the day after Hanukkah with a note, once again, that he didn't need it anymore and it should go to someone else.

"So, December rolls around. My brother says he's sure someone is going to buy the menorah again, but the days go by, we sell a few menorahs here and there but no one comes. I tell him I don't think it's going to happen this year. He bets me $50 it will … and now here you are, 15 minutes before we close the store."

Naomi stared at the man, tried to read his expression behind the thick beard and *payot*. She looked at the box again, and then she laughed.

"I'm sorry are … are you fucking with me or something?"

The man frowned. Naomi wondered if she made a mistake by using foul language in front of him, but he just said in response. "I do not fuck with people."

"So everything you said was true? You sold me a cursed menorah?"

"Cursed?" The man exclaimed. "Why should it be cursed?"

"You said nobody keeps it and one of its owners died. That sounds like a curse to me."

"She was going to hospice, of course she died," the man said with a shrug. "And we buy a lot from estate sales, including this piece originally. By that logic half of our inventory is cursed."

"Did any of them say why they bought it back?" Naomi asked.

Another shrug. "Just that they didn't need it."

"And you weren't curious?"

"Of course I was curious, but none of them wanted to talk. They just said someone else needed to have it."

Naomi groaned. *This sounds like some* Ringu *crap.*

"If it makes you feel better, nobody who brought it back seemed particularly upset or desperate to part with it, even the woman who lost her mother," the man said. "And if you want to exchange for one of the other two Hanukkah menorahs, you can. I mean ... it would save me $50."

Naomi looked down at the box again. She carefully undid the tape, then looked at it again — the Hebrew letters as numbers, the eye that seemed to be looking back at her, that word "*zachor.*"

She liked the menorah. It felt like hers. Maybe it was abandoned by all of its previous owners because it wanted to find her?

What kind of bullshit am I thinking? She asked herself. Was it idolatry to even think of the menorah as having some sort of wants or needs, or was this like that story in Hebrew school they told her about how every blade of grass has an angel above it imploring it to grow?

Naomi closed the box and pressed down on the tape. "I'll take it."

The man nodded. "Use it in good health."

Naomi exited the store, heard the man lock the door behind her as she left. She looked around the street for a moment, looked at all the shops with signs that she couldn't read. It was weird to be in a neighborhood like this. If her ancestors ever lived like this, those days were long gone. Even her grandparents had rejected this life. Where did that leave her in a place like this?

It leaves you the same place you'd be anywhere else, she told herself. *Thirty-seven-years-old and spending the holidays without your family.*

Naomi took a breath so long and loud it came out as a sigh. *Just a few steps,* she thought, *then I can just cry it all out ...*

"Wait!"

Naomi's back stiffened. Well, she couldn't cry now. She turned to see the man running toward her.

"You forgot to buy candles!" The man said as he approached. He placed a smaller box on top of the menorah box. "Here you go. Free of charge."

CHAPTER

TWO

SUNDAY, DECEMBER 18, 2022 — THE FIRST
NIGHT OF HANUKKAH

Well, that was a weird end to the night, Naomi thought as she walked into her new apartment. *Or day. This is the night, I guess.*

Naomi hung her keys up on the coat stand — one of the few things that she'd taken from the house — then hung her actual coat, hat, and purse on it. Anthony had suggested they should always have one place to keep and find everything important before they left the house, and while she'd occasionally left her keys on the coffee table or purse next to her bed, it felt like something she should keep up when she was alone.

For however long that would be.

It was a small place, a one-bedroom apartment above a small house not far from the beach. Since she didn't plan to stay there long enough to hit the more lucrative summer months, the owner of the house agreed to let her live there for less than a thousand dollars a month, which was a rent price she hadn't paid since possibly the second Bush administration. It was furnished, albeit very lightly. The couch and coffee table wasn't hers, and they both pointed toward a TV stand with no TV that also wasn't hers. The kitchen had a small table and two chairs that came with it, same with the fridge, and she'd bought fold-out chairs in case Shane and Sylvie stayed with her for dinner. The bed-frame was already here, but she'd had to buy one of those mattresses advertised on podcasts where the specifications were based on a survey that she never knew if she answered properly. (What type of firmness did she really like? Sure, she slept on her side but was that good for her, given her back problems?) After the mattress arrived at her house and popped out of its box, Naomi dressed it in the sheets that she'd rejected for their marital bed three years ago but had never quite thrown away.

Naomi set the boxes on the small table. She had about 20 minutes before it would make sense to light her Hanukkah candles, so she fired up the old hot water kettle she'd had since college and made herself some pumpkin spice tea that she didn't particularly like but felt compelled to use up since she bought it in October. The tea had reached the point where she was able to take comfortable sips when her phone rang. She picked it up, saw the word "Mom" in bright white letters, and sighed.

It's the holidays, she told herself. *You have to pick up.*

Naomi put down the phone and rubbed her eyes. She took a deep breath, then tried to put on her biggest smile — sure, her mom wouldn't see it, but the idea was to help her mood — before swiping on the phone to answer.

"Hi Mom!" Naomi said, trying to sound cheerful.

It didn't work. Naomi waited through the dead air for a moment — once or twice she'd hung up early, and her mother never let her forget it — then heard the quiet groan on the other end. "Hi, dear. I ... How are you?"

"I'm fine," Naomi lied. She set down her tea on the coffee table and started to walk around the room. "Actually, you're never going to believe this. After I saw the kids and Anthony off, I realized I forgot to bring a menorah to the apartment. So, I ran to this Orthodox neighborhood and I found this —"

"I don't know why you let them go with him," her mother said curtly. "It's your holiday, too."

Naomi rubbed her right temple with her free hand. She knew what she wanted to say next, but she also didn't want to say it, because it wasn't really how she felt but it was the ending of a long, drawn-out fight and a long, drawn out negotiation that she was still trying to settle in her mind.

"I know it's my holiday, but ...," Naomi sighed. She puttered toward the window, and pushed the bland white curtain aside with her free hand so she could see down the darkening streets to the Atlantic Ocean churning in the distance. "Look, Hanukkah just doesn't matter as much as Christmas."

Her mother scoffed. "Oh, bullshit."

"No, no, it's not bullshit," Naomi dropped the curtain and started trudging back toward the kitchen. "Yom Kippur is an important holiday. Rosh Hashanah is an important holiday. Passover is an important holiday. Hanukkah is this minor festival that's not even in the Bible that's been elevated in American culture because it's so close to Christmas."

"Honey, if I told you all that when you were four-years-old, you would have cried your eyes out and asked why we were less important than everyone else."

Naomi took a breath so hard her chest rose. "And that's what you think I'm doing, huh? Look, I don't like not being with the kids for Hanukkah but they haven't seen my in-laws' family for the holiday in two years. You're in Florida. My job is almost ending and if I quit now, I worry I'm not going to get a recommendation at a time when I really, really need it. I just ... I just need to give on this one."

The line went silent. Then her mother sighed in that one particular way, and Naomi remembered that it was the sad version of her mother that originally called. As much as she may have chafed against the nagging version of her mother, Naomi knew that she had to, that she wanted to, respect that sadness.

"I just don't want you to give too much, and I think you have here," her mother said.

"Maybe," Naomi admitted. "But it's just one holiday, isn't it?"

"It's never 'just one' holiday in this day and age," her mother said. "And you never know how many you have left."

Naomi felt a squeeze on her heart. She sat down at the table, reached her hand out to worry at the boxes.

"I miss Jan too, Mom."

"I know you do, dear, but ..."

But I'm never going to miss her the same way, Naomi thought. Not that she should have been expected to, but ...

"Look, I ... I didn't call to berate you," her mother said. "I just wanted to wish you Happy Hanukkah. I wish I could be there. I should have made the effort to be there."

"Times are hard," Naomi said. "And you've been through a lot."

Another sigh echoed from Naomi's cell phone. Naomi waited for her mother to talk for a few seconds, and when her mother didn't say anything more, her eyes darted to the window.

"Hey, Mom. It's getting dark ..."

"Right, right. I still have about a half hour here. Maybe I'll set things out."

"Do, um, do you want to Skype?"

"No, no, no. I'm sick of bothering with that stuff. It's one thing if it's your kids, but ... The virus is almost over. We should be living in the moment."

Naomi didn't think her mother was living in the moment very often these days. Not that Naomi could blame her ...

"I'll call you tomorrow," Naomi said.

Her mother let out one final sigh and they said good night. Maybe they both knew Naomi's promise was tepid at best.

Well, time to start your first holiday as a separated woman, Naomi thought.

She opened the small box of candles first and took a peek inside. In Naomi's experience, there were three types of Hanukkah candles — the short ones that dripped wax everywhere, the long ones that fell out of the sconces, and the long ones that did both. These were long, colored white and varying shades of blue. She picked the darkest blue for the *shamash*, the center candle that would be used to light the others, and a single white candle for the first night of Hanukkah, which she put on the sconce furthest to the right.

She lit the *shamash* and prayed, "*Baruch ata Adonai, Eloheinu melech ha'olam, asher kid'shanu b'mitz'votav, v'tzivanu l'had'lik neir shel Hanukkah.*"

It was an easy prayer to remember, similar to the one that started off the Saturday night services, and it came to her mind quicker than its translation ever would. ("Blessed are you Lord, Our God, Ruler of the Universe, who has sanctified us with your commandments and commanded us to light the lights of Hanukkah.") She lit the first candle. The second prayer came easily as well.

"Baruch ata Adonai, Eloheinu melech ha'olam, she'asah nisim la'avoteinu, bayamim ha'heim baziman hazeh."

She never remembered the translation for this one. (It was "Blessed are you Lord, Our God Ruler of the Universe, who performed miracles for our ancestors in those days at this time.") If this was a night later in the week she would essentially be thinking, "Now is the time when I light the other candles" while saying it.

She was about to sit down, but she remembered there was a third prayer on the first night. She unlocked her phone and quickly found a website that had it written out in Hebrew and phonetic English.

"Baruch ata Adonai, Eloheinu melech ha'olam, shehecheyanu, v'kiyimanu, v'higianu laz'man hazeh."

She read the translation written in English below, "Blessed are you Lord, Our God King of the Universe" — ugh, this site still used exclusively masculine terms for God — "who has kept us alive, sustained us, and enabled us to reach this season."

Well, that's certainly a prayer for these dark times, Naomi thought.

Naomi sat down at the table. The directive now was to enjoy the light of the candles, something that always seemed like a nice idea but hard to maintain. When she was in her 20s, she would sit for a bit, sometimes read a book. But it was hard not to walk away and go watch TV or do some sort of chore. And in the last three years, when every Hanukkah had been a desperate attempt to re-create the ones of her past, most of the time after the lighting had been trying to get the kids to dance, trying to get the kids to open their presents, throwing wrapping paper away.

Naomi opened her phone, tapped her thumb on the photo app.

She looked at the photos of Hanukkah from the previous year. In 2021, every Jewish holiday had come ridiculously early — she couldn't remember another time when Rosh Hashanah matched up with Labor Day — and Hanukkah had been no exception, coming only a few days after Thanksgiving. Naomi would set up her Hanukkah menorah — it was metal, plated in gold and silver, probably sitting forgotten in the china cabinet back at the house — on the stovetop so it would be safe if a candle fell out, and it made Naomi cringe a bit to see the empty cans of cranberry sauce and box stuffing in the background.

She looked at the pictures of Shane and Sylvie first, pictures of them singing in front of the lit menorah, opening the modest presents she had bought them, struggling through a game of dreidel that had been cute until they started yelling at each other that she or he had been the one to really win. It always struck Naomi how adorable they were — black hair that curled at every chance it could, brown eyes with a tint of gold, pale cheeks that turned red whenever either of them smiled. They could be a handful — Naomi was sure any set of twins were — when they weren't jumping on things they shouldn't or answering for each other, they were fighting over which identical toy was "theirs" or demanding that their particular slime video on YouTube be the one they watch on repeat. Still, they were sweet and full of life and whenever she was alone like this ...

Naomi scanned back through her Hanukkah pictures, the candles going from eight down to one, the present pile increasingly getting bigger. She swiped and she swiped ... and then suddenly stopped.

Anthony stared back at her, his arms wrapped around Shane and Sylvie. It always surprised and saddened her how few pictures she took of him these days. He was still as handsome as when they met. His hair was black, although nowhere near as curly as the kids'. Black bristly hairs grew from his toned arms. Usually he kept his face clean-shaven, but the holidays in quick succession had exhausted them both, and so stubble covered his face, moving down his neck to his muscular chest.

He'll find someone new fast, an ugly voice whispered in her head.

Naomi put down the phone. She tried to encourage the sensible voices. *He's still yours for now. This is just a break. Wasn't leaving your decision?* But none of them were strong, were convincing enough. She laid her head down on the table and wailed.

How the hell did I get here? She thought. This wasn't where she thought she'd be five years ago. This wasn't where she thought she'd be last year. How the fuck had her life led her to this point? How could she be going through a holiday like this …?

The cry was long and ugly — tears, snot, gasps from her mouth that she would never have let out if she knew there was anyone to hear her. She cried and cried and just as she was starting to burn out, she felt a chill slowly creep up her spine.

Naomi looked up and the menorah. The two candles had burned down to nothing, leaving only a blue smoke in the air. The room was dim, but the gold menorah nevertheless seemed to glow without the light. Naomi rubbed the tears from her eyes, unsure of what she was seeing, and when she looked again, her eyes zoned in on the word in the center of the menorah.

"*Zachor*," she whispered, not really knowing why. The whisper became a breath, then she slowly closed her eyes.

THREE

FRIDAY, DECEMBER 22, 1989 — BEFORE THE FIRST NIGHT OF HANUKKAH

W hen Naomi opened her eyes, she awoke in her bed.

It was not the bed with the mattress that had popped out of a box in her new apartment. Nor was it the California king bed with the dark cherry wood headboard that she had shared with Anthony. When she opened her eyes, she was looking up at a pink canopy held up on four large white bedposts.

Naomi sat straight up in bed, her mind reeling, her breath coming out in pants. She remembered the canopy, but everything else had been forgotten until this very moment: the pink sheet set with the lace-trimmed comforter, the rainbow throw rug, the duck and frog decals on the walls that had been left over from when this room was a nursery. But it was all coming back: the stickers she had put on her closet, the metal doll's bed. The doll's name was Susie. Oh God, when she looked at that brown toybox she remembered all the names of the toys spilling out of it.

"What's happening?" Naomi said, but her voice didn't sound like hers. It was so high pitched, so ... she looked down at her body, first noticing *The Little Mermaid* nightgown that had eventually turned pilled and itchy but now looked new, and then ...

Naomi screamed, and it was a child's cry that came out.

Her mother ran into the room. "What's wrong, honey? Did you wet the bed?"

Naomi turned her head to look at her. It was bizarre to see her mother this way again. On the one hand, she looked exactly the way she always did when Naomi closed her eyes and thought of her mother: a thin build, a slight smile, huge glasses that covered the top half of her face, and black, curly hair that circled her head like the trim on a hood. In recent years that black hair had deflated and gone gray. The glasses had been replaced by smaller, more stylish ones. The thin build had become bony. Yet seeing her mother like this again, Naomi was struck by how much she felt that this was what her mother was "supposed" to look like, and how much her mother, in many ways, looked like Naomi did now ...

"No, I didn't wet the bed!" Naomi shrieked. She was surprised at how upset she felt by the accusation, how hard it was to think up the right words when she tried to speak. "I'm ... I'm not supposed to be a kid! I'm 37 years old!"

Her mother just looked at her. Naomi recognized the look — the look that Anthony and she had shot to each other multiple times since their kids learned to talk — the "I'm really trying not to burst out into laughter because of the ridiculous shit my kid just said, but they're making it very hard right now" look.

"Oh, you're ... you're 37, are you?" her mom chortled, covered her mouth with her hand and coughed way too loudly into it. "That's ... that's incredible, sweetie."

Naomi frowned. She threw her legs over the side of the bed and tried to slide off, then immediately realized she'd misjudged how short her legs were and fell to the floor. When she hit it, she couldn't stop herself from screaming.

"Naomi!" her mother yelled and ran to her.

"Are you sure you want this?" her mother asked.

Naomi and her mother were sitting at their old breakfast table and her mother had just slid a plate of sunny side eggs and buttered toast in front of her. Naomi had wanted it, but upon seeing the slimy sheen she felt her gorge rise in her throat. She picked up her Winnie the Pooh fork and poked the yolk, watched it wiggle and split and bleed out yellow ...

"Why does it look so yucky?" Naomi asked.

Her mother sighed. "I didn't think you'd like this. Here, I'll switch with you."

She took away Naomi's Winnie the Pooh plate, slid the sunny side eggs onto her own (it was white with a thick, solid trim of loud aquamarine with red and purple splotches — God, they had those plates for years and Naomi had completely forgotten about them until now), and then scooped the scrambled eggs from her plate onto Naomi's.

Naomi tried not to pout as she speared the scrambled eggs with her silly little Winnie the Pooh fork. "You made these for yourself because you knew I'd eat them, right?"

"Ah, you're too smart for me," her mother said as she cut off a slimy slice of egg white. "Maybe you'll have them some day."

Naomi pouted as she chewed the scrambled eggs. They tasted good, like scrambled eggs should. "I ate sunny side up eggs yesterday," she said. "I ate them on toast spread with avocado."

"Avocado!" her mother laughed. "You had Pop-Tarts yesterday. I think I'd remember if you ate a guacamole sandwich."

Naomi wished she was eating Pop-Tarts. They always had strawberry with the icing and sprinkles, but she really wanted chocolate. She didn't know why — she'd had the chocolate before and they weren't very good.

God, was this going to be her reality from now on? Would she really be going through her whole life again with her grown-up — *adult* — memories and likes warring with her child's mind? Would she have to go through school again? Through puberty again? Would she be able to fix everything this time? Or would she still be hindered by her old self, the way she couldn't bring herself to eat those eggs?

"Mommy?" Naomi asked as she struggled to scoop the scrambled eggs up with her fork. (And when was the last time she called her mother "Mommy"? But that was the first word that came to mind.) "What year is it?"

"1989."

Naomi sighed and thought for a bit. "I'm four years old."

"That's right," her mother said with a proud smile. "And you'll be five at the end of February. I'm still so glad we didn't have you during a year when you risked being a leap year baby."

"I was so happy to be five," Naomi whispered to herself. "I remember waking up on my birthday and running around the room and shouting, 'I'm five! I'm five!'"

"You're so funny today," her mother said. She had already finished her breakfast, started collecting her silverware and drinking her last dregs of black coffee. "Anyway, hurry up on those eggs. You have to go to daycare soon."

Naomi's head shot up. "Daycare? I'm going to *daycare* today?"

This fucking sucks.

Her mother nodded. "It'll be fun, though. It's close enough to Christmas that they're going to be having their holiday party today. You'll get an early start on Hanukkah!"

Naomi's heart started beating hard. "Hanukkah? It's Hanukkah today?"

"That's right, the first night of Hanukkah is tonight," her mother put her dishes in their sink. "I need to go to the bathroom. When I get out, I want to see you eating those eggs."

Naomi started shoving the eggs in her mouth as soon as her mother left, her mind racing.

OK, so it was the first night of Hanukkah still. That meant she was probably going to go back at the end of tonight, right? She wouldn't need to re-live her own life all over. Just a day. She could do a day. It would probably even be fun! How many times had she looked at the pictures of her twins at daycare or their arts and crafts projects and tried to remember those days?

When her mother came back from the bathroom, Naomi had finished the eggs and was starting on the toast. "Good job," her mother said. "I'll remember to tell Daddy when he gets back from work tonight."

Naomi felt her heart drop into her stomach. "D-Daddy?" she asked. "Daddy is here?"

Her mother shook her head. "No, Daddy gets up early to go to work."

"R-Right," Naomi said. She put her toast down, said she was full and let her mother lead her back to her room to get dressed, trying her best not to cry or be sick.

Naomi had not seen or heard from her father in 30 years.

CHAPTER

FOUR

I t wasn't easy to be a kid.

Naomi supposed that on some level she had always known that, but the years had smudged the edges off her childhood, leaving a warm, nostalgic haze around her memories.

Now, in the thick of it, she realized how hard it had been. When they left the house to go to daycare, Naomi struggled to zip up her puffy pink coat with the yellow stars, and when they arrived, she found taking off her seatbelt impossible. (And God, she really had just worn a seatbelt in those days. Now she always drove with her twins in their booster seats.) She had to step twice as fast to keep up with her mother's long gait, lift her knees up to her hips to climb stairs. Everything was bigger and heavier and taller.

But there were good parts to being a kid again, too. She couldn't help but smile when her mother led her into her daycare classroom. Parts of it she had still vaguely remembered, like the alphabet banner and laminated cutouts of Mickey and Minnie Mouse on the walls, but the bright blue rug with sunflowers — each with a number from 1 through 20 on the brown seed disk — or the cubbies for her coat and blankets, she had forgotten.

She had forgotten how the room would change every month as well.

It was full on Christmas at this point. Green tinsel outlined the chalk-board and cork bulletin boards, with laminated cutouts of holly taped at every corner. There were pictures of Santa and Mrs. Claus up on the bathroom doors and cutouts of reindeer tacked up on the windows. And of course, there was the plastic Christmas tree. It was decorated simply. The ornaments were merely colored balls and candy canes, and the trim was a long string of popcorn. Still, Naomi couldn't help but be interested in the gift bags beneath the tree.

Naomi walked inside her classroom, and all of the names immediately came back to her again. There was Miss Kim, a young woman who dressed in huge sweaters over blue jeans and kept her dark hair tied up in a pink scrunchie with white polka dots. (Naomi had always liked her — she was sweet and kind and, as someone who had probably just gotten out of college, had plenty of energy to keep up with the kids.) There was Mrs. Anne, a stout older woman with a beaky nose who favored pastel plaid dresses. (Naomi had always liked her, too. But given how stern she was ... she urged the class that it was *time* to stop playing and could they *please* get in a circle, she wondered if the feeling was mutual.) And there was Miss Jenaye, a woman who had to be around Naomi's age, who was known for keeping her dark natural hair in cornrows with bright beads on the end of them. (Naomi hadn't remembered her much, because she was so quiet, preferring to redirect kids with a gentle touch or a whisper in her ear, but now that she was back here, she liked that too.)

Then there were the other kids. Nick and Matty and Joshua. Zachary and Kevin. Danny S. and Danny T. There was Jessica and Heather and Tiffany and also two girls with the same name, although one spelled it Ashley and the other Ashleigh, which sometimes got pronounced by the teachers as "Ash-LEE" and "Ash-LAY," even though in the second case that was wrong.

It was strange to be back among them again, among these kids she had seen every day but in 2022 couldn't remember well enough to even think of looking them up on Facebook. She did enjoy playing with them. They reminded her of the past but also her twins.

Still, it was odd to be here and feel like an imposter. She decided at one point to do a summersault just because she hadn't been able to do one in years, and then was scolded by Mrs. Anne for getting "too rowdy." She started playing with toys, but wondered if the way she stacked blocks looked too precise, if she didn't seem as engrossed with brushing a doll's hair or pretending to make a stuffed polar seal swim through the water as she should.

"Girls aren't allowed to play with trucks," Matty said as Naomi moved the ladder of a red Hess fire truck up and down.

"Girls can play with anything," Naomi said. *Ugh*, she thought, *things sucked in the 1980s.*

"Yeah, well you told me yesterday that I wasn't allowed to play with a Barbie because I was a boy."

Shit, Naomi thought. "OK, then I was wrong yesterday. Anybody can play with anything. The teachers would probably agree with me."

"Well, I wouldn't play with dolls anyway because they're stupid," Matty said and walked away to play with Nick and Joshua.

Naomi sighed and went back to investigating the truck, rolled the wheels, and inserted her finger into a slit in the back, realizing this was a bank as well. *Maybe he learned better too, eventually,* she thought.

Circle time came next, and Naomi began to remember this now. After the hellos and the exercises and the singing, Mrs. Anne would bring out a wooden calendar, one where she could change out the month and days with special tiles. They'd go over what month it was and the days of the week and occasionally even count all the days in the month. And then, of course, they would talk about the holidays.

"We're very fortunate to have two holidays coming up this week-end," said Mrs. Anne. "The first, of course, is Christmas, which will actually come this Monday, but we get to celebrate it with all of you in class today."

Someone — it may have been Heather — responded with a "yay!" which set off a lot of the kids into cheering and clapping. Naomi clapped politely, feeling weirdly drowned out as the kids started talking to each other about what Santa was going to bring them.

Mrs. Anne clapped a few times to bring the kids back to attention. "But we have another holiday that's happening tomorrow, too," Mrs. Anne said. "It's called Hanukkah — can we all say that, class?"

The class repeated "Hanukkah" back to her.

"That's right. And it's the Jewish people's Christmas. It just lasts for eight days and kids get one present per night." Mrs. Anne then looked directly at Naomi and smiled. "Naomi, you're Jewish, right? Are you excited about getting your first present tomorrow?"

"I get it tonight, actually," Naomi said. "Jewish holidays always start the night before the calendar says they do."

Mrs. Anne looked a bit surprised. "I ... I don't know if that's true."

"Sure it is," Naomi said. "Unless the calendar says it starts that night."

"Hmmm," Mrs. Anne said, then she smiled again, a little less pleasantly than the first time. "Well, I'm sure you'll enjoy your first present whenever you get it."

Circle time ended after that, and Naomi had to admit she was still a bit sore as Miss Kim ferried her and a couple of the other girls to a low table. "'The Jewish people's Christmas,'" Naomi said under her breath. "Dumbass."

Miss Kim looked at her funny as she helped push in the chair behind Naomi. Naomi cringed and tried to smile back at the teacher, as if to try to send the message *No, no. I'm still a sweet little kid. Pretend I didn't use a swear word that I shouldn't have known until I was 12.*

To Naomi's relief, Miss Kim walked away. When she and Miss Jenaye came back, they started to hand out green pieces of construction paper. A simple picture of a pine tree was on each of them, the branches coming out as three triangles on each side.

"Excuse me," Naomi said when Miss Jenaye was about to hand her one. "Can I have a blue or gold piece of paper instead? I'd like to make a menorah."

Miss Jenaye bit her lip. "Well, that's not the assignment ..." she looked around a bit. "But this is just about practicing cutting with scissors and gluing, anyway."

Naomi had planned to take care of the whole project, but Miss Jenaye insisted on helping her out, drawing a crude representation of a menorah on a baby blue piece of paper, then drawing little yellow teardrop lights she could place on top of it.

"There's a holiday for people like me this month that uses a candle holder similar to this," Miss Jenaye said. "It's pretty new, though. Maybe when I get older I'll celebrate it."

"I hope you do," Naomi said. "Trying to start new traditions for holidays that your family never celebrated growing up is hard."

Miss Jenaye looked at her with a smile. "How do you know a thing like that?"

Naomi realized what she'd done and inwardly panicked for a moment. Should she lie? Tell Miss Jenaye the truth and then risk her old self not knowing what she told Miss Jenaye the next day? Then Naomi realized how her own twins had gotten out of these uncomfortable conversations.

"Oh, I, uh ... just know things like that because I am a very smart little girl," Naomi said.

Miss Jenaye laughed and left Naomi with her craft.

It turned out Naomi still needed that scissor practice. It was hard for her young hand to hold even the small scissors made for it, and occasionally her hand shook or the scissors fell from her hand as she tried to cut on a curve. And the purple Elmer's glue was as mediocre as she remembered. Occasionally the purple would bleed through the yellow construction paper lights.

"Naomi, that's so beautiful!" Miss Kim said as she came around to collect everyone's projects. "You did a great job!"

It's OK, Naomi thought. *I fucked up on making the lights straight.* But she said thank you for the compliment.

The teachers put up her menorah on the bulletin board with the Christmas trees. Then they had the party with lunch. First there was a special pizza — Naomi didn't remember what the regular pizza was like back in daycare, but she assumed it was something frozen because this pizza was basically a slice of delivery pizza cut in half. (That was about all Naomi could eat right now, anyway.) Then there was the party food and ... well, Naomi had to admit this was probably a good part of being a kid in the 1980s and 1990s. The party had pretzels and popcorn, cupcakes and cookies and an assortment of chocolate candy. When it was Naomi's turn in line, she asked Miss Jenaye to give her one of everything. As she was led back to her chair, she thought of the expensive no-allergen cake balls she had to buy for the twins' class last year and missed this time.

"You have a Snickers?" Tiffany asked when she sat across from

Naomi. "I really like those, too, but when I eat them I feel like a bunch of ants are crawling all over my lips."

Naomi decided she'd eat the Snickers when she got home.

Nap time came afterward, and Naomi was surprised that even after the excess of sugar — and oh, it had been so, so nice to eat all that crap on a digestive system that wasn't prone to heartburn — that she wanted to go to sleep. Then again, she'd heard experts say a sugar rush wasn't real.

"You shouldn't have let Naomi change her assignment," Naomi heard Mrs. Anne whisper from across the room.

"I'm sorry," replied Miss Jenaye. "It's just because of her religion ..."

"If you let one of the children do something different, soon they'll all want to do something different," Mrs. Anne whispered back. "Besides, a Christmas tree is barely about Christmas, anyway. Soon these people won't be satisfied until we can't do anything more festive than a snowman."

Naomi made a big show of waking up after that. When she wouldn't go to sleep, they let her color for a while. ("You've improved so much!" Miss Kim exclaimed.)

By the time the kids got their presents, the day was almost over. It made sense, Naomi figured. It would have been a distraction if they'd had them earlier in the day. Naomi opened her bag, which was red and white and had a drawing of a snowflake on it. Inside she found a candy cane and a small bag of Christmas cookies (she noticed one of them was a peanut butter blossom — she hoped Tiffany didn't get that one), but she was happy to find they'd also included a dreidel and *gelt*. And she also saw that everyone had gotten a potpourri bag, only Naomi's was blue whereas the other kids' were green and red plaid.

"You know, I don't think your bag is as pretty," Jessica said to her.

She and Naomi were the last two kids on their side of the room. Most of the kids had already been picked up by their parents, and the ones that remained had the chance to play.

"Well, I like it," Naomi said with a shrug, although something about this conversation felt familiar. She really hadn't remembered this day too well, and was sure that some things, like asking to make the menorah, had to be new. And she'd known Jessica's name when she saw her, but looking her now — with her pale, flat face and wavy hair tied in pony-tails by thick red and green beads on either side of her head — she wondered if there was a deeper memory involved.

"So, you don't celebrate Christmas?" Jessica asked.

"No," Naomi said, and she instinctively tried to fumble with the dreidel in her bag. "My mommy and daddy are both Jewish."

"Is that because Santa Claus doesn't like you?" Jessica asked.

Oh, Naomi thought. Yes, she remembered this. She remembered the crying and running into the bathroom, the assurances from her mother that Jessica just hadn't known any better, that they would have a wonderful time at home with Daddy and forget all about this by the end of the night.

The child part of her wanted to run into the bathroom and cry, but instead Naomi tried to push that child self down, tried to answer the way she would if someone had said this to one of her kids.

"No, Santa likes everyone. It's just not his job to visit me. It gives him more time to see kids like you."

Jessica crossed her arms. "Well, I think you're on the naughty list."

Well, takes one to know one, you fucking brat, Naomi thought. It would have been tempting to say that, or something about Santa Claus not being real, but it was probably better to tell the truth.

"You know you have no way of knowing that," Naomi said. "And you know that you're just trying to be mean."

"I am not!" Jessica yelled with a stomp of her foot. "You're the one who's not getting any presents!"

Jessica went off to play with something else, and Naomi wondered how it was that kids could be so absurd in their cruelty, how something that would come off as nonsensical to her now could be so devastating in the moment.

But maybe every fight looked that way after a long time had passed.

CHAPTER

FIVE

FRIDAY, DECEMBER 22, 1989 — THE FIRST NIGHT OF HANUKKAH

Naomi's mother was the last parent to arrive at daycare, and as she helped Naomi into the back seat and buckled her in, Naomi tried to think about what she was going to do and found that she couldn't. There were times throughout the day that she felt more like the child she had been, and other times when she felt painfully like the adult she would become. That adult was looking forward to some confrontation, to some sort of reckoning, but that child only wanted to see her father.

But hadn't Naomi — the adult Naomi — wanted to see her father, too? Was that why as soon as her mother opened the door, Naomi ran to him, so happy she had tears in her eyes.

"Hey ... sweetie," her father mumbled in her ear. "How ... How was daycare, honey?"

Naomi was so overcome she couldn't answer. She had barely remembered him. He was still in the suit he wore when he went to the office to do ... Naomi couldn't even remember, something with insurance? But it fit his tall, lanky build very well — she could feel the muscle in his shoulder as she cried into it. He had light hair, the type that looked almost red in the light. When Naomi wiped her eyes and looked up at his face, she saw the hint of freckles on his skin.

He looked ... young. But why wouldn't he? He had been younger then, compared to her age now.

Her father smiled at her briefly, then patted her on the head before turning away. "Deb, what's for dinner?"

"Oh, we'll just throw in some TV dinners in the microwave after we light the candles," Naomi's mother said. "Tomorrow is Saturday. I can make latkes then."

"Aww," Naomi said. What if she was back in 2022 by then?

Her mother raised an eyebrow. "What are you talking about? Last time I made latkes you hated them."

That was probably true, Naomi thought. "Well, I like applesauce!"

Her mother laughed. "Be right back. I'll get the menorah."

As her mother left for the china cabinet in the back room, Naomi was left alone with her father. She followed him as he walked through the kitchen, desperate to talk to him.

"Daddy, we had a party at daycare. It was mostly for Christmas, but they mentioned Hanukkah and —"

Her father picked up a newspaper and started rifling through it.

"Daddy. Daddy!" She called out.

Her father looked over the newspaper at her. "Oh, I'm sorry," he said. "What did you say?"

Naomi's lip pouted. *He's just tired,* she tried to tell herself. *How many times have you gotten home from work and just wanted to crash and look at your phone when your kids started talking to you?*

And yet ...

"Hanukkah time!" her mother called out.

When her mother came back with the menorah, Naomi gasped, partly with childhood happiness and partly because she hadn't seen it in years. It was tiny and made of brass. The branches had intricate braids running up them, with beads in red, blue, green, and yellow beneath each candle holder. It wasn't very pretty, wasn't very impressive, but it was theirs.

Naomi's mother took a half-empty matchbook out of a kitchen drawer and used that to light the *shamash.* They said the first two prayers — her mother had never said the third — and then sang

"Hanukkah O Hanukkah" and "Ma'oz Tzur." The lyrics for the first song always came naturally.

AND WHILE WE are singing
The candles are burning bright
One for each night, they will shed a sweet light
As we dream about days long ago.

THEY NEVER REMEMBERED the lyrics for the latter, but her mother had cut out the backs of old Hanukkah candle boxes where they had been printed, and they read them from there.

Well, her mother and father read them. Naomi didn't get one, presumably because she couldn't read yet. This would have been, perhaps, the first time she'd ever sung these songs straight through, these songs that now came second nature, these songs that had been a throughline through the years. The first one was corny, the second one she barely understood even now, but being back here, at this point where most of her memories began ...

Naomi reached out and held her mother's hand, felt her mother squeeze back with her familiar warmth. She reached out to hold her father's, and he squeezed back, too. And yet ...

The child in Naomi was happy. The child had wanted this moment where the three of them were together and a family, where she could be with them and just feel enveloped in both of her parents' love in a way she hadn't felt in years.

And yet the adult couldn't help but keep looking, keep searching both of their faces, keep wondering, *do they know? Are they happy? Do they feel this love I'm feeling, or are they just going through the motions, just tolerating each other until ...*

She wished, if this had to happen to her, that she could have just been in this moment, could have forgotten her current life and her family and her marriage and ...

"Naomi," her mother said with a smile, "It's time to open a present."

They always did Hanukkah in the kitchen for safety's sake, but the presents were always kept in a basket in the living room. In the years to come, Naomi developed a tradition of picking the smallest presents for the first few days. It proved useful, especially when she realized what a letdown it was to open a present on the last night of Hanukkah and find it was something like colored pencils or a tiny box of candy. But she hadn't developed it at this point, and she didn't know if she'd be back here again.

"I want that one," she said, pointing to the biggest present.

It seemed like her mother hadn't been able to find specific Hanukkah wrapping, so all of the presents were in blue and silver paper with blue bows. The one she picked was tall and thick, boxy at the bottom but lumpy at the top. She opened it clumsily, her small hands not being able to rip off the paper the way she expected them to, but quickly as possible, the paper coming off in small little bits.

"Oh ..." she whispered when she saw what was inside.

It was a lot to process, seeing this toy again. In a way, her sudden wash of nostalgia felt gauche and stupid. How many children had asked for this toy? How many of these were in someone's closet? She could get another like it on eBay back in 2022 if she wanted to, and yet ...?

What would it have been like, she wondered, if the boy in *The Velveteen Rabbit* had somehow managed to see his beloved toy again, not as a real rabbit in the forest but as it once was before it had turned shabby and balding — its shape restored and the pink back in its ears. Would he have been happy to see it back again? Would he have recognized it without its lumps and stains?

In looking at the toy, seeing it brighter and shinier than she ever remembered, she felt the childhood excitement at seeing a toy and imagining all the games she would play with it, only this time she knew for sure what those games would be. When she saw this shiny, pristine new toy she could remember the imaginary adventures in the clouds, the tea parties, the show-and-tell sessions, the snuggling up with it watching movies and the many, many nights when she would sleep with it by her side. And she'd remember when those times were over, when the bear — now faded and lumpy — would be placed in a new box of cardboard and packing tape in her closet, no longer needed but never forgotten.

"Thank you," Naomi said, stroking the bear's yellow fur, the smiling sun on its stomach. "I know I'll treasure this."

Naomi's mother gasped and put her hand on her heart. "Naomi, that's such a beautiful thing to say. I'll get you scissors and help you get it out of the box."

Her parents both left the room. When they were gone, Naomi laid on her stomach, kicked her feet behind her as she looked at her bear. Despite that, though, she could hear their voices from the kitchen.

"I don't get it," her father said. "You can get a pastel bear anywhere."

"Well, this is hers," Naomi's mother answered.

"It's a lot more money than the ones at the drugstore."

"It'll be worth it. She's worth it."

Naomi sat up, took her hands off the bear. She would have said the same of buying something expensive for her kids, and so would Anthony. And yet ...

"Am I?" Naomi whispered.

The TV dinner didn't taste any better in 1989 than it did in 2022, but there was still something special about finishing everything and finally being able to eat the brownie in the top center square, still too hot on the inside. The family ate while watching TV, too, which was nice. The television was small and still had a cord remote to change the channels, and they didn't have cable so all that was on was an episode of *Full House* and *Charlie Brown's Christmas Special*, neither of which really held Naomi's interest very much. ("They're laying it on a bit thick with the Jesus stuff, aren't they?" her father said about the latter.) Throughout this, Naomi tried to wait for a moment when her father would leave the room, where she could conceivably follow him, and they could talk away from her mother. But by the time *A Very Brady Christmas* was scheduled to come on, Naomi's mother said she had to go to bed.

"One day, we'll have Hanukkah specials," Naomi told her mother as they walked hand-in-hand up the stairs to Naomi's bedroom. "Not too many, and they won't be very good, but we'll have them."

Naomi's mother nodded noncommittally. "That sounds nice."

They went through what Naomi now remembered was the evening routine. First her mother would watch while Naomi brushed her teeth, then they would go to bed and her mother would read her a story. It wasn't a very good one — a picture book about Hanukkah that tried its best to compress the history of the holiday in a way that could be digestible to kids — the cruel reign of Antiochus, the Jews who would hide their Torah scrolls in favor of dreidels whenever a soldier came to investigate their house, the Maccabean revolt, the restoration of the temple and the miracle of the oil that burned for eight days — and just left Naomi with a kind of vague impression of everything that happened. (She wondered when *Herschel and the Hanukkah Goblins* was published ...)

But it was nice to have her mother read to her again, and, when the story was over, to be tucked back into her canopy bed, to feel her new yellow bear in her arms, to be young and feel her mother's hand stroke her hair.

"Did you have a special Hanukkah?" Her mother asked.

"Yes, Mommy," Naomi answered. It didn't feel weird to call her that anymore.

"Good," her mother said. She leaned down and gave Naomi a kiss on the forehead. "It will probably be better tomorrow, when we have time to make a nice meal and everything like that. I'm glad it was special, though. It can be hard, especially when the holiday is so close to Christmas, not to feel a little left out, but I want you to enjoy it."

"I do ..." Naomi said.

As she left, Naomi stared up at the canopy, hugged her first gift tighter. So, this was the first day of Hanukkah when she was four — at her home with both of her parents.

She remembered that conversation that she had with her mother in 2022, right before she came here. Her own twins would never be left out of Christmas, she thought. Their father celebrated it, so they always would, no matter what they chose to be when they grew up.

But she wondered if it had been right to leave them out of Hanukkah. Would they have other years when they chose to take part in this tradition? Or would it all fade by the wayside as those other holidays

— the ones she had called more important but in this society were ulti-
mately less convenient — had?

Her door opened, and Naomi took a deep breath in. She kept
staring at the canopy, kept girding herself for what would come next, as
her father approached the bed. He kneeled down and stroked her hair,
just as her mother had done, but Naomi did not look at him.

"Good night, Naomi," he kissed her cheek. "See you tomorrow. I
love you."

He was already turning to go. Naomi closed her eyes, took a sharp
breath before she said. "Are you already thinking of leaving?"

When Naomi sat up in bed, her father turned back to her, confused.
"Leaving ... the room?"

"Leaving Mommy," Naomi insisted.

Her father laughed uncomfortably. "Sweetie, I'm not going
anywhere."

"Yes, you are," Naomi said. She tried not to cry, tried to be calm, but
there was a hint of a crack in her voice. "You have to go. I get that. I
understand that."

"Naomi ..."

"But you don't have to leave me!" Naomi tried not to yell, started
pounding the comforter in front of her instead. "You leave in four years
and then I never see you again. Why? I get that Mommy's a lesbian, but
why didn't you call me? Why didn't you send me cards?"

"You —" her father shook his head. When he spoke, his voice was an
angry whisper. "You shouldn't know a word like that or insult your
mother like that. What's wrong with you? Did another kid in school say
this?"

"What is it, Daddy?" Naomi stood up in her bed, was actually
crying now. "Are you a homophobe? Do you hate being here? Did you
not want to be a father? Did you find another family and forget all
about me? Is that it? Is this all a mistake? What is it? *Why did you
fucking leave me?*"

Her father backed up from her, looked at her with a deep, deep
loathing and horror. As much as Naomi had forgotten his face over the
years, she knew with a sick resignation that she would never forget his
face ever again.

He ran out of the room. "*Deb!*"

As he screamed her mother's name, Naomi grabbed onto her bear and cried into its neck. Why had she done that? What had she hoped to accomplish? But ... but ...

Naomi squeezed the bear harder, tried to stifle her tears, but the tighter she grabbed, the more she felt it fade away.

CHAPTER

SIX

SUNDAY, DECEMBER 18, 2022 — THE FIRST NIGHT OF HANUKKAH

When the bear — her beloved bear — had completely faded, Naomi's arms rested on solid wood. She lifted up her head, and the menorah she had bought earlier that day sat in front of her. The smoke had cleared. The glow had faded.

I'm back, she thought. It was a relief, an enormous relief, a relief she'd expected but also ached to feel. And yet she was already missing the freedom and ease with which she had used her old body, already felt nostalgic for the comfort of her own bed. Already felt regret for ...

Naomi rushed to the box of candles, opened it up with shaky hands and put a new candle in the branch furthest to the right. She picked out a second candle for the *shamash* and lit it, then brought the *shamash* to the new candle.

The *shamash* immediately went out. She tried a second time, then a third. She took the first candle out of the holder and used the *shamash* to light it. Finally, the flame caught, but when she put both candles back in the menorah they went out.

Naomi let out a long sigh. "Well, I guess I know the rules now."

But did she really? What had happened? Was that all an illusion? A dream? Had she really gone back in time?

Naomi thought about it for the rest of the night. She made herself a dinner of sunny side up egg (which tasted great now) on rice mixed with avocado and soy sauce. After she finished eating, she paced around the room. Occasionally the phrase *predestination paradox* would come to mind and she would think about calling her mother

She did call Anthony, but the call went to voicemail. *Can you give the kids a hug from me?* She texted. Then for the next hour she checked to see if Anthony had read the message.

Around 10:00 p.m., she finally settled down in her bed to sleep. She stared up at the blank ceiling. When that didn't seem to help, she looked for something to watch on a couple of streaming services — Netflix, Tubi, the Criterion Channel — but the thought of getting lost in some other world right now seemed overwhelming. She flipped through the pages of her old copy of *Jane Eyre*, and then when that didn't work, she listened to the soundtrack from *Solaris.*

Is this appropriate? She asked herself as she listened to the electronic dirge. *Isn't this about Jesus? Was the original composer an anti-semite or was that just Wagner?*

She wondered what her 4-year-old self would have thought of this music, what her kids would think if she had them listen to it. She wondered what her father was doing now. She wondered about that Snickers bar she'd saved from daycare and never ate. But mostly, she thought about tomorrow, and wondered where she would be going tomorrow night ...

NAOMI'S STORY WILL CONTINUE ...

ABOUT THE AUTHOR

Rebecca Henely-Weiss is a former journalist and occasional author/critic. Her fiction work has appeared in the zine *Secrets of the Goat People* and previous Tarina Anthologies. In addition to writing, her hobbies include baking, going for long walks, entering movie watching challenges and drafting fantasy casts for drag competition reality shows. She lives in central New Jersey with three cats, two sons and one husband.

A Demon's Scorn

Kate Seger

No one wants to ask their ex-girlfriend - who happens to be a demon they summoned by mistake - for help. But when Kael learns a malevolent beast conjured in 600 AD is about to devour the galaxy, he isn't left with much choice. Now, the fate of the world rests in the hands of a grumpy warlock with dubious skill and his jilted lover, wandering ancient Rome. And Kael isn't sure which is more terrifying, the looming apocalypse or a spurned woman's scorn.

CHAPTER I

YOU WOULDN'T DARE

In a fickle world, in a town that was forever reinventing itself, the antique shop was a constant. It had presided over the corner of Abbott Street and Lillian Lane for nearly two centuries. There had been subtle changes, of course, but they were minimal compared to the upheaval that had taken place in the pastoral town around it. It was not, Kael realized, so rustic anymore. He marveled wistfully at the transformation as he drove through the outskirts towards Laurel's Antiques and Oddities... where Lorelei would be waiting.

She always was.

Where once there had been rolling meadows and farmland, Kael now sped past pool supply stores, fast food joints, and car dealerships. The town appeared to have succumbed to rampant urban sprawl, and then, as was often the case, sudden collapse. The roller skating rink, bowling alley, and mega mall that had burst forth in a wave of euphoric boom-town development decades earlier now stood vacant and dejected. Humanity had folded back in on itself as the antisocial era of one-click shopping, on-demand streaming, and social networking ushered in their demise.

But the shop... Kael could hardly believe how little it had changed as he parked his silver Mercedes at the bottom of the winding drive. The building looked almost identical to how he remembered. Apart from one painful change to the wooden façade; What had once been a stark gray, was now painted over in egg-yolk yellow; a hue Kael intensely disliked. He couldn't say it surprised him to see it, though. For all her demonic prowess, Lorelei had always been a summer creature at heart. Left to her own devices, it stood to reason that she would paint over everything in the color of sunshine.

According to the sign, the Victorian manse that currently doubled as Laurel's Antiques and Oddities had been many things in its long years, but it had never before been yellow. This peculiarity of Lorelei's also extended to the rows of sunflowers, great golden heads turned up as if in greeting, lining the walkway as he trudged up the drive.

Kitschy, Kael thought, clucking his tongue.

Apart from the nauseating coat of paint, the place looked exactly as it had on the day he'd left, seventy-seven years ago. Back then, it had been a tea shop, now it sold antiques, but it was still... the shop. That was the thing about change. No matter how much shifted, some things stubbornly resisted the pull of time. The shop, and Lorelei, who was evidently Laurel for the moment, were amongst those who stayed the same. They could change their faces and their names, yet something of their essence always remained. Their true nature did not change.

Not until they were destroyed.

Kael hesitated on the sprawling porch. His hand hovered over the brass door knocker without touching it. There was no doubt in his mind that Lorelei—Laurel, he corrected—knew perfectly well he was standing on her front porch. They were bound. She could sense his presence in the same way he could sense hers. It seemed she had just made up her mind to be difficult.

This, too, did not surprise him.

He took the knocker in his hand and banged it against the heavy door. No response came from within. Kael sighed, running a hand through his tousled dark hair. He knocked again, louder this time, then frowned and shoved his hands into the pockets of his tailored slacks, waiting. Still, the door did not open. But he thought he could hear a sound, a footstep on a creaky floorboard. Old houses gave up their secrets easily—some of them, anyway.

"Lorelei, I know you're in there. Open up," Kael called in a tone that he hoped meant business.

"What are you doing here, Kael?" came the muffled reply from behind the closed door.

"We need to talk." His words were clipped. He didn't have time for these games.

"About what?"

Kael rolled his eyes at her petulant tone. "Lorelei, let me in or, so help me, I'll break this door down." His voice was flat. Calm. The kind of calm just waiting to explode.

"You wouldn't dare."

"Trust me, Lorelei. I would," he assured her.

Apparently, Lorelei recognized that, yes, Kael would, in fact, break the door down. And he could do it with a single muttered word. Locks clicked, and the door opened just a crack. Wide blue eyes peered out at him through the slit. Eyes that never changed.

And still haunted his every dream.

Kael grabbed the door by the knob and yanked it open, bringing himself face to face with Lorelei. She was tall and pale as ever, but it seemed she'd elected to be a buxom blonde in this incarnation. Plaited coils of platinum hair were piled high in a chignon atop her head, a few wisps falling free to frame a freckled, heart-shaped face. The vision of schoolboy fantasies, clad in denim and a plain white tee with a deep v-neck.

Kael snorted and rolled his eyes. "Oh, that's a fine look for you. Very Betty Sue, the farm girl."

Lorelei folded her arms across her ample chest, pouting. "What's that supposed to mean? What are you even doing here?" she snapped.

Kael didn't answer her. He didn't want to piss her off and be forced to go through this pantomime again if she slammed the door in his face. Or worse. Even if Kael tore the door from the hinges, Lorelei had other ways to bar him from the shop if she really wanted to.

"Nothing, Lorelei. Or should I call you Laurel?" Kael smirked. "May I come in?" He kept his tone as even as he could stand to.

He thought Lorelei would deny him for a moment, but she acquiesced, stepping aside so that he could enter.

CHAPTER 2

I NEVER ASKED TO BE BORN A DEMON

K ael crossed the threshold and was hit with a wave of nostalgia so intense that it made his stomach clench. Though the furnishings had changed, the bones of the house were as they'd always been... and that scent... lemon verbena and spicy clove, underlaid with the earthiness of sage and something far darker. Something that was not of this world and did not belong in it.

Kael clamped down on the sentimentality blossoming within him, taking stock of the array of antique wares to distract himself. Lorelei had always had an eye for aesthetics, and this particular repurposing of the shop seemed to suit her quite well. She'd only acquired the finest pieces throughout the ages, and had arrayed them in such a way that, despite the busyness, the result was still inviting.

But he wasn't here to admire Lorelei's collection. The goods were all a front, anyway. A pretty illusion hiding something sinister.

Just like Lorelei.

"We need to talk," Kael repeated.

Lorelei sighed and gestured towards the door on the left.

"Then let's talk," she said in a deceptively airy tone. Kael knew she had no interest in speaking to him. She was clearly still pissed.

He watched her saunter into the living room, and tried not to notice the alluring way her hips swayed as she walked. She was doing that on purpose.

He exhaled slowly. He could not let her get under his skin, or all hope was lost.

Lorelei gestured to a divan, which looked to be a relatively recent acquisition. Kael sat on it, acutely aware of her eyes on him as he did so. Now it was his turn to watch as she lowered herself gracefully onto a decidedly familiar-looking Victorian fainting couch, arranging her curvaceous body seductively upon it. An image of her nude flashed in Kael's mind, posing for a portrait long ago when she was a raven-haired beauty who wore a different face. He tried to slam the door closed on that vision but couldn't get the thought of her body–

"Kael." Lorelei cleared her throat.

"What?" He blinked, slipping out of his reverie.

"You said you wanted to talk to me, not stare at me. Are you even listening?" She gave him a pointed look.

"No—yes. Sorry, now I am." He stammered, cursing himself silently. He'd sworn he wouldn't let her enchant him again. He was doing a fine job of failing at that.

"Why are you here?" Lorelei enunciated each word slowly, as if she were speaking to a child. "What sort of trouble are you going to start?"

Kael groaned internally. What sort of trouble, indeed.

"The big kind, of course," he replied with a wry smile. Lorelei did not seem amused. "But I'm not here to start it. I'm here to put an end to it."

Lorelei let out a huff, blowing a stray tendril of hair from her eyes and drumming her fingers on her denim-clad thigh. It was peculiar, seeing her in blue jeans. The visions still burned in his mind were of her wearing gowns, corsets, satin, and lace.

"And you think, after seventy-seven years, you can just waltz in here and ask for my help? After everything? That's asking for a lot, Kael."

She wasn't wrong. He had left her here, bound to this house, while he'd gone off globe-trotting at the behest of his handlers. But he was a warlock, conscripted to the Arcane Circle, bound to do their bidding. Sure, he could have asked for some gigs closer to home, but he'd never tell Lorelei that.

Kael gave her a pleading look. "Listen, I'm sorry for what happened. You know I didn't want to go—"

Lorelei scoffed, unimpressed. "You could have taken me with you."

Kael shook his head, tamping down his rising irritation. "You know I couldn't. The Circle doesn't allow demons—" He bit off his words and clamped down on his tongue in the process—hard enough that he tasted blood. He shouldn't have said that.

"You know, I never asked to be born a demon, Kael." He'd heard this song and dance before.

"And I certainly never asked for you to summon me to this backwater town in this hole in the universe and trap me here *forever.*"

Lorelei's eyes blazed, and her irises flashed blood-red. Kael winced, praying she didn't do anything rash. He'd already had to put new windows in the house once after a row when they were still 'an item.'

"You're right, Lorelei. I know. I'm a jerk. And I'm terribly sorry for all the trouble. If I could set you free, you know I would. I wish I could take it all back."

It was the truth. Not out of any pity for her, but because Lorelei had been a thorn in his side since the day he summoned her. Accidentally.

He had been trying to summon his cleaning lady. A friendly little ghost named Muriel. He wondered how Muriel was doing these days.

"You're the only one who can help me, Lorelei."

She didn't answer, only gazed at him with those sky-blue eyes, lips set in a thin hard line.

CHAPTER 3

FREEDOM

"You have not told me what you need help with."

Lorelei's color was rising, cheeks blazing scarlet. Kael sensed she was close to dropping the facade and giving her inner demon free rein. He would have to be careful.

He cleared his throat, folding and unfolding his hands in his lap. "Do you remember how I told you about that *thing?*"

Lorelei stared at him. "*The* thing?"

Kael nodded. "Yeah. The thing. The thing that wants to eat the world."

Lorelei nodded, eyeing him warily.

"Well, the thing is, I need to go back in time to stop it. Back to when the Arcane Circle summoned it."

Lorelei let out a sharp bark of laughter, then groaned. "You can't do that, you idiot. It's too late. You can't avert an end by altering the beginning. That's not the way it works. You'll just make a bigger mess of things."

Kael shot her a nasty look. Did she always have to be so superior? He'd never met a bigger know-it-all. "What do you know about it, anyway?" he challenged.

Lorelei sighed. "Kael, I am three billion years old. You may think you're worldly and knowledgeable, jetting around at the behest of the Circle. Summoning ghosts and–" She broke off. She hated the word demon. "*Things.* But I remember a time when the earth was in its infancy, and I'm telling you–"

Kael interrupted her esoteric speech on the intricacies of the universe by slamming his fists down on the antique coffee table, splintering it. Fragments of wood flew across the living room and a blue and white chlorite vase shattered as it hit the floor.

Lorelei frowned. "What the hell, Kael? That was ancient Sumerian. You know, irreplaceable? Unless you want to go back to Sumer and get one. Since time traveling is your new *thing.*"

Kael squinted at her and shook his head. "Don't you understand? The world is going to end!"

Lorelei shrugged and stuck her tongue out at him. Actually *stuck her tongue out* at him, then said, "Worlds are born and die every second."

"Not my world!" Kael boomed.

Their gazes locked as a steely war of attrition raged between them, neither willing to back down.

"I've seen what this thing can do, Lorelei, and–"

Lorelei smirked. "Where? In your crystal ball?"

She had never taken much stock in divinations, calling them parlor tricks for mortals who wanted to play at understanding gods and other beings beyond their conception. But Kael *had* seen the monstrosity the Arcane Circle had conjured up. They'd been trying to sweep it under the rug since 600 AD. But it was still out there. And it had been moving through the universe, chewing up galaxies and spitting out the pieces for centuries.

Now it was coming for them.

"Lorelei, this thing that's coming, it's not like–"

"I know what it is," she snapped, then got to her feet, pacing, her boots hitting staccato notes on the wooden floor. "You would go back... to before the Circle's ritual?" she asked, her voice flat with indifference again.

"I would."

"You know how long ago that was, right? It is not the same world you know. You won't know the language. You won't know the customs."

Kael threw his arms in the air and snarled. "For god's sake, Lorelei. I'm not going there to have tea and chat with the locals."

"And what would you do once you got there?" She arched a pale brow.

Kael opened his mouth to answer, then snapped it shut. He wasn't sure. Not exactly. In fact, he had no idea. But he'd figure something out. "Whatever I must," he finally said.

Lorelei snorted out a laugh. "You're a fool, Kael."

She crossed the room and stood before him.

"I loved you. And you left me here to rot. Now you want me to help you save the pathetic world I'm bound to and trapped in?"

Lorelei leaned in close and Kael caught a whiff of her scent, gasoline and verbena, citrus and smoldering fire, as her lips pressed to his ear. "What do I get out of it?"

Kael twisted around and narrowed his eyes at her. He didn't like where this was going. Negotiating with demons was never a good idea. Bargaining with one who used to be your *lover*...

He scooted farther away on the sofa so he couldn't smell her heady, intoxicating scent and so her creamy white breasts weren't right there, just waiting for him to reach out and–

"What do you want from me?" Kael growled. Tension was building in his groin, his cock straining his gray linen pants.

Lorelei didn't answer. Instead, she climbed up onto the sofa, kneeling on all fours. Her plump ass stuck up in the air, her full breasts swaying pendulums as she crawled towards him.

"Lorelei, knock it off," Kael warned.

But she didn't.

Kael wasn't even sure how it happened. One minute, he was scrambling to get away from her; the next, he found himself pinned between the arm of the couch and Lorelei's body– that incredible, nubile, curvaceous body. Before he could react, she had crawled up onto his lap and straddled him. His head and heart sounded an alarm as her thighs pressed against his, plump but powerful. Kael could imagine how soft her skin was beneath the denim and his rebellious dick twitched. *Traitor.*

"What... do... you want." He barely managed to get the words out between deep breaths.

His self-control was slipping. Again.

Lorelei took his face in both hands, pulling it close to hers, and breathed the word into his mouth. "Freedom."

Then her lips locked with his.

CHAPTER 4

A FEW STIPULATIONS

Lorelei's tongue traced Kael's teeth, then darted between them, teasing as it twined with his. Kael felt like he had fallen into a dream. No, not just a dream. *The* dream. The one he'd been having for centuries. The taste of Lorelei exploded in his mouth—strawberries and brimstone, wine tinged with petrichor—a bittersweet forbidden fruit.

But then her claws dug into his shoulders, and Kael's eyes flew open. He winced as trickles of warm blood coursed down his back from the punctures in his flesh.

This is a 400-dollar Burberry Sherwood Motif shirt, he wanted to scream, but that wouldn't get him anywhere. Lorelei had never understood the value of money, being able to conjure it on a whim.

Instead, he said, "You know I can't unbind you, Lorelei. It's against the rules. The Circle would take away my magic, and then I'd age 400 years in a heartbeat and die. Is that what you want, Lorelei? Because if I die, you won't be bound to me anymore—"

She smirked. "Oh, what a pity..."

Kael ignored her and went on. "But you'd still be bound *here*. To this house. That was the Circle's doing, not mine. And what happens when the *thing* devours the world, and you're still bound to it because there's no one left to release you? You're just gonna float around a dead world. Alone for the rest of your days. You think you're lonely now, well—"

Lorelei still straddled him, her face inches from his, unfamiliar with its freckles and button nose except for her eyes, and pressed a finger to his lips. "You're an asshole, Kael. But, surprisingly, I don't want you dead. So, fine. I guess I'll have to help you stop the apocalypse." She heaved a world-weary sigh.

Her breath still smelled like strawberries, and Kael's rebellious dick twitched again. He hoped she didn't feel it.

"You-you will?" he asked, head cocked to the side, looking at her uncertainly. This had to be a trick.

Lorelei nodded and nuzzled his neck, running her tongue down his carotid artery. Her fingers moved, unbuttoning his shirt, tickling him with her long nails as she stroked his chest, toying with the wiry black hair.

Kael was afraid he would melt into the sofa as her demon heat radiated into him.

"I will," she purred. "But there are… stipulations. I promise to help you save the world, if you make a vow to me, too."

Kael's body went rigid, his muscles tensing. He trusted Lorelei about as far as he could throw her, which wasn't far. Particularly not at this moment as, while she spoke, Lorelei had deftly grabbed his wrists in her hands, yanked them over his head, and held them there, demon strength readily apparent.

Kael contemplated lobbing a fireball right at that pretty, *fake* face of hers, then reconsidered. Everything in here was *old*, and he suspected it wouldn't take more than a stray spark to start a whole conflagration.

Then there would be firemen and cops. More wasted time. Plus, she'd really be pissed. He'd have to build her a new house… if the world didn't end, anyway. And she was more likely to help him save the world if he didn't set her on fire, Kael decided.

He kept his voice even. "Okay, Lorelei. Tell me your stipulations."

She released one of his hands, looking thoughtful, then brought her index finger to her lips. Lorelei sucked on it, her pink tongue swirling around the digit like a lollipop, and held it up.

"One...You move back here."

Kael tried his hardest not to grimace, but he could feel his lips pulling away from his teeth. "For how long?"

The look she gave, hard, eyes gone red around the rims, left him with no doubt that she meant forever. An eternity. It certainly wasn't how Kael would choose to spend eternity, but he figured, *Oh well, I'm rarely home anyway. Circle business keeps me–*

Lorelei interrupted his thought, holding up a second finger.

"And when you travel, I go with you."

A sheen of sweat broke out on Kael's brow, and he opened his mouth to speak, but Lorelei's dark glower silenced him. "I already know what you're going to say. *Girlfriends* aren't allowed on official business."

That wasn't strictly the case, actually. The Arcane Circle didn't care who you fraternized with, as long as they weren't, well...a *demon*. But Kael thought it best not to point that fact out at the moment, so he only nodded for Lorelei to continue.

Which she did.

"Honestly, Kael. If I *save the world*, don't you think they'd grant me a little latitude? I'm not asking to be released to reap souls and eat the hearts of babies, for Satan's sake. Just to follow you on your trips. Maybe I could even help you!" She brightened at the notion. "I'm certain they'd allow it. As a reward."

Kael wasn't too sure about that, but he figured he could cross that bridge when he got to it. Something could be arranged, even if it wasn't exactly what Lorelei imagined.

"Fine, fine," Kael grumbled. "Anything else?"

Lorelei squirmed on his lap, and even through her jeans and his slacks, he could feel the burning heat of her Godforsaken lady bits.

"Marry me."

She dropped the final bomb with a huge smile plastered across her face.

Kael blinked and shook his head, then swallowed so hard he choked. When he finished sputtering and found his breath, he stared at Lorelei in disbelief.

"You've got to be kidding. Why? Why the fuck would you want to marry *me?* If there's anything the past 200 years have proven, it's that you and I *do not* get along."

Lorelei's grin remained, and she nodded enthusiastically. "I know! That's what makes it so fun! Kael, I must admit, it's been so *boring* around here without you. There's no–"

He cut her off before she could wax nostalgic and detail all the wonderful—*horrible*—times they'd shared in their past, taking a different tactic.

"Yes, but why marriage? It's so... cheesy. Mundane. Ordinary. Couldn't we just, you know, live together? Like we used to? There's paperwork, silly traditions. Wouldn't you rather, I don't know... live in sin? You are a demon, after all, isn't that kind of your thing?" he suggested.

Lorelei's face fell into a pout so childlike that Kael nearly laughed. He was less amused when she answered.

"Because, Kael, I want you to be bound to me. Like I am bound to you."

CHAPTER 5

HARRY POTTER ISN'T REAL

"Fine," Kael agreed. Because he had to. What else could he do? The fucking world was going to end if he didn't.

Lorelei leaped off his lap and clapped her hands together. "Perfect! Let's do it!"

Her enthusiasm was utterly absurd. This was why she drove Kael insane. She'd been sulky when he'd arrived. Then she hated his guts... until she wanted something, at which point she tried to seduce him. Now, suddenly, they were BFFs and *getting married*—God help him.

Maybe I should just let the world end, Kael thought. *It might be less painful.*

But Lorelei was already grabbing his hand, pulling him to his feet so aggressively he almost went airborne. She crossed the room with him in tow and pressed the false wall. With a creak that reminded Kael he'd need some WD40 if he survived this, it slid open, revealing a staircase that seemed to disappear into the black depths of eternity itself.

They descended together, Lorelei tugging at Kael's hand like a toddler anxious to get on an amusement park ride. He measured his steps to keep up with her, praying he didn't fall and break his neck. Immortality potions didn't cover incidental injuries; an eternity of paralysis in Lorelei's care was a daunting prospect indeed.

Finally, they reached the bottom. It was black as the bowels of the earth—because it basically was. Kael muttered a quick spell, and a dozen torches burst to life along the walls. Yeah, it was kind of old-fashioned. He could have replaced them with a switch and a light fixture years ago. But he kind of liked the nostalgia...

Except it wasn't nostalgic.

Not at all.

Because when the flickering torchlight illuminated the chamber, everything was... "Yellow? Are you fucking kidding me?"

Kael's eyes darted from the sunshine-hued walls to his divining table, once clad in black velvet, now dressed in a yellow gingham print tablecloth. Silk sunflowers and marigolds. "Bee Happy" prints. Figurines of fluffy baby ducks. Even the chalk of his summoning circle had been traced in paint the hue of a school bus.

Lorelei at least had the decency to look chagrined as Kael glowered at her.

"Oh right, that. Well, you know, you were gone for a really long time, and I was just trying to make the place... homey."

Kael almost demanded to know what she had even been doing down here in *his* magical lair, the warlock version of a *man cave*. But upon further consideration, he decided he didn't want to know.

He slapped his forehead and shook his head.

"Are you mad?" Lorelei's eyes had a wicked gleam that told him she'd done this just to spite him.

Keep calm. Don't let her get under your skin. She'll get bored and stop tormenting you if she can't get a rise out of you. Kael coached himself like he'd done a thousand times before in Lorelei's presence.

But he couldn't quite bite back a sarcastic response. "No, it looks lovely. I hear shabby chic is all the rage for dens of black magic this year. And I'm sure lemon yellow will be Pantone's color of the year."

Lorelei scoffed. "If you're going to be mean, you can just get out. "

"I live here! It's my house!" Kael boomed. Then he sighed deeply and did his best to sound *nice*. "It was just unexpected. Let's drop it, Lorelei."

His jaw ticked and he ground his teeth, changing the subject to prevent the fight. "So, how does this time travel thing work? Tell me how we do this."

Lorelei batted her lashes at him, and he noticed her eyes had gone blood red, with shadowy black vortexes swirling where her pupils should have been. Even after all these years, it still creeped him out.

"Say please and I'll tell you," she chided in a saccharine sweet voice that seemed truly bizarre, coming from a creature sprouting devil horns on her forehead before his eyes.

"Please," Kael growled.

Lorelei smiled and two large, yellow fangs popped out, curving over her lower lip. "I can channel power to you, but you need to cast the spell. Because, you know, I'm bound." She glared at him, which was particularly disconcerting, considering her eyes looked like two embers of hell fire.

"Yeah yeah." Kael rolled his hand in the air, urging her on. "So what's the spell?"

Lorelei frowned. "You didn't learn this in Warlock school?"

Kael balled his hands into fists at his sides to prevent himself from strangling her. "There's no such thing as Warlock school, Lorelei. Harry Potter isn't real."

Lorelei snorted.

"Tempus flectit ad nutum meum et defert me ad punctum desiderium meum."

Kael was not one of those old-school warlocks. He did his spellwork in English. Like normal people. His lips drew down into a scowl at the prospect of getting those words to come out of his mouth properly.

"Is that Latin?"

Lorelei shook her head. "High Valyrian."

Kael blinked and scratched his head. *High Valyrian.* It sounded so familiar, but he couldn't quite place it. Was it one of the demon tongues or–

"Game of Thrones isn't real, Kael."

Lorelei's cackles echoed off the stone walls. She doubled over, clutching her stomach, and laughing so hard tears poured from her glowing eyes, rolling red as blood down her cheeks.

He wanted to strangle her. "It's not funny. We don't have time for your little games."

"You said you'd be nice."

She stuck her tongue out at him again, and Kael wondered what he'd done in a past life to deserve Lorelei.

CHAPTER 6

I NEVER WORSHIPED URANUS

"What color candles?" Kael asked, rummaging through the large iron chest in the corner of the room.

"Blue-green. It should be obvious. Your god of time, Kronos, is associated with Uranus and—"

Kael turned around and squinted at Lorelei. She was in full demon form now, her blonde hair coal gray, skin ashen, two red horns spiraling off her forehead. He was annoyed that he still somehow found her hot.

"I don't need the song and dance. I never worshiped Uranus, or any God, for that matter. Religion is for the unwashed masses. I just need to know which candles," Kael growled.

"Uranus isn't a God. It's a planet. Kronos isn't really a God either—he's a demon too, but your people insist on likening—"

Kael didn't have time for a lesson in theology.

"Blue?" He held up a blue candle in his right hand. "Or green?" He picked up a green one.

Lorelei sighed. "Fine, stay ignorant, Kael. You know, that's always been your problem. You always want to go, go, go. Do, do, do. You never stop to reflect on—"

"BLUE?" Kael boomed this time, waving both candles in Lorelei's direction. "OR GREEN?"

Lorelei shrugged. "I guess if you don't have blue-green, logic dictates you would use a combination of both."

Kael caught her sticking her tongue out and waggling her fingers behind her ears in his peripheral vision as he reached back into the chest, pulling out more candles. He ignored her, carried them over to the yellow summoning circle, and lined them up, staggered blue and green at each connecting point of the pentacle.

She was such a little brat.

He placed the last candle in the center of the summoning circle, then turned back to Lorelei. "Look good?" he asked, though he wasn't particularly interested in her opinion. He might not be the best warlock in the world but he could certainly arrange a summoning circle.

Lorelei scanned the circle. Her nose crinkled in dismay, but she said, "It would look better if they were blue-green, but I guess beggars can't be choosers. You never seem to be prepared."

A thousand responses flitted through Kael's mind, but in the end, he just grabbed Lorelei's hand and hauled her to the center of the circle.

"So, what now? Just repeat that Latin gibberish?" He was running out of patience.

Lorelei glared, and twin flames kindled where her pupils should have been. "You're the one who asked me for help, and now you're being a miserable curmudgeon *as usual.* Do you want to do this yourself?" she snapped.

Yes, Kael thought.

Unfortunately, he couldn't. Traveling a couple thousand years into the past wasn't like hurling a fireball or summoning a ghost to clean your house... and somehow, he'd even managed to screw that up.

He was a warlock, sure, but he wasn't a great warlock. Maybe even not a *good* warlock. The Arcane Circle was only convinced of his prowess because he'd slain a couple of demons in the 1800s.

Only he hadn't.

Not really. Lorelei had. He was only the conduit.

Some things never change, Kael thought.

"So, do you remember the *gibberish*? Because if you muck it up, we could wind up back in a world full of toxic gasses and amoeba. Which would be fine, for me, but you would die because– "

"I know, I know. Immortality potions don't cover incidentals." How many times was she going to remind him? "I memorized the words."

Lorelei nodded and stepped into the circle next to Kael. She was all business now, her blue-black lips pursed together, her eyes swirling with demonic power. When she took Kael's hand, there was a sizzle. He smelled brimstone and felt a surge of dark energy run icy-hot through his veins.

"Light the candles," Lorelei ordered.

"Lux at petua illuminarte."

I'll show her, Kael thought as he spoke the words in Latin instead of English.

For a moment, nothing happened. Kael furrowed his brow.

"Kael, you—"

Before Lorelei could finish, the sleeves of Kael's very expensive suit burst into flames.

He shrieked, shaking his arms.

Stop, drop, and roll was forgotten in his panic until a force like a semi-truck plowed into him, sending him crashing to the ground. The carefully arranged candles flew every which way as Lorelei pounced on him, her demon skin devouring most of the flames.

Kael thrashed around under her until, at length, the fire was out.

He took several deep breaths, got to his feet, and dusted himself off, more embarrassed than hurt.

"Idiot. Pronunciation matters. Do that with the *real* spell, and you'll be amoeba food. Or worse," Lorelei warned as she walked around the summoning circle, picking up and righting the candles.

Kael didn't answer. What could he say? He brushed the soot off his arms to the best of his ability, mourning his ruined shirt and muttering curses under his breath.

"Let flames illuminate," he grumbled.

The candles sprang to life.

CHAPTER 7

THE PORTAL

Kael rejoined Lorelei in the center of the summoning circle. The flames danced, throwing more shadows on the lemon-hued walls, and casting the room in an ominous ambiance despite the French country accouterments. Kael found it much improved.

"So? Are we going to do this?" Lorelei tapped her foot impatiently.

Kael nodded. He opened his mouth to recite the Latin words to the best of his - admittedly limited - ability, but before he could speak, Lorelei clapped her hand over his lips.

"Why don't you just repeat each word after me? So we don't have any... mistakes," she suggested.

Kael muttered something incomprehensible and fought the urge to bite Lorelei's fingers. What did she think he was, a child? A novice? Incompetent?

But when she removed her hand, Kael growled, "Fine." Because he didn't want to wind up being amoeba food.

Do amoeba even eat people, or is she making that up? Aren't they microscopic? Kael wasn't sure he even knew what an amoeba was, let alone whether they were carnivorous, but he also didn't think he wanted to find out.

Lorelei took his hand and held it. Kael felt that powerful charge run through him again, like his blood was simmering beneath his skin.

One by one, she recited the Latin words. Each time, Kael repeated something that must have been at least reasonably close because she didn't correct him. Lord knew she'd happily take advantage of any chance to inform him he was wrong.

"Meum!" Kael declared the last word, dramatically raising his bare, ash-covered arms above his head. He had no idea if the final flourish made the spell more powerful, but he liked to think it did.

For a moment, nothing happened, and Kael assumed he had done it wrong.

But as he waited for Lorelei's impending reprimand about what a terrible Warlock he was, he suddenly noticed a strange blue glow about an arm's length away.

The air around it rippled and churned as it expanded, resembling the static on a television set with no reception. It started as an orb the size of a baseball but rapidly expanded until Kael and Lorelei had to step back to avoid being sucked in.

Kael beamed, pride bolstering him. "I did it!" he exclaimed.

"You made a portal!" Lorelei golf-clapped, and Kael deflated.

"Yeah, well, let's not celebrate until we see where it spits us out," he muttered with thoughts of caustic methane and ammonia wasteland populated by amoeba plaguing him.

"I'll go check it out."

Kael shook his head emphatically. "Oh no, you won't. You're not leaving this house without me." That was just what he needed, his rogue demon gallivanting across space and time unsupervised. The Circle would have his head if he lost track of Lorelei.

"Fine," Lorelei sighed, pouting.

"You're not going like that, are you?" Kael assessed Lorelei's sickly gray skin, sharp horns, and red-rimmed eyes with a raised eyebrow.

"Of course. I figure we want to scare the idiot ancestors of those wing nut warlocks in the Circle out of summoning the big bad *thing*, right? So what better way than by letting them think they summoned the little bad thing?" She struck a pose, like Madonna doing *Vogue*, her hands up, her butt popped out. "They think they accomplished their goal, which appeases their frail mortal pride. We stave off the *thing* and save the world. Right? Did you have another plan?"

Kael had no plan. His plan had been to wing it and see what happened.

She might be a pain in the ass, but he had to give her credit for thinking on her feet. He wouldn't tell her that, though.

"What if it doesn't pop us out exactly where we need to be? You want to traumatize all the local peasants? Let them see a demon running amok in the streets?"

Lorelei shrugged, but Kael saw a little gleam of excitement in her eyes. Whether she would admit it or not, he knew some part of her liked that idea and thought it would be great fun. There was no sense arguing with her about it.

He cleared his throat. "Right. Well, we'll stick with your plan," he conceded. "But I'd appreciate it if you'd change back into human form."

Lorelei gave him a surly look and crossed her arms over her chest.

He wasn't going to win this fight, so he gave up.

"So what next?" he asked, resigned.

"Just think about where and when you want to go, then step through." Lorelei pointed at the auspicious swirling vortex that presumably functioned as a portal.

"That's it?"

Lorelei nodded. "That's it."

CHAPTER 8

OH NO YOU DON'T

ere goes nothing.

Kael gripped Lorelei's fingers so tightly that the bones probably would have snapped if she didn't have preternatural strength.

His first two steps toward the portal were long and confident, but he hesitated with inches left to close. Sweat beaded his brow, and tension knotted his shoulders. The amoebas flashed through his mind again. Kael was pretty sure they were microscopic and almost as certain they didn't eat people, but his brain still conjured up images of tiny, blind worm-like creatures with rows of shark teeth swarming like piranhas.

He tried to envision Rome. The Coliseum. Chariots. Marble sculptures. All the things he remembered from *The Gladiator.*

It didn't help. The amoebas expanded, swimming through his thoughts, large as cats, then elephants. Giant man-eating amoebas swirling in his mind's eye.

"What are you waiting for?" Lorelei demanded, exasperated.

Kael gave her a side-eyed look.

"Nothing," he said, but he still didn't budge. His legs felt weighed down, like his shiny black leather Gucci Jordaan loafers had been swapped out for concrete blocks.

Lorelei sighed. "You really need to get your shit together, Kael. Do you want to save the world or not?"

He didn't. Not really. The Circle overlords had talked him into this, but if he had a choice – one that wouldn't result in the end of days – he'd still be drinking wine on the Riviera.

Kael whipped around just as Lorelei's skin flashed bright red.

His hand, still clutching hers, *burned* like he was palming hot coals, and Kael shrieked, dropping the appendage like a hot potato.

A demon can never be fully tamed. You can dilute their power by binding them, but their essence will always remain. And with it, power.

The Circle's warning flashed in Kael's mind at the same moment Lorelei acted. It happened in the space of a blink.

One second, Kael was saying, "Lorelei, what the fuck is your prob—"

The next, before he could complete his thought, she disappeared from his line of vision, and he was shoved – hard – from behind.

Kael staggered forward, crashing into the portal.

As it crackled, static electricity zapped through Kael, and his skin prickled as every hair on his body stood on end at once. He whipped around to see Lorelei standing there, her hands on her wide hips, her face twisted into a vindictive, taunting sneer.

"Bye-bye, Kael! Have fun in Rome. Bring me back a nice wedding gift...if you make it back, that is."

As Lorelei raised her hand to wave bon voyage enthusiastically, Kael snarled, "Oh no you don't."

Against the pull of the portal, which was desperately trying to drag him to Ancient Rome - or the prehistoric world of man-eating amoebas, as the case might be - Kael reached for her. Sparks exploded in the air, hissing, as his hand shot out, wrapping around Lorelei's wrist.

Her shriek could have broken glass and probably did. Kael immediately thought about the windows upstairs and whether they would need to be replaced *again* as he hauled a surprised Lorelei, kicking and screaming, into the portal with him.

"Think about Rome, you asshole," Kael heard Lorelei shout as everything turned topsy-turvy.

She sounded far away, though he still clutched her by the wrist, and

Kael suddenly felt weightless. Like he'd left gravity behind in the basement of the old house on Lily Lane. Lorelei was floating too, Kael noticed, kicking her feet and flapping her free arm like a featherless bird in the thick miasma of... whatever time-space was made of.

"ROME!" Lorelei shouted again.

Nausea rolled in Kael's guts, a byproduct of the strange off-balance feeling. He slammed his eyes closed.

"Rome, Rome, Rome," he muttered.

And just as he was about to blow chunks, the spinning sensation passed, and Kael felt solid ground beneath his feet.

Around him, strange sounds. The clang of metal. Grunts. Feral, untamed-sounding grunts. And Lorelei's quiet voice near his ear:

"Shit."

Kael echoed Lorelei's muttered curse in his mind. He really didn't want to open his eyes.

But he did.

And immediately regretted it.

CHAPTER 9

IT WOULD BE LATIN

T he stone and concrete ellipses of the Colosseum spread out around them, rows of tuff seats soaring four stories high from the packed earth ground. Several thousand spectators sat in the tiered cavea, most silent, with their jaws slack, gazes boring into Kael and the horned, red-skinned demon standing beside him.

Worse yet, were the gladiators on the floor of the arena itself. At least a dozen burly men with bronze skin, clad in loincloths with leather armor fastened to their arms, surrounded Kael and Lorelei. The occasional clash of metal against metal could still be heard, but it quickly quieted. Within a few moments, most of the warriors' weapons dangled at their sides as they gawked at the duo that had appeared by magic in their midst.

They, too, stared at Kael and Lorelei with stunned expressions plastered to their faces, frozen for the moment, in uncertainty.

They were also humongous.

"Do something, Kael," Lorelei hissed, her red eyes flicking around at the scarred and pockmarked faces of the gladiators.

Do something? Oh, that's rich, Kael thought. What the hell was he supposed to do? Ask them if they'd be so kind as to let them go along their merry way because they had an apocalypse to stop? Surely a band of ancient warriors from an era when superstition and fear of magic were rampant would be just fine with that.

But one of them had to do something.

And Kael could tell by the pinched look plastered on Lorelei's face that she certainly wasn't going to stick her neck out for them. After all, she was basically immortal. Whereas he...

Immortality potions don't cover incidental damage.

As the last clanging of arms rang out in the Coliseum, a silence so complete that Kael could hear his own blood rushing in his ears fell like a pall over the crowd and gladiators alike.

Kael dropped his gaze to the ground, taking a moment to ponder which was worse - super-sized amoebas or Roman gladiators - and determined they were about even. The sinister clumps of brown and red that could only be blood and entrails strewn across the stony ground further hammered home the necessity of getting out of this jam - fast.

Kael redirected his attention to the crowd of spectators, trying to pretend the gladiators weren't slowly converging in a ring around him and Lorelei.

Clearing his throat, he raised his voice and, hoping he sounded authoritative, declared, "FRIENDS, ROMANS, COUNTRYMEN!"

The crowd's expressions became even more baffled, and the silence was broken by murmuring from the stands. The gladiators remained silent, but their expressions hardened.

"They don't speak English, Kael," Lorelei hissed.

Well, fuck...

"What language do they speak?" he asked Lorelei through clenched teeth.

She gave him a look that could curdle milk. Meanwhile, the din slowly crescendoed to a roar, and the gladiators continued closing the space, forming a loose ring around the warlock and the demon.

"Some ancient dialect of Latin, you ingrate," she growled.

Latin. Of course. It would be Latin.

Kael had always thought Latin was pretty obsolete and pointless. After all, almost all spells were translated into English in modern-day America. It was kind of like learning algebra. Why bother when you've got a calculator on your cell phone and Google? But he suddenly rued his ineptitude and lack of interest in foreign languages.

"You were the one who said we wouldn't be dropping in chat," Lorelei reminded him, her voice sing-song with 'I told you so.'

Kael reeled on her. "Well, you speak Latin! You talk to them!" he exclaimed in exasperation as the crunch of boots in blood-wet sand sounded, the circle tightening around them.

Lorelei tilted her chin up, looking indignant. "And just what am I going to tell them? 'Hi, I'm your friendly neighborhood demon, and I was hoping–"

Kael cut her off. It was his turn to say 'I told you so.' "I warned you not to come here looking like that. I told you to stay in your human form. But you wanted to play 'scare the peasants." His gaze raked down her plump but muscular form, her bouncy crimson-skinned breasts peeking alluringly from her white t-shirt.

Despite the fact that he could very well be about to meet his maker, he found himself struck by the urge to rip off the shirt and take her right here on the floor of the Coliseum.

A pair of sandaled feet stomped into view, loincloth swinging in the breeze, as one of the gladiators appeared less than a foot away, breaking the spell of Lorelei's body.

He didn't look curious anymore. He looked pissed. And scared. And his beefy hand was dropping to his hip, where an ax half the size of Lorelei hung from his belt.

"Unbind me," demanded Lorelei.

Kael hesitated. If ever there was a time to have the monstrous power of a demon at his back, this was it. But...

"No." Kael shook his head.

Who was he kidding? Unbinding her powers would unbind her from *him*. And no way would she stick around to help him once her freedom was granted. She'd be off, cackling all the way into some other space and time.

Lorelei's face reddened further, turning as bright as a tomato now, and flames danced in her pupils.

"Well, you have to do *something*!" she shrieked.

The arena trembled slightly with the power of her shout, and the greasy-haired ax-wielding barbarian froze with his ax half drawn, his eyes wide with terror. Gasps and screams from the crowd echoed off the stone walls.

The panic wouldn't last for long, though. For once in her, however many-billion, years of existence, Kael had to admit Lorelei was right.

They had to do something.

Right now.

CHAPTER 10
GLADIATORS

T he foot, which was just visible through a gap in the wall of bare thighs and lightly armored limbs surrounding them, spawned the idea.

Kael recognized that it might not be the *best* idea he'd ever had. In fact, it might be terrible and end in disaster since he had never used the necromancy spell before.

Not intentionally, anyway.

He'd learned to raise the dead by accident years ago when Lorelei had run into the room screaming that her beloved guinea pig Floofy was choking on a sprig of alfalfa.

Kael had never liked the damn rodent. It hadn't been fond of him either, and bit him every chance it got. But he cast Breath of Life to appease Lorelei and get her to shut up before she broke all the windows screaming.

He didn't know the filthy rodent was already dead. Furthermore, he didn't realize that casting Breath of Life on something deceased works a little differently.

And that was how he got saddled with a black and tan undead guinea pig minion that only ate raw red meat. It had taken him five years to get rid of the damn thing.

So it wasn't a spell he was particularly confident casting. However, short of calling lightning or conjuring a fireball - both of which could potentially result in the destruction of one of the architectural wonders of the ancient world - he didn't see many other options on the table.

The gladiator was on the move again, battle ax now in hand, and the telltale *tsssks* from all around told Kael more weapons were being drawn.

Lorelei was in a frenzy, hopping from foot to foot and ranting, "UNBIND ME! Please! Listen to me, Kael. I don't know what happens to me if you die when I'm bound to you, and I did not survive for countless millennia only to be banished because you—"

Her chirping made Kael want to throttle her, but he restrained himself, holding up a hand and hissing for her to be silent. "I have a plan," he announced, hoping he sounded more confident than he was.

Lorelei looked surprised, which irritated Kael. Why was she so shocked that he'd come up with a plan? She never had any faith in him.

"KAEL, look out!" Lorelei shrieked.

It almost sounded like she really cared about his well-being, but he suspected her bigger concern was the prospect that if her master perished, she might too.

Kael ducked and staggered gracelessly to the left, slamming into Lorelei. The closest gladiator's ax sliced the air so close to his face that he felt the wind of the blow against his skin.

Now or never, he decided.

In his best omnipotent Warlock voice, Kael bellowed, "BREATH OF LIFE!"

The ax-wielding maniac hesitated, seemingly confused by Kael's apparent shouting at a dead man. Kael stared at the corpse's foot, willing it to show some sign of life.

Nothing happened.

Kael cursed. Did he have to touch the body? He'd been holding Floofy.

He scrambled towards the fallen warrior and then barked, "Distract him!" over his shoulder at Lorelei.

She opened her mouth, most likely to protest that he wasn't the boss of her, but slammed it closed. For once, she seemed to recognize this wasn't the time to argue.

Lorelei sighed. In the space of a heartbeat, before the gladiator could even think about taking a swing at her, she had transformed into her human skin in all its bountiful, blue-eyed beauty.

"Salve Pulcher," she purred, placing a hand on the aggressive behemoth's shoulder.

The gladiator's eyes bulged. He lowered his ax, cocking his head to one side, mouth hanging open like a fish out of water. It was like the gladiator transformed from a feral pit bull into a puppy dog with one glance at Lorelei's demure smile and heaving bosom. Kael would have laughed if he wasn't so concerned he might be moments from death.

Why didn't she do that immediately? Kael wondered, but let it slide. He had bigger problems to deal with.

Kael had made it within reach of the body, but his frantic sprint had been enough to jar several other gladiators out of the reverie Lorelei had them under.

As they bull-rushed toward him, Kael threw himself to the ground and grabbed the corpse's bare foot.

Gripping it tightly in his hand, he tried again, "BREATH OF LIFE!"

The pounding of footsteps on the ground sounded like war drums in his ears.

"Breath of Life, Breath of Life, Breath of Life," he whispered, shaking the foot.

The men's heavy breathing was a war cry.

"Breath of Life," he whimpered in a desperate plea.

The barbarians were close enough that he could smell their sour sweat. Wasn't Rome famous for its bathhouses? They obviously didn't frequent them.

He heard the grunt as one of the gladiators hefted his ax.

And then the dead man's toe twitched.

CHAPTER II
DEAD MEAT

At first, Kael thought he had imagined the movement - that it was wishful thinking. Then it happened again. Not just a twitch this time, but a violent spasm of the dead gladiator's entire leg. The corpse's foot shot out, connecting solidly with the bridge of Kael's nose.

The bone made an unpleasant crunch with the impact like an egg cracking, and the sharp pain made stars pinwheel in Kael's vision. He yelped and scrambled backward on his hands and knees, warm blood streaming down his lips and chin, splattering on the packed earth.

Well, that's definitely broken, Kael thought.

He didn't have a particularly handsome face to begin with, and this likely wasn't going to be an improvement. He would have been annoyed had the timing of the assault not been so fortuitous. While he was blinking back the tears in his eyes, an ax blade came down a hair's breadth from his head.

Kael marveled at how timing was everything in life as he scampered farther from the grunting gladiator, who was struggling to pull his ax free to have another go.

A broken nose was a small price to keep his head attached to his shoulders, he decided.

Kael was still thanking whatever gods, guardian angels, or demons were looking out for him when the low, mournful moaning started.

His skin prickled with goosebumps and the hairs on the back of his neck rose.

"Kael. What the hell did you do?" Lorelei demanded, hauling him to his feet and pointing at

the previously inanimate corpse.

It had risen - all six-foot-plus and 300 pounds of him - and was now quite animated, indeed, flailing its arms around and stomping its feet. Entrails spilled from the grievous wound in its abdomen that had ended its mortal life.

No one could survive such an injury. And the other gladiators seemed to recognize that. They paced nervously, their gazes shifting between Kael and Lorelei and the monster they - no, he... Kael hadn't needed her help this time - had created.

The eerie groans it issued made Kael grind his teeth in dismay. But they weren't half as alarming as the single word it began repeating over and over:

"Meat. Meat. Meat."

Most of the gladiators threw in their towels at this point, watching a safe distance, moving closer to the exits as a group.

But of course, there's always one. The would-be hero rose from the ranks of the stunned warriors, charging toward the grisly reanimated corpse.

Perhaps someone would write a poem or a song about this brave young warrior one day... but he wouldn't be around to hear it. The undead thing reached out, grabbed the gladiator's arm, and ripped it off at the shoulder.

The young warrior collapsed, dead before he hit the ground, blood gushing in spurts.

The undead gladiator proceeded to lift the severed arm, examined it, then took a big bite out of it. Once it had chewed and swallowed, it flashed its viscera-coated teeth in a broad grin and contentedly muttered, "Mmm meat."

With this, the circle of warriors around Kael and Lorelei fractured completely, and chaos reigned. Some gladiators backed away from their fallen comrade, while others turned and ran without shame. The whole arena became a cacophony of screams and shouts as the spectators fled for the exits in a stampede, crushing anyone who got in their way.

"Well, solved that problem," Kael announced with some satisfaction as he wiped his bloody nose with the back of his hand, watching the gladiators flee.

Lorelei gazed at him with an expression that was one part wonder and two parts consternation.

"What the actual fuck, Kael? Your *plan* was to make a goddamn undead gladiator? And you think everything is hunky-dory now? Forget the *thing* in outer space... *This* thing you've created is gonna make *more things*. They'll eat half of Europe. And that will just be breakfast. I mean, it's *your* world, not mine, but I don't think starting the zombie apocalypse is the best way to go about saving it."

Kael rolled his eyes. She kind of had a point, but did she always have to be so damn dramatic? "That only happens in movies," he assured her, though he had no basis whatsoever for this beyond hope and idle speculation.

The red hue started leaking back into Lorelei's skin, and her eyes glowed red.

"How do you know?" she demanded.

Kael paused to consider and decided she was being hysterical again. Even if it *could* multiply or procreate or whatever, surely, if he *made* it, he could control it.... Right?

"It's my minion," he informed her.

"Your minion?" Lorelei dead-panned. She didn't sound convinced.

"My minion," Kael affirmed with a nod.

But as he watched the undead warrior rip his fellow gladiator's leg off at the knee and start munching on his foot, Kael wasn't so sure about that either.

"Prove it," Lorelei fired back, crossing her arms over her chest.

Kael scratched his head. "What? How?"

She glared at him like he was the dumbest man in the world. Watching the zombie dig into the dead man's calf like a chicken wing while grunting and rocking back and forth made Kael briefly wonder if she was right.

He consoled himself with the fact that while, yes, the undead gladiator put a bit of a wrinkle in their plans, and no, he wasn't entirely sure he could control it, the guy it was currently devouring hadn't yet turned into a zombie.

That was a good sign. Maybe he was right and that really *did* only happen on TV.

"Make it *do* something, dummy. Like have it put that half-eaten leg down," Lorelei suggested.

Kael wiped more blood off his upper lip and forced a smile that he hoped didn't look as phony as it felt.

"Of course."

He nodded to Lorelei, then turned to address the zombie. "Put that leg down at once," he ordered sternly.

The undead gladiator glanced from Kael to his meal and blinked.

Then it went right back to gorging itself.

CHAPTER 12
FRANK THE MINION

K ael frowned at the creature he'd created as it disregarded his command and resumed sucking the marrow from the dead would-be hero's femur. The slurping noises caused his already queasy stomach to twist into a knot.

Why couldn't anything ever be easy?

With a sigh, Kael turned to Lorelei and said, "I might be a little out of practice."

She barked out a laugh and shook her head. "You think controlling a sentient undead being is the same as taking care of a zombie guinea pig? That whatever brain cells are left up there are gonna bow to your will, just because you resurrected him?"

Kael tilted his head to the side and stroked the stubble on his jaw, looking confused. As a matter of fact, he *had* thought that. "But... he's a minion. Isn't that what minions are supposed to do?" he mused.

Lorelei clucked her tongue. "Kael, technically, *I'm* your minion. I mean, you summoned me. You bound me to you. It's basically the same thing, right? And do I *ever* listen when you tell me what to do?"

Kael didn't have to ponder that one. She most certainly did not. Truth be told, he hadn't stopped to consider what would happen *after* he cast the Breath of Life spell. He'd just assumed the gladiator would leap to the defense of its maker and then kind of... wither and disappear, like in a video game.

Apparently, that wasn't the case.

He grimaced. "Okay. I see your point. So what do we do now? We can't just leave him here to terrorize the countryside."

Lorelai shrugged and twirled a strand of blonde hair around her finger. She looked incredibly attractive, with just a blush of her red demon skin tinting her face. Some utterly irrational part of Kael, that was just happy to be alive despite the zombie problem, wanted to bend her over and rail her right there on the blood-soaked earth of the Colosseum.

He could imagine her plump ass bouncing beneath him and the strangled cries of ecstasy echoing off the stone–

"Hello? EARTH TO KAEL!" Lorelei waved her hands in front of his face, shattering the delicious daydream.

"What?" he grumbled.

"I said, you're right. We're gonna have to bring your *minion* with us."

Kael snorted. "Oh, a fine group we'll be, strolling down the Roman roads. A warlock in a singed, blood-stained designer suit, a demon who refuses to wear her human skin, and a gigantic undead gladiator with his guts leaking out of its stomach."

Lorelei bounced on the balls of her sneaker-clad feet and clapped her hands.

"Yes! It's just wonderful. It's so nice to be out and about again, not cooped up in that stuffy old house. What an adventure!" She gazed thoughtfully at the zombie, still docile and immersed in devouring the dead gladiator. "All we need to do is make sure we have a stockpile of meat, and everything will be fine."

Kael thought that was a bit of an optimistic assessment of the situation, and he found her blasé use of the word 'meat' to describe dead people more than a little disconcerting. But he kept his mouth shut. Mostly because, quite honestly, he thought bringing the zombie with them might, unfortunately, be their only option.

The last time he'd cast the spell, Lorelei had refused to tell him how to release a minion. Because she wanted to keep the zombie guinea pig, of course. She'd tied a little yellow bow around his neck and lovingly fed him ground hamburger three times a day.

The skeleton of Floofy would probably still be following Kael around if he hadn't left his cage door open. Alas, Floofy 'wandered' out the front door – and into a sewer grate. He was pretty sure Lorelei still hadn't quite forgiven him, but being rid of the undead guinea pig was worth her continued ire. And all the windows he'd had to replace when she'd learned of the 'mishap.'

And now, watching her skip around like a schoolgirl, he could tell she was forming the same 'bond' with his zombie.

So he wasn't the least bit surprised when she chimed, "We should give him a name."

And with that, Kael knew that she'd never let him banish it, even if he could figure out how.

"Frank," she suggested with a decisive nod.

Kael's eyes rolled heavenward, and he silently beseeched whatever God had spared him from the angry gladiators to again come to his aid and rid him of both Lorelei and *Frank*.

Aloud, he said, "What kind of name is Frank for a zombie? That's the most ridiculous thing I've ever heard." Kael shook his head. "Furthermore, it's not a pet, Lorelei. It's an undead monster."

The zombie affirmed this fact by coughing up a small bone, which it spat on the ground before muttering, "Meat," again.

Lorelei's eyes had shifted to blue, and she blinked at Kael with that pretty, pleading expression he'd never been able to deny. *That* was the face that had convinced him not to send her back to whatever hell she belonged in.

"But we can keep him, right?" she asked.

Kael grunted and kicked a rock. As it skittered across the hard-packed earth, the zombie dropped the femur and chased after it, more like a puppy playing catch than a bloodthirsty, all-devouring abomination.

"Grab an ax," Kael grumbled. "Help me cut up the body because I don't want it eating me. We'll bring him to the Circle. They'll know what to do with him."

He bent down and picked up an ax.

It didn't register to Kael that he had already gone from calling Frank '*it*' to '*him*'.

To Be Continued...

AFTERWORD

Want to know what happens next? What are Kael and Lorelei going to do with an undead Roman gladiator? Will they save the world, get married, and live happily ever after?

Follow *A Demon's Scorn* and find all Kate's other works here! Linktr.ee/kateseger

ABOUT THE AUTHOR

Kate Seger's writing interweaves fantasy and mythology unto unique tapestries. An introvert, dog mom, and freelance editor, when she's not searching for fairy circles in hopes of being transported to an enchanted kingdom, Kate is immersed in the chaos of her writing process.

She lives with her husband and her rescue dog Gracie on the banks of the Hudson in Westchester County, NY, where, alas, she has found few portals to magical Realms.

Links:
Facebook page: www.facebook.com/katesegerauthor
Facebook group: www.facebook.com/groups/Courtofdreams
Instagram: www.instagram.com/katesegerauthor
Twitter: www.twitter.com/katesegerauthor

THE SOLSTICE LEGACY

LORE NICOLE

CHAPTER

ONE

T he smell of books tingled Emily's nose as she checked in each book from the drop box. Personally, she disliked the drop box. Whether one book was dropped, or several, damage could happen to the covers and pages. Emily hated seeing bent covers. Growing up, books were her escape from the school bullies. The adventures and characters within them were precious gems that should be cared for, not disrespected with creases, tears, and stains. Maybe being a librarian and seeing books come in with damage was not the best career choice for her mental health.

It did come with a few perks. She was able to see all the new books as they came in. The library was usually quiet, which helped on days she had migraines. Lastly, she would rather be home and a recluse, but working here was the next best option, besides working at a morgue or cemetery. She couldn't handle dead bodies. Even when her grandfather passed away a couple weeks ago, she couldn't go to the wake because her family had decided on an open casket, despite knowing her feelings about it. She did go to the funeral out of a sense of duty. The coffin was closed tight, so she felt less anxious being there.

She was just checking in the last two books when her phone went off, playing Carol of the Bells. Taking it out of her jean jacket pocket, she barely glanced at the caller ID before clicking the power button to silence and ignore it. Lawyer Avery Moores had been calling multiple times a day since her grandfather's death. Something about his will. While Emily loved her grandfather and the crazy stories he used to tell, she knew he wouldn't have much to pass on. Leaving the calmness of her daily routine to visit with a lawyer held no appeal, and she didn't see the value in it.

Hearing the little tinkle from the bell over the library door, Emily didn't bother looking up, since it was probably just another regular coming in for another book to read.

"Hello, Emily," a man's voice rang out. It was meant to sound pleasant and light, but it grated on Emily's nerves.

"Hello, Mister Moores," she mimicked back. She knew she sounded childish, but being only eighteen, she knew she could play it off as being young. It wasn't like he knew what maturity level she had.

"I figured if you were going to ignore my calls, I might as well find you in person," he started. "I believe you misunderstand who your grandfather was and what his estate holds."

"My grandfather liked to tell tales of grandeur, Mr. Moore. He lived simply and invited my family over if he felt like it, or was even around."

"When was the last time you were at his place?" he asked.

"Probably five years ago," she said. Trying to ignore him, she started to wheel around the returns cart to put books back out on their shelves. Emily hoped he wouldn't follow, but she was not that lucky.

"Over the last five years, your memories could have changed based on input from others. They could be altered by time and showing you things that seem less valuable, dark, or boring." She had stopped the cart to place a few books and was pleased when he ran into the back. A pained groan escaped his lips, and he grunted. "Please, I will leave you alone if you just meet me at the estate after you are done with work."

Emily figured nothing would change her mind from seeing the place, and it would be a waste of time. However, if he would finally leave her be, then the short trip could be worthwhile after all. She turned his way and gave a strained smile. "Fine. Six o'clock it is."

CHAPTER

TWO

At five o'clock, she reluctantly closed up the library. Before leaving, she had turned around to see if any books needed to be put away first. She didn't see any and gave up trying to procrastinate. She got into her older dark blue car and began the half hour drive from town to the countryside where she remembered her grandfather living. It had been long enough since her last visit to make her cautious enough.

With it being Summer, she at least had more hours of sunlight to see the roads with. If she was lucky, she would head back home in it, too. The country roads could be dangerous during twilight and hours of darkness. Not only could a corner be missed or wrongly judged, but loose gravel could drag a car into the grater ditches, and animals had a tendency to run out into the roads. She'd rather make it back to town with her car in one piece and still lacking dents.

She pulled up in front of a large house. It could be described as a mansion with its many windows, turrets, and fencing all around that was trying to keep an overrun garden corralled. In her memories, she could see a dark home that was nowhere close to this size. There was a garden, but not all of this old scroll-decorated fencing. *Am I in the right place?* she thought to herself as she double-checked the map on her phone. *It says I am. Could my memories really change this much over five years?*

She was still staring at the house from the driveway, trying to decide if she should walk in when Mr. Moores pulled up beside her. He got out and came around his car to stand beside her, staring at the house in solidarity. "Does it look like how you remember it?" he asked with a smirk.

"Not at all," she replied softly, still in disbelief. "How could my memories be this far off?"

"I cannot tell you for sure since I am only the lawyer for the estate. What I can tell you is that things might be explained by a letter your grandfather left behind for you. It is inside, on top of his desk in the office." He took a moment to let his words sink in. "This place is now yours," he stated, handing her the keys. She took them automatically and just stared at them, lying in the palm of her hand. *Hers?* "Your grandfather left the entire estate to you. The house, bank account, his cars, the land, everything that is here and at the bank is yours, including the safe deposit box. You were the one he decided would carry on his legacy. He said you earned it, but don't ask me what he meant because he didn't explain. I will take off and let you decide if you go in or not tonight."

He quickly got into his car and left just like he said, leaving her to her own thoughts out here with no one else but the wild animals and plants. *This is all mine? But what about my mom and brother? They were grandpa's relatives too. I wonder what grandpa meant by I earned it. My memories don't match the place I'm even seeing right now. How can I earn something I don't remember?*

Her thoughts raced as she tried to decide what she was going to do. Even though it was summer and she had a couple hours of daylight left, she didn't want to be out here in the dark if she lost track of time. She often lost time as she read books, so she knew it could happen if she explored this place. Tomorrow was Saturday. The library would close at one in the afternoon and not reopen until Monday morning. Perks of small-town living. *Tomorrow,* she told herself. *I'll come back tomorrow.*

CHAPTER
THREE

Yet, she did not return that weekend. She felt some sort of apprehension she could not place. She thought about the house and her grandfather all week, trying to fix her memories but not succeeding. It was the next weekend when she finally resolved that she must figure the mysteries out.

After closing up the library, she went to the local gas station to grab an already-cooked pizza and some drinks and snacks. She didn't know what was in the house for appliances and figured she shouldn't trust any of the food there to still be good. While pizza and snacks weren't the best food choices she could make, it was only for the weekend, she tried convincing herself. Although she knew she made bad choices all the time. That's why she had the weight she did. She read books over exercising, ate easy food over fresh cooking, and enjoyed watching television on her time off work.

She wasn't concerned about having a romantic interest and told herself that she was fine with herself the way she was. Even if that was a lie. She just refused to dwell on her self-esteem issues and the emotional ones that lay in the dark recesses of her past. Her weight was more like her personal armor. If she didn't attract attention, then she could ignore past events and not have to deal with them.

However, her grandfather's estate was a part of her past that she couldn't ignore any longer. She was completely confused by the contradictions between her memory and the actual place. The confusion bothered her all week, no matter what she tried to do to put off visiting it again. She had to get it done and over with. Maybe she could sell the place and forget all about it. She just needed to work out why her grandpa chose her for it all. *If I sell it, I would feel obligated to share anything earned with my mom and brother, no matter if their names were on the will or not.* Not only were her memories at war, but her own ethics on the situation she was presented with were too.

It didn't take long before she was standing in front of her car, holding onto her food and staring at the front door. Emily had a feeling this was going to be a pivotal moment in her life and was slightly afraid of what she might see and learn inside. She read about discoveries; she did not do them well herself. Well, then again, in her short years, she didn't have much experience with shocking discoveries or mind-blowing revelations, either.

Whatever happens, my grandpa thought I could do it. He left this place to me, so let's hope I live up to what he expected.

She straightened her shoulders and grabbed the bags and pizza a little tighter. She hastened through the front gate, up the porch steps, and stood in front of the large wrought iron double doors before losing what courage she had. There was a bench beside the doors on which she sat her pizza and bags so she could grab the key from inside her purse.

Once she slid the key into the lock and turned it, the heavy-looking old doors slid open with surprising ease. Not wanting to chance the nearby animals with her food, she gathered it all up to take inside, hoping the kitchen or dining rooms were close. She was able to shut the doors with her feet for now without setting anything down. She noticed the office on the left and the living room on the right as she walked through the entry hall. There was a closed door she assumed was a bathroom before she came across a large open kitchen that flowed into the grand dining room. Her arms were straining as much as her eyes were to take it all in, and she almost dropped everything down with a harrumph on the island counter.

The outside looked like a historical mansion, while the inside was grand and updated. The kitchen even had hanging pots and pans over the island, a double wall oven, and what looked like a huge gas range with a copper range hood. Everything was dark or wood-toned but felt warm. Even though her grandfather had passed away a month before, it didn't look like there was dust anywhere. Emily wondered if someone came around to clean like a maid or if it just happened to remain clean. She made a mental note to ask the lawyer about any staff and bills.

Emily took her time in the kitchen. She ate a slice of pizza as slowly as possible while it was still half warm. That didn't take long enough before she was placing her drinks and the rest of the pizza in the fridge. After closing the fridge door, she stood there and stared up the hallway in the direction of her grandpa's office. Her mind played tricks on her eyes as the office looked like it was getting closer. *Why am I so afraid of this? I just need to buckle down and get it over with. If it is going to change my life, it's better to know sooner than later. Right?*

As she was talking to herself, Emily made her way to the office. She replied to her own "right?" with an echoing "right" as she stood over the desk. Sure enough. Right on top was a letter in a fancy envelope, complete with a wax seal.

CHAPTER
FOUR

E mily stood there for a moment, having a staring contest with the wax seal as if it would blink in loss and she could leave. She let out a sigh before picking it up and trying to gently lift the seal without tearing it. Once it released itself from the lower part, she lifted the top with the seal dangling and removed the letter from inside. Even the letter was fancy! Creamy, rich, textured paper and what looked like penmanship was done using a quill and inkpot. *Hopefully, I won't be expected to uphold these fanciful letters,* she thought before she began to read.

My dear Emmalynn, it started off with. Only her grandfather ever called her by her given, and lengthy, name. Since she was young, people would think they heard Emily when she told them her name, and after a while, she decided to just go with it. It was much simpler nodding than trying to spell it out for them to pronounce it correctly.

My dear Emmalynn,

If you are reading this, it means that I have passed on from this life at age seventy-five on the Summer Solstice. You are probably wondering how I knew the day that I would die. That is the burden of being a timekeeper, but you do not know about that yet. Your memories have been altered over the years to keep you safe from those who wish to have our abilities by any means necessary. However, now that I am gone, you must take up our family's legacy and keep our present lives safe from those who would wish to change things.

I know. None of this makes sense right now. You most likely believe this letter to be the insane ramblings of an old man. Trust me. I know. I, too, thought my grandmother was crazy when I got my own letter many years ago. But I hope you keep reading, and trust in the old man you can remember bits enough of, to consider what I am about to ask you to do.

I hope you are curious enough to want your actual memories back; for that foggy film over them you have to be gone. I hope you wish to remember the stories I told you and the adventures I took you on with me. Memories that will help you remember all I have taught you about being a time-keeper. Please, do not give up our family legacy and let it fall into the wrong hands.

If you have read this far, I would hope it means that you are intrigued and willing to continue. There is a drawer in my desk that only opens willingly to the appointed timekeeper. It's the shallow one on the top right side; a person could overlook it, as there is no handle. Just touch your fingers upon it for a moment, and it should slide open. Inside is a pocket watch that I wish for you to hold between your hands, close to your chest, as if you were praying. Then all should be made clear to you.

I love you, my Emmalynn. You may think of yourself as only an adventurer in books, but from the journeys we took together, you can do so much more. I chose you to be the timekeeper from the time you were four, and my tales would light up your eyes. Taking up the legacy means you get our family estate and everything with it. Ask Mr. Moores any questions about our family home and holdings, but beware. He does not know of the meaning behind you being a legacy holder.

You should tell no one about being a timekeeper, a Protector of Time. That is, unless you can fully trust in them to keep the secret, such as a soul mate that you marry. Just know that some of those who wish to change things may disguise themselves in your life as friends and lovers. Please, be careful, my dear. I have complete faith in you and your instincts. Trust your mind and heart over your eyes, as seeing can be deceiving, and everything will turn out in the end.

Forever with you,

PopPop
Lawrence Carnell

CHAPTER
FIVE

Emily stared at her grandfather's penmanship for a long while before slowly setting it down. If what the letter said was true, she should probably place it in the secret drawer so no one else could ever see it. Well, if she opens the drawer. She really wanted to just think of her grandpa as senile in his old age,too ignore everything he wrote, but it bothered her that her memories had been altered.

She was not sure if the altering scared her the most or the idea that people were basically hunting her for something she had no idea about. She also didn't know if she wanted her original memories. Emily was certain that there would be bad memories because life was never just about the good parts. The bad had to even them out, or nothing was ever learned. It was tempting to think that she could remember her own adventures with him, but it also scared her that she could be solely responsible for her current time. So many conflicting emotions, Emily wasn't certain of anything.

Just a week ago, she was just a librarian. Just a young adult with her own apartment and bills. Her only responsibilities were work, paying the bills on time, and remembering to eat if she got lost in reading a book. No children. No pets. Yet, now, it sounded like she was essentially responsible for the entire world.

What if I don't want that responsibility? Will someone out there really change time? Would I even know if they did or just think things went to hell on their own? Even if I wouldn't know, do I currently feel like I could let those things happen? The self-debate was both emotionally and physically draining, and she flopped down into the plush office chair, grabbing hold of the desk when the wheels tried whisking her away.

Just as she grabbed onto the edge, her ring and pinky fingers just barely brushed that shallow drawer front. It seemed to glow as it slowly slid open, as if it were afraid she would slam it shut. Although that was tempting to do, the glow mesmerized her, and Emily realized it was not the drawer but what was held inside that was beckoning her. She thought she heard her name being whispered. *"Emmalynn. Emmalynn."*

Thoughts no longer racing in her mind, her hand reached towards the pocket watch as if on its own accord. Emily gently picked it up and held it in front of her to examine the swirl design on its shell. The swirls made up something similar to a sacred tree design, but with smaller swirls filling in what would have been the blank areas. It was certainly interesting to look at, but did she think it held the power alluded to in the letter? *Well, let's just get this over with and find out, shall I?*

The letter told her to hold it between her hands as if she were saying a prayer. While it had been a while since she had been to church, she could at least remember how she held her hands together in front of her chest during silent prayer. Some people placed their hands closer to their faces or down into their laps, but since her grandfather seemed to know her well, she knew he meant for her to do it her own instinctual way.

Emily held it between her hands as they rested on the desktop, surprised that the metal watch was warm and not cold from sitting inside the desk. She slowly raised her hands up to her chest, not sure of what she expected to happen. She definitely didn't expect what happened next.

CHAPTER
SIX

A blinding light flashed from between her hands as Emily was thrown backward. It was a good thing she had been sitting when she held the pocket watch. Just sitting caused the chair to roll, and its back struck the fireplace, her head just inches from hitting the mantle. Even without striking her head, she was still in shock. As the glow faded, all she could do was stare at her hands as they now lay open, showing the watch off in their center.

Once the glow was completely gone, the watch looked perfectly normal, and she questioned her sanity. The noise of a bird pecking on the window to her right startled her, and her hands flew up. The pecking cut off abruptly. In fact, the whole bird just sat staring at her. Emily returned the stare until she realized leaves were no longer moving with the wind out in the garden. *Are they frozen?* she thought in awe. It slowly sunk in that she actually stopped time.

She found herself having a flashback. When she was twelve, she was looking to participate in her school's small science fair. Back then, Emily was into fossils and wanted to create something about dinosaur fossils, like a poster with pictures. She was excitedly telling her grandpa about her project when he told her they could use real fossils. She thought he meant those small ones found in rock shops, since the bigger, more real ones were in museums.

How could she know he would whisk her away through time? When they stopped, they had arrived inside a nest of pterodactyls, a mom and her babies. She remembered him throwing his hands up and the babies' beaks all froze in place. Everything went silent and still, except for them. Around the nest were small bones from other, smaller creatures. He told her to quickly grab a few, and they tucked them into her messenger bag. Next thing she knew, he placed one arm around her and readied the pocket watch. He waved his spare hand to let time restart as they disappeared back to their own present day.

She remembered opening her back and finding the bones still in there. Except these bones were not clean and new looking anymore, but stained from time. They were as if she had found them in the ground and cleaned them up. Her grandfather helped her figure out the animals from which they came just in time for her mom to come back to get her. Her mom asked where they found the fossils, and she remembered her grandpa telling her they had taken a quick trip to an exhibit. While it was a lie, was it really? Emily smiled at him as they shared the secret.

How did I ever forget about that? she wondered. The letter had mentioned her memories being tampered with and foggy. But to actually have forgotten that science project and time with her grandpa completely? She had no words. *Oh! The bird!* she thought as she remembered the reason for her flashback. Her grandfather had waved his hand to release the pterodactyls, so she waved her hand toward the bird... and nothing happened.

Am I supposed to do something else? Hmm, what do the characters in fantasy books usually do in this situation? she asked herself as she stood there, the only living thing in the currently still world. *FOCUS!* she thought suddenly. *The characters always think about their intentions and then push them out through their magic. Do I actually believe I have magic, though? Obviously I do, since I froze a bird and the rest of the world in time. Unless I'm dreaming. In that case, I should have magic and be able to do whatever I want in my dream. Might as well enjoy this in case I wake up soon.*

She decided to give the hand waving another try, except while trying to envision the bird and plants moving this time. Trying to keep the vision while attempting to push out magic and wave her hand was harder than she thought it would be. She was focused so hard that it surprised her when the bird started pecking again.

Why does the pecking sound like it's knocking at me?

SEVEN

Convinced that there was no way a bird could be knocking, she walked up to the window, expecting it to fly away. Up closer, she could tell that it was a raven, which she rarely saw around here. It also stayed in place on the windowsill and tilted its head at her as if she were the odd one. They both remained still until the raven gave one more tap with its beak. Maybe it really is knocking. It wouldn't be the strangest thing to happen to me today.

She reached over, unlatched the window lock, and slid it up. There was no screen, and it was as if the bird knew that. As soon as it was up far enough, the raven took quick steps toward her and into the house. Emily gasped as it flew off the ledge and went to land on the desk.

"Well, aren't you just a curious little thing?" she questioned out loud.

"Me?" it replied. "It took you long enough to let me in." It sounded like an older boy's voice as it spoke.

Wait, it just spoke? she thought for a second and then collapsed to the floor.

~

I MUST HAVE FAINTED, Emily thought as she realized she was lying on the hardwood floor. She turned her head from side to side, eyes still closed, to try and remember how she ended up down there. *Pocket watch. Blinding light. A pesky bird. Froze the world. Talking bird. Talking bird?!*

Her eyes popped open, and right above her was the raven, looking down at her from the corner of her grandfather's desk. In case she hadn't recovered yet, she didn't want to risk standing when she sputtered, "You talked. B-but, you're a bird!"

"Came to that conclusion yourself, did ya? If you are this slow, how in the world will you keep the world safe? I always trusted your grandfather's judgment, but he might have needed to think you through a bit more..."

"There you go. Talking some more. Either I'm dreaming, or I've completely lost my mind."

"If you were dreaming, you wouldn't be waking up from fainting then, would you?"

Considering what the actual bird was saying, she had to agree she wasn't dreaming. "Okay then. I've just lost it."

"Sorry. I wish that were the case, but it's not. Your grandfather chose you to take over the legacy as a Protector of Time, and I am the unfortunate Guardian of Time that was given orders to aid you. Well, aid your family lineage. Maybe I can ask for a trade..." the raven mumbled more under his breath.

"If you are to help me, and you seem to know who I am, who the heck are you? Or what are you?"

"You've read books," he started. "You've probably read about witch familiars that could talk, right?" She responded with a nod, not wanting to say anything else that caused him to doubt her intelligence. "I am like that. A familiar but for Protectors like you, your grandfather, and your great-great grandmother. The name is Tobias, by the way," he said, interrupting himself. "I am to help get you up to speed and remain at your side in case I am needed. These first couple of days, your memories will slowly return, and then we can get down to business."

"I take it I won't be returning to work or my home then?"

"Now you are thinking smart! You will want to stay here in case you accidentally use your powers before you get them under control. This estate is paid for through the legacy your family built, and you don't need to worry about money or bills. There's plenty of money to last in the bank." He paused to preen himself. *Maybe he had an itch?* "You have a much more important job now, although you won't be able to talk about it to anyone. Hmm. Maybe you can say you inherited this place, since you did, and that you are pursuing a dream of writing. If I remember you correctly, you were always reading and writing as a child, so it wouldn't be too far-fetched, right?"

I knew him as a child? she wondered. *Gosh, I really hope my memories return quickly so I don't have any more surprises. This fainting does not help with headaches at all...*

CHAPTER

EIGHT

E mily was thankful she was not the only librarian. Besides her, there was the head librarian and another who was new and part-time. When she called the head librarian Mary to explain her inheritance and needing to get things in order, she recommended that Michael take her full-time spot. He was kind, efficient, and loved books as much as she did. She felt that he could handle the extra hours well. Luckily, Mary agreed and accepted the sudden resignation.

Emily was both sad that she was leaving as a librarian and also excited for her future. As long as she wouldn't be expected to run, unless being chased. Then again, she would probably chance playing dead instead if it came to that. Hopefully, she would be a great protector and live up to her grandfather's expectations. If she went on as many successful adventures as he had, maybe she could be a writer after all and not let it just be her cover for family and friends. No one would really believe the stories were real, especially if she changed up details, as time travel was thought of as pure fantasy.

Emily had resigned on Sunday when the library was closed so Mary could work out the schedule before the new week started. Her food and drinks had lasted her through the weekend, but she would need to return to town for more on Monday. She also needed to begin packing and moving things from her apartment. She wouldn't need the furniture, so maybe she could leave it furnished so the landlord could find a tenant faster to replace her. They were only contracted for a month at a time, but she still felt bad giving him short notice. Barry was older and quite nice. He was one of the few willing to rent to her before she had the chance to build her credit and rental history.

So much to do and so little time! Emily thought that not having her library job would open up her schedule to take care of everything. However, Tobias had other plans. He didn't want to wait for all of her memories to sink in before starting her training. So far, she'd only had a few memories come while sleeping in her dreams. Just little trips she had taken with her grandfather, like visiting Salem to watch an actual witch trial for her history class creative essay in eighth grade. It didn't hold much for her, as far as learning how to use her powers, but it was a great memory she loved having back, nonetheless.

These dreams weren't enough for Tobias. He seemed to be really impatient, and Emily often wondered how her grandfather had reacted to him when they first met. *I'll have to ask the cranky old bird sometime,* she thought, meaning Tobias, not her dead grandfather. *Although, if I go back in time, could I actually ask my grandfather? Maybe I have to ask Tobias about it, or would he freak out?*

These thoughts ran through her mind as she was trying to pack up all of her groceries, hygiene essentials, clothes, bedding, knickknacks, books... So many things she hadn't thought of needing to move! She left home with only the bare amounts and now had to move ten times as much stuff. One car trip was quickly turning into five. How could she have accumulated all of this in less than a year?!

It took all of Monday and most of Tuesday to transfer it all. The rest of Tuesday was spent getting things she needed from the grocery store and trying to organize the kitchen, so she knew where everything was. Emily hadn't even started unpacking anything else except for things like her toothbrush, which she had put in a travel bag. Even her clothes were still in suitcases lying open on the guest bedrooms floor.

Emily didn't know where or how her grandfather had died, so she refused to take over his room without thoroughly cleaning it first. Since she had the guest bedroom, it might take a while before Tobias would quit pestering her enough for a deep clean. Exhausted and ready to fall asleep that night, Tobias had finally reached the end of his patience. "Tomorrow, you will train," he said. "Hopefully, hands-on learning will spur your memories. Unless you happen to dream them all up tonight, which I highly doubt."

Now she was tired yet wide awake with apprehension. *Great,* she thought. *Please let me get some sleep. If I could just get all the memories back by tomorrow, that would be fabulous,* she prayed, not sure to whom. *If I'm a protector with magic, does that mean I'm not a Christian? What would my mom think?* Different scenarios played out in her mind before her body gave in, and she finally dozed off...

CHAPTER
NINE

She woke up to a very sharp pain on her head. Emily was rubbing at the spot on her forehead as she reluctantly opened her eyes. Squinting, she made out the shape of Tobias perched on her chest. Thankfully, there was a comforter between her and his sharp claws. "Did you seriously peck me?" she said, shocked.

"As a bird, I don't have many options," he replied. "You didn't wake up when I landed on you or called your name. Trust me. Pecking you wasn't my first choice. Now I have the taste of your sweat on my beak," he complained as he feigned retching noises.

"If you ever do that again, I will start waking up swinging," she warned.

"Yeah, yeah. If you are quick enough," he taunted back. He flew off from her and landed on the dresser. "Well, get up! What are you waiting for?" he questioned and started preening himself.

"For you to leave? You might be a bird, but you said 'as a bird' if I recall correctly. That means you have other forms, and one could be human. I refuse to get up with you watching me."

"Fine," he huffed. "I'll go to the kitchen and wait for you to come down for breakfast. Don't take too long, or I will return!"

She watched him fly out her doorway and cautiously sat up, trying to see out her door if he was perched outside. Seeing the way was clear, she climbed out of the nice, warm bed and stretched in her fuzzy unicorn pajamas. *I would have been less embarrassed if he saw me naked than seeing me in kiddish PJs,* she mused, giving herself a chuckle. She knew he was serious about returning, so she quickly took a tee shirt and jeans out of her suitcase and went to the bathroom to get dressed and ready for the day. Whatever the day would bring, she figured a comfortable outfit would be her best choice.

As she stepped into the kitchen, Tobias spoke up from the island, making her jump. "Make sure you get enough protein. Never know how long we will be away and if there will be food. A wee bit jumpy today, are we?" he teased.

Emily gave him a glare before walking to the fridge. She opened the door and spotted the eggs and cheese. Getting sausage links from the freezer drawer, she took the items to the counter and then grabbed tortilla shells from the cupboard. She cooked up cheesy scrambled eggs as the precooked links warmed in the microwave. She tossed them together into the tortilla and added a little salsa before rolling it up into a breakfast burrito.

She pretended to watch out the window while eating as slowly as possible. He made her jump so she would annoy him back by being slow. Maybe one day he would learn not to irritate her if he wanted her to actually do things on his time. As Emily reached the last bite, she heard a low grumble "finally" from behind her. She couldn't help but smile as she took her plate and glass to the sink and started the faucet. Usually, she hated washing dishes. Today the task would give her pleasure knowing it would get to him as she took even longer. Then, after dishes, she had to return the perishable foods she didn't finish using back to the fridge. This, too, she did slowly and tried not to look his way.

When all the tasks were complete, Emily sighed internally and started up the hallway to the office. Almost to the door, she looked over her shoulder and saw that Tobias was preening himself again. She crooked her brow and asked, "Well, are you coming?"

"I don't know," he replied. "Are you finally ready?" She watched him take off, and he flew straight for her. Afraid of what he might do, she quickly ducked into the office. "Oh, now you can move," she heard.

Emily walked around the desk and touched her fingers to the secret drawer front. She watched it slide open for only the second time. Packing and taking care of different things over the last few days allowed her to stay away from the pocket watch after she had returned it to its dark home in the desk. Now she gingerly picked it up, afraid that it was going to send her flying again. It was still warm in her hand like before, but when she placed her hands together, nothing happened.

"You already received the transfer of power," the annoying black bird reminded her. "It's not like it will give you more." His feathers shook a bit, and she realized the sounds she thought were coughing were really him laughing at her. She crossed her arms in indignation and crooked an eyebrow his way while waiting for him to finish.

"It's not like I know what it can do. I don't even know what I can really do. If you are finished mocking me, want to tell me your plans?"

"I don't really have a plan," he confessed. "The best way to teach protector ways is just to have you do things."

"So. You don't have a plan. Anything can happen, and we just have to figure it out?"

"Yup! That's pretty much it," Tobias said cheerfully, which made her nervous. "I'm going to land on your shoulder if you can raise an arm up." Staring at his shiny, black claws that could tear through her skin, she raised her arm slowly and trusted that he needed her alive. He surprised her by landing softly, and his nails barely poked in. He was heavier than he looked, though, and she let out a small grunt.

"If you are ready," he continued, "push down on the watch button to start the time on it. Then place your hands together like you had when you received your power. Just please keep your arm up as you do it, so I don't lose my balance and hurt you." He waited for her to do as told and then said, "Think about a time and place, really focus on it, and direct magic into the pocket watch."

She couldn't help but close her eyes to help focus. Trying hard to think of a time and place while pushing magic through her hands and into the watch was challenging. Emily almost thought it didn't work because the environment didn't change temperature and was eerily quiet. At first.

Emily felt hands pat her shoulders and then heard a young lady's voice. "Milady? Are ye well? It wilnot be good to fall ill for ye wedding day."

Oh shit.

AFTERWORD

Was this enough to capture your attention and ensnare you to read more? You can read more about Emily by visiting AuthorsoftheQuill.com for the link to the serial version or subscribe to the newsletter to find out when this story will release in ebook and print. While visiting her website, look into the other stories by Lore Nicole, as well as those from her other pen names she sweetly calls her "other personalities."

About the Author

Lore Nicole lives on a family dairy farm with her husband and three children in Southwestern Wisconsin. Books were always her escape in childhood, and she hopes to provide that escape for others through her writing. She may also include hard situations, based on personal experience, in hopes that the stories help readers feel less alone in their own lives. One example is her battle with endometriosis, which is the basis for her newest novella titled "Moon Contract." You can find it here: https://www.books2read.com/Moon-Contract . You can also discover more from her at www.AuthorsoftheQuill.com or follow her on Facebook @writerlorenicole.

As Many Times As You Wish

THOMAS VAN BOENING

E verything felt heavy, and everything ached. I recognized my family around me, but I could not get my brain to spark the right neurons to get my mouth to speak. My breathing was on autopilot, and each time it took what little strength I tried to muster to get a word out was taken in an ongoing cycle of struggle.

I tried and tried to say anything. A mutter, a single syllable, anything to tell my loved ones that I was alright, despite laying in a hospital bed.

Doctors and family tried coaxing a response that would have been considered alert and aware. My grandkids tried playing music from some of my favorite records, but I couldn't hum along like they were hoping. I appreciated hearing The Beatles, Buddy Holly, Fats Domino, Sha Na Na, The Beach Boys, and Jimi Hendrix. It was better than the consistent beeping of the machines I was hooked up to and the droning of ongoing chatter from the doctors and nursing staff.

Then they gave up with the rock and roll after a few days.

I knew if Cheryl was here, I could get out of this. But she wasn't, and I had a good feeling I was going to be joining her in the hereafter very soon.

Except it was soon. Days and days of this agony went on. I attempted one or two genuine efforts to get my eyes to blink whenever doctors asked questions, but even this was beyond my capacity.

This horrifying predicament was like being stuck in concrete, except nothing covered me but the hospital bedsheets and the various cords monitoring me and feeding my body nutrients via an IV tube. To me, that little amount was heavier than the world, making everything I could do, say, or control seemed impossible. The paralysis gave me more and more anxiety as though I were locked out of my own nervous system, and the key to unlocking it could be in bumfuck Egypt for all I knew.

After so many attempts and so many dead-ends in my brain, I just couldn't mentally gather the energy to do anything.

There was no more fight left in me.

The kids and grandkids took turns visiting with me. Playing my records again and singing old rock and roll tunes to comfort me. All the while, someone was holding either of my hands as I slept, hoping it wasn't the last time.

My family, I thought as my vision faded. My wonderful, loving family.

Then silence.

More silence.

Then a moment of silent bewilderment and vibrant color and sensations is what I remembered next.

The relief was incredible. Like I'd just awoken from the best rest I've had in decades, or just shed the worst hangover ever with a simple catnap.

I could move my arms and hands for the first time in weeks as I rubbed my eye sockets.

My vision came back into focus. Except, that wasn't quite right. It was more like a pixelated screen catching up to the visual data from a 2000s HDTV screen. Except, there was no monitor in front of me, and I checked my face and eyes for a VR headset that wasn't there, for sure.

And I wasn't lying in a hospital bed as I had been for weeks. I was sitting in what looked like a mid-century office. Something like a 1960s corporate high-rise executive room. Something that was once futuristic, but looked comically retro, like the furniture of the old Jetsons cartoon I watched as a kid.

The desk in front of me had all four legs coming out at an angle to match the space-age style everyone was doing in the late 50s and early 60s. And my brown leather chair looked like an odd basin with an oval-shaped back to it.

Perhaps I was just dreaming in a coma, I thought. Like a really bad fever dream.

"Hi dad," a familiar voice said while leaning through an open door in the adjoining room to my right. "Feeling better?"

I truly was. Then I looked at my hands and saw no IV hooked into my arm, and I fully realized I wasn't struggling to move from my stroke.

Seeing Tristan like this was surprising because he looked a lot younger. Forty entire years younger, I estimated.

My son repeated the question as he walked to the other side of the desk. He was still taller than me, a little heavier set, and was wearing the same frameless glasses he had since 2011. And he still had his hair buzzed. I never hated the look, but I wish he'd get a professional barber to give him something in style.

This is all familiar somehow, I thought. That stroke did a number on me.

"Tristan, I've never been better. What did the doctors do to me?"

"Dad, there's only one thing I can tell you, and why you've recovered this well. You're dead."

It was curious to receive that kind of news so casually. It was like I had heard this news before. And it was completely unsurprising that I wasn't bothered by this news. I was just elated that I could move again.

"Oh. Well, that's alright. So... is this-?"

"Not heaven," my son said. "It's better. At least, I think it is."

"Better?"

"Oh, yeah. For a true afterlife to be a paradise for everyone, this place is catered to every individual code in the digitized world."

"Code?"

Tristan smiled. "Call it your code, spirit, essence, soul, avatar. Whichever term you prefer, you're correct. It's all the same here inside the world of After."

I had an initial urge to rub my temples, but I wasn't that confused.

"So, what is this place?"

"'After' is the name of the place," Tristan said. "It's not the afterlife, but it's an extra step toward it anyway. It all depends on what you decide. But I'm getting way ahead of myself. Come. Walk with me, won't you? I bet you've been wanting to move around for some time."

I did. I stood easier than I had in decades. I was nearly shocked when my knees didn't ache, pop, or crackle, and thrilled when I kept stride with Tristan like I was his age. I followed him from the office to the door he came in, and on the other side I saw a long white hallway with thousands of dark gray doors. It looked like it went on for miles, and I was sure I couldn't see the end of it.

"What is this, the Matrix?"

"Hold that thought," Tristan said as he closed the door behind us.

Then he opened the first door to his left.

Inside was an old hospital room. A woman was in labor, howling as the doctor between her legs instructed her to just give one more push.

The woman panting and screaming was someone I remembered well, but she was also someone that died almost thirty years ago.

"Mom?" I asked. "Where's dad?"

I realized the question sounded preposterous.

Tristan put a hand on my shoulder. "While you were born, grandpa was frantically pacing in the lobby. It was 1949, after all. It wasn't usual for spouses to be in the delivery room back then. Luckily for grandma, she was in labor for only twelve hours to bring you into the world."

"How interesting," I said. "So, time travel is possible after you die?"

Tristan closed the door as the baby's head entered the world and cried its first sound.

"This hallway is your life," he said. "And as you can see, it's a pretty long one. What we saw just now was a rendering of your memory. So, yes. Time travel is a possibility in the world of After."

My son didn't open every door as we conversed. I did notice on each brass plaque there was a date inscribed.

"That's not possible," I said. "That had to be one heck of a performance to make someone who looked like my mom-"

"It looked like grandma because that *was* grandma," Tristan said. "I promise everything you are seeing is real. Virtual reality on this scale is as real as you want it to be. It's alright, though. It's common for everyone to not believe what they see at the end of a life-loop."

"Life-loop?"

Tristan closed his eyes and instead of irritation, I saw patience as he gave a soft sigh. Then he curled his finger for me to follow him.

"Alright, Dad. What's one of your favorite memories as a kid?"

"What does that have to do with anything right now? This is the strangest dream I've ever had."

"Please, trust me on this. I will prove it to you. I'm sure you have many favorite times as a kid, but what's the first memory that came to mind just now?"

"Oh," I started. "My childhood? That was so long ago."

"Think it over," Tristan insisted. "I have a pretty good idea what it is, but I'll let you say it anyway."

"Oh... Probably the time I stood up to Alan Lowe. I never told you about him, but he'd torment and pick on other kids every day because he was held back a year when I was in third grade. In retrospect, I feel like he was an unwanted child from a very poor family, and he took his anger out on others. But I still stand by what I did to him."

Tristan hummed. "Right this way."

After a minute, he opened a door on the right. Instead of another room, the doorway led to an open field on a playground. The same playground I spent many morning and afternoon recesses. I smelled the faint odor of cattle feedlots with the breeze blowing toward town.

Memories of my dad came, calling the reeking stench of distant cow shit 'the smell of money' on many occasions. I snicker at this, but Tristan doesn't notice.

The trees were turning, and I guessed it was early October as it was still warm outside.

While walking I saw plenty of kids in fifties clothing or patched-up forties clothing if they were hand-me-downs. Near the end of the muddy football field, I saw a commotion of several kids surrounding two others.

I saw a pudgy pimple-stricken kid that could still stop in my tracks. The same kid that gave me plenty of Indian burns, wedgies, and every other schoolyard mode of roughhousing just because he could. Alan Lowe stood on top of another boy in a red and white striped shirt with blue suspender pants. That boy was me, in fifth grade. I had a bloody nose, and I had the immediate goal to avenge the new clothes my parents had spent good money on.

I saw the world of Hastings, Nebraska, in 1960 as kids hollered at the tumult between Alan and me. The screaming turned into cheers when my eleven-year-old counterpart kicked upward and struck into Alan's gonads, and he was down with his voice squealing an octave higher, and squirming in a fetal position for a good minute as my younger self walked away to the nurse's office while the other kids cheered.

"He never hurt me again," I said. "This is weird."

"It's your life," Tristan said. "Again, what you're seeing is a rendering of your memory, and every door we go through contains another to witness. After is a perfected simulated replica of everything. Down to the flecks of dirt on your face and the breeze in the air."

129

"How is this possible?"

Tristan closed the door and beckoned me to follow further down the hallway. "The world of After is one of humanity's best inventions. Several generations of research and development finally catching up to everyone's dream to live forever."

"But I'm dead," I said.

"The afterlife is where you spend the rest of eternity," Tristan said. "Digital or otherwise. Your brain was scanned and preserved a week before your death, replicating every connection between every neuron within your amygdala, your neocortex, your hippocampus, and all that stuff. Every one of your memories and the memories from millions of others is responsible for recreating the past in perfect detail."

Once again, I had that strange sensation I had been told this before.

"I got another memory for you dad. You'll love this one."

As soon as the door opened, a burst of amplified sound blasted a tune I recognized in an instant. A song I loved more than anyone.

"My band days," I said.

We were in a dark school gymnasium, and on the stage, I saw my mop-top haircut as I strummed beautifully on my sunburst Fender bass and sang harmonizing vocals as we did a cover of The Zombie's *She's Not There* in front of a packed crowd. I read Mankato High, one of our favorite stops on our weekend tours.

But it's too late to say you're sorry,
How would I know, why should I care?
Please don't bother tryin' to find her,
She's not there.

The Kansas kids loved every moment of it. They came for our original songs, but they stayed for the many covers we played. In the tri-state area, teenagers were starved for rock and roll they could only get on the radio and black and white TVs unless they were rich and had some of the first color TVs. Even back then, all fans knew the best was seeing a band in person.

"You were too good for that band," Tristan said. "And you earned more money on the road than grandpa could hope to get on the farm. Heck, you bought your dream car with your road money."

I smiled. "I loved my 1964.5 Ford Mustang Fastback. Things never looked better, even with the cold war and Vietnam on everyone's mind. I could outrun everyone and everything in that red beast. I almost cried when I sold it."

Tristan closed the door as the song ended.

"Why are you showing me this?" I asked.

"There's a good reason, I promise. At the end of everyone's life, we give your coded avatar, or soul, a choice to truly end your existence on this earth, go on existing in a separate paradise simulation, or go back and live your life all over again with another life-loop. After is a true masterpiece."

"If I do a life-loop, would I remember things if I went back?"

"It's impossible to completely erase memories," Tristan said. "The human mind, organic or digital, tends to want to remember something. That's where most people get the sense of déjà vu or that feeling like they've known someone for years despite meeting for the first time. Also why some have an old soul. The researchers that created After may be able to incorporate a reincarnation option, but despite the simulations, many millions of zettabytes of code... that's about a quadrillion megabytes. By the way, we cannot quite figure out that option yet. Perhaps it'll be one more great innovation in both our futures."

"Can I see the future?" I asked.

Tristan pointed down the hallway, which still had no discernable end to it.

"What date do you think it is right now? As in... *right* now."

I tried to think of the last date I saw. I had a stroke and was in the hospital for the longest time. The rest was a blur before this place.

Then I finally realized what I was suffering on my deathbed. I was so confused at the time, but it was crystal clear now. I wasn't in a coma, and I wasn't in a vegetative state either. Perhaps a sort of aphasia or partial dysphasia.

"It's June thirtieth, 2045," I said. "Or... that's what I last recall. I remember because I was admitted to the hospital the day before Serina's birthday. It was on the doctor's whiteboard. I couldn't say anything, but I remember."

"You died July nineteenth of 2045," Tristan said. "You went peace-fully in your sleep. No sign of pain or delirium whatsoever. You almost made it to your ninety-sixth birthday if you had held out for another month. Ninety-five is a respectable age, but 2045 was a very long time ago."

"So, what year is it?"

"It's 2429," Tristan said. "You've had four lifetimes repeated, all ending at ninety-five years, ten months, three weeks, and two days."

"I'm sure I'd know if I was in that far in the future."

"You can travel up to the present if you wish to," Tristan said. "It'll take you a while, but you'll be able to meet the great-grandchildren of your great-grandchildren and onward."

"So why haven't I yet?"

Tristan laughed. "Good question. Perhaps you won't go through it again."

"Go through with dying again?"

Tristan shook his head. "The last few times, you've always chosen a life-loop to relive your life. You find more comfort in the past. Nostalgia is the most addictive concept devised by human consciousness. Finding comfort in a place that no longer exists. Except, that was how people thought in the twentieth century and before. In this simulation, you truly *can* go back, if you wish."

"Can I go back to a time before I was born?"

"You always ask that. Yes. With all the options you have in After, you can go back to times of antiquity. The Renaissance, the Roman Empire, the times of Christ, all the way back to ancient China, prehistoric Morocco, and Mesopotamia. However, the further you go back, the more guesswork there is. After isn't perfect, but the simulation developers have a whole department on historical accuracy. Even with all the research at our disposal, it becomes more fictional than factual. A fake tree here, a shallow lake there. That kind of stuff. Sorry, I rambled a little. The short answer is 'yes.'"

"Amazing," I said. "I thought if I traveled back in time, I'd have a DeLorean, or at least Rod Taylor's time-traveling sleigh with all the bulky brass tubes and levers."

"Interesting," Tristan said. "Last time we had this chat, you brought up Doctor Who's Tardis and Skynet's time displacement equipment.

The time before that, you brought up the weird box from Primer, and Bill and Ted's phone booth."

"And, like you said," I started. "I get to choose what comes next for me?"

"Just like before," he said. "And just like everyone else."

"Are all my old friends in this place?"

"Of course they are. Everyone is. It wouldn't be much of an afterlife if they weren't. The real question is, are you ready to move onto a bigger experience than reliving your life."

"Do I have a limit?"

"In the world of After, you can relive your life as many times as you wish," Tristan said. "Keep that in mind for later. So what will it be, dad? Will you join everyone in the simulation to see the true future and a simulated past? Do you wish to unplug and find out what truly happens afterward? Or do you want to do yet another life-loop? The trick with that option is you're unaware of After's simulation, and once you decide, it'll be another ninety-five years before we talk again."

Neither option sounded bad, and yet I couldn't really decide.

"Can I see Cheryl?" I asked. "I'm overwhelmed. I want your mother's input."

Tristan smiled and opened a door. My nostrils were bombarded with an old familiar diner from Grand Island. The jukebox speakers were fuzzy, but I heard Diana Ross and The Supremes singing *Someday We'll Be Together*.

Hey, hey, hey,
I long for you every, every night
Ooh, just to kiss your sweet, sweet lips, baby
Hold you ever, ever so tight,
And I wanna say,
Someday we'll be together.

I saw Cheryl walking my way.

Walking?

I couldn't believe it.

Because of gout, my wife was unable to walk without pain for the last three years of her life. That was in 2036.

I hadn't seen her in nine years, and I also noticed Cheryl was thin and eighteen years old again. I figured this must have been how she wanted herself to appear to others. She was wearing her favorite bell-bottom jeans with red and white lilies she embroidered herself and a golden flower power shirt with her top two buttons opened just the way I liked.

She also was wearing her waitress apron. The same one she had the day we met.

"1972," I whispered to myself.

"Tell you what, dad," Tristan said as he put his palm on my back and encouraged me forward. "I'll let the two of you decide together. Either way, I'll see you later."

"Can I interact with the past?"

"On a life-loop, you can't," Tristan said. "But your life-loop is over, and this is just a simulated past with your memories. Mom's code... er, her spirit is right there, and she's been waiting for you. It's not just mom who is looking younger now, by the way. See for yourself."

Tristan pointed to a mirrored sign for Coca-Cola. Instead of the happy couple drinking, I focused on my face, which was now without worrylines, crow's feet, and other wrinkles and thin white hair.

It was the first time I had genuine anticipation since waking up in After.

"See you soon," Tristan said as he closed the door behind me, and I sat at the closest open booth.

"Hello Ritchie," Cheryl said.

I looked down and noticed my hands were youthful. I noticed I no longer had saggy skin, dark visible veins, liver spots, and bruises I used to get, no thanks to the occasional bump, and the blood thinners I was taking. I could see why I chose the life-loop option so many times."

"How long have you been waiting for me?"

"It feels like yesterday," she said.

She sat across from me and put her hands on top of mine as she sat back against the red cushion.

"Still," she continued. "It has been a while."

I heard Spiral Staircase singing on the jukebox. I couldn't place the name of the song, but I recognized Pat Upton's voice.

"It's been a while since I last sat here," I said. "God, I could go for some eggs and hashbrowns. I can't believe this exists again. They closed this down so long ago."

Cheryl smiled as she wrote my order on her pad. "I'll get you the maple sausage links you love too."

"With fresh squeezed orange juice?"

"Only the best for you."

Here's the true test if this is real, I thought.

"Wait," I said.

She turn back, and I stood to stand. She looked up at me, and I had the first kiss in countless years.

Spiral staircase's song was ending. I realized it was *More Today Than Yesterday.*

Every day's a new day, every time I love ya,
Every way's a new way, every time I love ya,
Every day's a new day, every time I kiss ya,
Every way's a new way, oh, how I love ya,
Every day's a new day, every time I love ya,
Every day's a new day, every time I love ya.

"Hey," she said between kisses. "You'll get me fired at this rate."

Simulated or not, I felt everything I should have felt with my arms around her back.

I could never grasp how much I missed the warmth of her skin and the scent of her perfume.

"Ritchie," she laughed between kisses. "You never change."

I moved my hands down the small of her back slowly before she stepped on my foot. It was always her flirty warning whenever we were in public.

"It *is* you," I said as I cradled her face in my hands. "I had to be sure. My *God*, I missed you so much."

She poked her glasses up the bridge of her nose and put on her wide smile, and tilted her chin down. "You get more patient the longer you're in this place. But, we'll talk more when I come back. My shift is almost up."

Cheryl winked and I sat back down, enjoying my surroundings. Watching other couples flirt over ice cream floats between two straws, or laugh loud enough at their private jokes as the *Return To Me* by Dean

Martin started playing.

It's a song like this you wouldn't hear in a grocery store, I thought to myself. Times change, but classics never die.

Dean sang the Italian refrain as Cheryl returned, and the food smelled amazing. I unwrapped the knife and fork from the napkin and ate the sausage links first.

"Cara mia," I said while chewing.

Thoughts of *The Matrix* came to mind again as the delicious greasy taste of the sausage satisfied my stomach with each tender swallow. Then after several bites of hashbrowns and eggs, and I no longer cared if it was artificial. I believed it, and it was all I needed to accept everything in the world of After.

"Do you want to spend the rest of time with me?" she asked.

"Is there a difference if you and I spend a lifetime together all over?"

"You've always wanted to see the future. Every time you finish your life-loop, you are taken aback by what has happened in 95 years. It's a large chunk of time, by human standards at least."

"Okay," I said. "So what's the biggest pressing thing for humanity in 2429?"

I thought it was a wild thing to ask. I'm talking about the future, which is now the present while sitting with my wife in the past.

"Same as usual. Humanity causes problems, so humanity fixes them. Nowadays we're just doing it on other planets and colonies."

I smiled. "You've told me this before, haven't you?"

"Last time I talked about the first moon colonies."

"How many are living on the moon now?"

"About twenty million," she said. "It seems like a small number compared to the population of Earth. But consider that in the year 2000, absolutely nobody was living on the moon."

"You mentioned other colonies?"

"Of course," she said. "There are plenty of floating sphere cities between Venus and Mars. Venus is a hopeless cause to colonize, but Mars is on the brink of habitable soil and terrain. All thanks to the terraforming programs of the twenty-second and twenty-third centuries."

"No kidding," I said.

"They're planning on opening the first cities of Mars in 2500. Drones are constructing eco-domes, solar farms, artificial rivers, and all sorts of infrastructure on the Martian surface, and both moons."

"I remember when I was a kid, I thought Mars would be colonized by 1999. How simple we were, back then. Tell me more about Mars."

"The trees have been planted by drones, and within a few decades, Mars will have forests and jungles. Some insects are spreading and pollinating, but not all have accepted the Martian atmosphere. Something to do with the converted oxygen and the lower gravity. It's a struggle, but we're taming the Martian frontier. Man-made climate change can be a positive, if aimed in the right direction."

"What else has happened since 2045?"

Cheryl laughed, and her eyes went wide, a clear sign she didn't know where to begin.

"Ritchie, you really should join us and catch up with me and the last twelve generations of our family. You'll get to hear stories from so many of humanity's advancements. Just like Audrey's side has a long lineage in academics. Plenty of them could explain better than me."

There still seemed to be no wrong answer, and yet I was under the impression I had to choose soon.

"What's say we both catch up next time?"

Cheryl rolled her eyes. "That's just it, Ritchie. The memories of my life are recorded. My time has been documented and relived by everyone I've come into contact with. Every friend, every stranger, every birthday, every social media post, every Christmas card, you name it. Just because I remain here, doesn't mean you won't get to see me again."

"So there are multiple versions of you?"

Cheryl made a fist and playfully knocked the top of my skull.

"Hello? Hello? Anybody home? Think, McFly. Think. What did Doc Brown always say?"

"Great Scott?"

"No the other thing."

"1.21 Gigawatts?"

"No," Cheryl said. "You're not thinking fourth dimensionally."

"Oh yeah."

I realized I hadn't seen the Back to the Future trilogy since all the kids moved out of the house. Trenton finally moved out in 2010, several years after high school, and Back to the Future was constant repeated viewing.

"Anyway," Cheryl continued. "My old preserved self is here and now. I'm interacting with you via the present simulation. Our past selves are forever kept in our past. And I've got to admit, I'm missing you more and more as the long years go by. But… what is another 95 years when you have the rest of time together?"

"But," I started. "Wouldn't you enjoy witnessing the moon landing for the first time again? Going to see Star Wars with fresh eyes again? To experience the rush of falling in love with each other again? See our children grow up and end up happy, despite all our struggles? Again? And again?"

"Ritchie, you can do that as many times as you wish. We already have. But at some point, you must come to terms with the fact that the past is set, and the temptation to change things never goes away."

I pondered her words. "I'd travel back and try to save Kennedy. Maybe prevent 9/11. I'd definitely try to save movie stars that were gone too soon, like James Dean and Marylin Monroe."

"It's not like you can time travel to change the past in real life either. Stephen Hawking himself proved that with his chronology protection conjecture, stating that the past is irrevocably gone. We've had a lot of technology come and go since we met in the 1970s; outside simulated time travel, there hasn't been anything that has gone back in time except for a handful of tachyons, and those were only a mere minute into the past and required far too much energy to make anything count, so sending humans back would be impossible for the time being."

I noticed an irritating inflection behind her words.

"When I was on my deathbed, I didn't exactly see much to look forward to."

"Whoever does look forward to the end?" She said. "But we live on in After. We're codified into this place, and we'll get to live on in the digital hereafter. Now we only have to look forward to everything in the future as more and more people every single day join the afterlife."

"It is amazing, granted, a little odd to get used to."

"You've said that after every life-loop."

Cheryl caressed my hand as she reached across the table.

"You have done four life-loops, by the way. That means it has been almost four hundred years since you looked at current events. Just imagine what seeing the next four hundred years will be like. You can do that by experiencing everyone's memories. The best thing of all, it never ends. That is, as long as humanity doesn't blow up the world."

"Really? We still fight wars in the year 2429?"

"We fought wars thousands of years ago," she said. "And we'll fight wars thousands of years from now. Some still wage war over resources, but ever since Astro-mining took off in the 2250s, we stopped fighting for precious metals, but you'd be surprised how many times wars were fought for rocket fuel to get to those off-world resources."

"Is America still America? Oh, please tell me that the greatest nation in the world is still America."

"I'll save a few spoilers for later," she winked. "But we were talking about warfare in the future. Yes, plenty of people still find a justification to wage wars. Most of the time, it's for stupid reasons."

"Isaac Asimov said it best. Violence is the last refuge of the incompetent."

"You don't read Asimov."

"No, but Trenton did. And quoted him often. He always traded sci-fi paperbacks with friends. Wish he read a few school textbooks with the same interest, but he did alright in college."

Cheryl looked at her wristwatch. "My shift is up. I'll take over your tour from here."

The door to the hallway opened.

"Show me something I would love here and now... or, well, you know what I mean. Something amazing that I wouldn't have seen in the 2040s."

"In due time," Cheryl said as she stood. "We can see it and the end of your hallway."

I took a few quick bites, filling my mouth with scrambled eggs and hashbrowns, and washed it down with the rest of my orange juice.

She took my hand and the door to the long hallway closed just as the jukebox changed to The Dave Clark Five's *I Like It Like That*.

"Dang," I said. "I'm always on my way out when a good tune comes on. We truly had the best generation of music."

"You'll have the rest of eternity for every song you could ever wish to hear. This is paradise, remember."

"You don't have to show me anything else," I said. "I'm leaning toward staying with you. It's just... How do you not get excited to go back? I'm glad there seems to be no wrong answer in the afterlife."

"If you're done seeing memories of you and me, perhaps more memories with the kids?"

She stopped at a door to her right and opened it.

It was dark outside, and loud pops and bright lights were in the sky with a faint haze of smoke.

"Your mom's house," I said as I held Cheryl's hand.

I saw the night sky fill with the occasional bottle rocket popping in the sky, and saw the younger kids lighting off Flashing Signals and Roman Candles.

"It's amazing how we taught the kids about fire safety," I said. "And then one or two days during each summer, we give them matches and lighters and tell them to go nuts."

I saw Cheryl's mother picking up paper plates and Styrofoam cups from the picnic table with her flashlight. I got a fresh cup and enjoyed pouring some of the homemade lemonade from the special glass pitcher.

It was cold and tasted as good as I remembered.

Then I saw Cheryl's sister Lucy show up with her boyfriend Frank Schuster, a South Dakota boy who had no business around anything that could explode.

"It's 1986, by the way," Cheryl whispered in my ear.

"Oh, not *this* Fourth of July."

"You've told this story so many times, and it was the first time we celebrated with all the kids."

Hearing a boom, I turned to the sky and saw myself shooting artillery shells one after the other a good twenty paces away from the farmhouse.

I watched Frank step my way, and I facepalmed when I saw what was coming.

My 1986 counterpart talked with Frank for a little while, and I went back to blowing up my last two shells. Then I saw my younger self hesitate to let Frank do one before the evening was done.

Knowing what was about to happen, I looked in disbelief as Frank took an artillery shell in his hand and said, "Ya wanna see something *really* cool?"

His intention, Frank would explain later, was he was going to drop the lit shell into the launching tube like it was somehow the coolest trick possible.

It didn't happen that way, and it wasn't cool.

He got it lit for sure. Being a chain-smoker most of his life, there was nothing wrong with Frank's skill with a Zippo lighter. What didn't go right was when a few cinders from the fuse burnt his hand, and he dropped it next to the tube. Not on top. Not remotely close to inside it. But completely outside its intended place, with just about anywhere to go but up.

"Everybody down!" The 1986 version of myself screams to all the attending family and friends just before the colorful boom.

I ran to cover Cheryl, who was holding the twins in both arms, and Audrey was playing with the other cousins.

The artillery shell's initial bang propelled itself toward the farmhouse, and the second explosion spread its bright, colorful shower of white and golden sparks a mere two or three feet off the ground.

The front porch of the farmhouse was spared, and didn't burn like I feared it would.

The relatives sitting in lawn chairs weren't as lucky. Nobody was seriously hurt, save for a burnt arms from the older aunts and uncles, and one of Cheryl's cousins had a burnt sundress, which left several holes in inappropriate places. The last bits of the disaster spooked a few of the kids with warm soot and hot embers landing on them, which led to frantic mothers patting them down from head to toe.

All of this happened within a few seconds.

Cheryl and I just turned to each other and laughed as we got back into the hallway.

"How did we survive some of these holidays?" I asked. "I swear the

Schuster clan all inherited Frank's daredevil antics. Lucy put up with him for almost forty years. It was bad enough for holidays."

"Oh, come on. That was the worst of them. And we all laugh at it now."

"Only when you consider all the other near-misses. Black cats with short fuses and roman candles that tipped over are tame compared to being stupid enough to light a shell outside the damn tube. That could have gone way worse. Honest to God, until I met him, I never understood how kids lost fingers while celebrating America's birthday."

"Mother would say lots of prayers for just about everyone to keep all of us safe," Cheryl laughed. "Especially Frank. Remember how mad they were at *you* for that mishap?"

"It was dark," I said. "And they only got mad at *me* because I didn't feed Frank to the wolves. We were already married. If they found out it was Frank's screw-up, I know your sister would never have gotten married. Despite putting everyone in danger, I had a soft spot for the kid. I always called him 'kid' too. It didn't matter if he was twenty when we first met. He never thanked me for that, either. That... *that's* the crap I never forgave. He just shrugged his shoulders and thought, 'oh well, no harm done.' Carefree arrogance is not the same as gratitude, and we both knew it."

"He always liked you, at least," Cheryl said. "And when I told mom a few years later, she was so concerned about him that I saw his name many times in her many prayer journals. She had a bible in every room of the house, and she always prayed to keep everyone safe. She believed that was why things always turned out well. I suppose I got that from her too."

That surprised me. I wasn't completely devout in life, but I didn't really expect her to still be religious.

"You still believe?"

"I always will. Just because we're in After doesn't mean we won't be in Heaven eventually. Who's to say we *aren't* in Heaven already? Our digital souls are just here as long as we feel like it, and my memories are recorded elsewhere in this simulation forever. I don't have any intention to unplug from After anytime soon, but I think eventually I'll become content with this existence and be ready for whatever comes next."

I smiled. "You know, I kept pondering reliving the good old days, but if I've already done so, I'm choosing to enjoy catching up in the simulation for a few hundred years instead. Before we get too off-topic, isn't it a little weird that this is essentially heaven... but not heaven?"

"Is there much of a difference?" she asked as she walked back to the hallway.

"There is a huge difference for all who died before the world of After was created," I said. "To those who lived before computers were everywhere."

"If all those people are waiting for us in heaven, then we'll still meet them in heaven. I hope we do. Until then, we still exist. Nobody says it's unfair that the average life expectancy in 2429 is one hundred and thirty years when humans in the stone age were lucky to live past their thirties."

I kept looking back and forth at the dates etched into the door plaques. I realized we passed the year 2000 already.

"I wasn't the best Sunday school student, but I'm sure God wouldn't like humans meddling in the afterlife like this."

She held my hand tighter.

"Without blaspheming, God hasn't intervened yet," Cheryl said. "If God made the scientists and engineers smart enough to accomplish this sophisticated level of virtual reality, then God isn't going to care if we show up to whatever is next in a hundred years, or a hundred thousand years, for that matter. If God made the world billions of years ago, a hundred thousand years is a drop in the bucket. God and the workings of the universe didn't give us time travel, so we created our own method."

She stopped at another door.

"Where next?" I asked. "Or... when next?"

"I picked a fun memory," she said. "You love it each time you see it."

We continued for a long while. I wish I could remember the other meetings from before, but I was happy holding her hand for the long walk until she opened the next door.

"2021," I said. "Oh, Audrey was supposed to graduate in 2020 before everything in the entire world was put on hold."

I recognized the Texas A&M University campus.

Cheryl and I watched our 2021 counterparts at the college pre-ceremony meet and greet with her professors. We followed the crowds and watched the guests of honor make their speeches before the Dean read the names of all the graduates.

"We got old," I said. "And I forgot how skinny I was after I quit drinking."

"I think that saved your life for as long as it did, and giving up smoking back in the 90s deserves a lot of credit too."

The dean called Audrey's name, and we cheered at the same time our 2021 counterparts did.

"To think we raised such a smart kid," I said. "The highest we achieved were our bachelor's degrees."

"You don't shed tears often," Cheryl said. "But you were so proud of her. The first doctor in the family."

"The first doctor," I laughed. "Of course I was proud. I wouldn't be much of a father if I wasn't. Some parents get to see their kids become ball players, and some see their kids become actors. Audrey getting her Ph.D. and teaching university courses was just as big a deal. Very few athletes and actors earned what she earned."

"She's still doing research to this day," Cheryl said.

"From here?" I asked. "From inside After? How?"

"Some residents of our make special requests to have their code implanted into either a drone or robot to still exist in the real world."

"That's wild."

We watched Audrey step off the stage with her Ph.D., and I followed Cheryl out into the hallway.

"They don't allow such requests to everyone, or else Earth and the colonies would be overrun with digital souls in metal bodies. Some parts of the world think the whole concept of a digital afterlife is technology run amuck, and the living powers that be considered the possibility of sabotage to the supercomputer mainframes to be a risk not worth taking."

"The middle east?"

"Not even close," she said. "It was Americans, ironically enough. A lot has happened since President Levitt. Where was I? Oh, yes. The robots with digital souls started in the 2070s for scientists to continue research too important for mortality to put a stop to. That way, we don't lose brilliant minds at inopportune moments. Because of that, we've time and again solved so many crises over the centuries."

"The future sounds amazing."

"We'll get to the end of your hallway soon. Should you choose to stay, you'll get to see the world of 2429. I can't make you choose anything, as you'll see shortly. That said, I can't wait to see your face when you see what humanity has accomplished."

For the first time, I could see the end of the hallway as Cheryl opened the next door.

"When is this?"

"2032. Probably one of our last great memories together."

"Except for the ones we are going to make going forward," I said.

"For sure? You're deciding to stick around this time?"

"To be honest, I've no idea why I hadn't sooner," I said. "Granted, I probably will again, just not until I catch up with the future. I *do* have that choice, right?"

"As many times as you wish," Cheryl said.

"I can't wait to see everything in the future."

"You mean the past," Cheryl laughed. "You'll get used to this. You have almost three hundred and eighty years of past events to see."

I saw a wide open range with a long field of solar panels and wind turbines.

Then I heard the bleating of sheep as they walked next to us.

"Our retirement ranch," I said. "You and I went all in with solar energy, and you got bored and wanted to raise sheep for wool to spin on your looms. After winning that lottery ticket, you still wanted the country lifestyle. We could have retired in Hawaii or Samoa, but you thought Texas was perfect. And I have to admit again, you were right."

"And I loved every last morning, afternoon, and evening we spent on that last decade of our lives together. Eighty million dollars could still buy a lot back in the 2030s."

"Before we got there, Culberson County was still one of the more remote parts of the United States, and after buying twenty thousand acres of Texas wilderness, we built and rented solar power to just about everyone willing to pay for electricity. As time went on, we understood the electric economy would never be a loser as long as humanity kept using electronics."

"The people of Van Horn hated us because you flaunted your Husker jacket whenever we went into town," Cheryl said. "But they warmed up after you offered to foot the bill of modernizing the football field for the high school, and setting up college scholarships for the team."

"They liked football just as much as we do. In fact, I think some loved the sport more than some people love their spouses. They just can't help but support the local team. It wasn't *my* fault my local team was back in Nebraska. Oh, and it wasn't just the football stuff. It was also making sure nobody in the county lost power on the grid whenever bad storms came along. The only other rich guy in town owned an oil field and never did anything like that."

"That solar farm is still there," Cheryl said. "It's not only been upgrading with the times, but it's thrice as large now. We also own thrice as much land in Brewster County and Big Bend County. Our investment turned us into one of the longest-operating solar farms in North America. You'll have to meet our descendants who last took care of the place."

I knelt down to pet one of the sheep, picking a few stickers from its fleece. I was impressed that a place with artificial intelligence could have that much detail for me to register.

"We did good," I said. "Sometimes you look back at all the struggles, but only remember the good times we had to make the struggles go away."

Cheryl leaned on my shoulder, giving me a slight massage as she kneaded my muscles. She still knew where best to dig and press her thumbs along my spine, shoulders, and neck.

"We had each other, Ritchie. And after a lot of prayers, we had that lottery ticket. That didn't hurt either."

I chuckled. "We would have done well without it, but I get the point."

I stood and, for the first time in ten years, from my perspective, watched the sunset, glinting off the solar panels before the sun disappeared behind the mountains.

"Well," Cheryl said. "I don't intend on seeing our 2032 selves. That's when our health began to wane. Trenton is waiting at the end of your hallway, typing away on one of his novels."

I figured that's how my other son would spend his time in the afterlife.

"You can make your final choice when you get to the end," she continued.

We returned to the hallway, and after a couple minutes of walking, we saw an open lobby. At one of the plush waiting room sofas, I saw Trenton on an ancient tangerine Apple iBook laptop. The same clamshell laptop we got him for Christmas in 1999.

Despite being Tristan's twin, he went out of his way to appear nothing like him. Trenton had a long beard and had a few pounds of broad muscle on Tristan.

I sat down next to him, remembering his insistence to not be interrupted. But interrupted he was when he looked out of the corner of his eye and smiled my way.

"Hi dad," he said. "What kept you?"

"The usual," I said. "New story, I presume? How's that coming along?"

"It sucks," he said. "But they always do until I fix it in a later draft."

He tapped a few more keys before shutting the lid.

"Mom says you're still writing," I said. "Isn't the afterlife when you put that aside to enjoy paradise."

"I'm still selling in the physical world," Trenton said. "Every time I finish a book, I consider unplugging, just to see what comes next."

"Oh," I said. "Well, what keeps you here?"

"Every time I release a posthumous work, it has tens of millions of people waiting to enjoy it. By the time I think of pushing the big button to unplug, I bring myself back to my laptop. I tell myself if nothing comes, and if I stare at a blank screen for a half hour, I have nothing left to offer the world. Well, clearly something has *always* come, if I'm still here."

"That's wonderful, though," I said.

"Fulfillment is a tricky thing. Following a book release, for a good while, I feel like I've acquired fulfillment in all its glory, and a little while later, I have that urge to keep typing to find fulfillment all over again. It's not like my digital mind is going senile, even after all these years in After."

"Do I dare ask how many novels you've written since you got here?"

"I passed a milestone of two hundred posthumous books in 2385. Still averaging one every other year. All thick enough to make Tolstoy, Hugo, and King smile."

"I suppose paradise is doing whatever makes you happy."

"Joseph Campbell said to 'follow your bliss,'" Trenton said. "And so, here I am. Granted, it gets harder to write science fiction when I'm literally living in the realized dreams of science fiction's past. But I still find a few mind-blowing ideas every now and again. I have to still consult Audrey on fact-checking. But enough about me. Did you enjoy the tour of your contributions to After?"

"My contributions?" I asked.

"You had specific memories of several rural places of Nebraska, Kansas, and Missouri from the 1950s onward. Of course, your contributions help make After a much more realistic paradise for those to remember simpler times."

Opposite the long hallway was a desk with several comically large buttons the size of the palm of my hand.

Cheryl led the way. "This is The Choice Room. And these here are your official end-of-life options for your soul. You have the choice of the Repeat button, which we have come to call the "life-loop" option. Then you have the Remain button, which you push if you choose to stay in After's post-life simulation until you wish to come back to the hallway of your life. And last but not least, the third choice is the Unplug button, which removes yourself from the After simulation entirely, but only you can make that decision."

"Well, I don't feel like unplugging," I said.

Trenton smiled as he put his hand on the 'Unplug' button.

"Wait!" I said. "What are you doing?"

I reached out to stop Trenton, but he hit the unplug button with a slapping sound, but the button remained still as stone.

"Gotcha," Trenton snickered before erupting in laughter. "Your reaction is priceless right now. Like mom just said, nobody else here can press your button. Look."

Trenton slapped all the buttons several times, and not one would be pressed. I sighed in relief when they wouldn't budge while Trenton leaned to put his body weight into it.

"That's not funny," I said.

"Oh, come on. It's a *little* funny."

"If you were alive, I'd ground you," Cheryl said. "What if your dad hit the button by accident?"

Trenton stopped laughing. "Alright, alright. I suppose we leave dad alone to choose for himself."

"Let's wait for everyone else," Cheryl said.

Then I saw Tristan come through a door on the other side of the desk. Right behind him was Audrey, who shoved Trenton out of the way in a run to put her arms around me.

"I missed you," she said. "I had memories upon memories but seeing you, but holding you here and now is so much better."

She looked older than Cheryl and I, which was odd considering we brought her into the world when I was thirty-one years old. I figure this image is how she preferred to be seen, just like one of Tristan's old video games.

Trenton put his arms around Audrey and Tristan. "We all miss you in our own ways. So, make the right choice this time."

Cheryl gave me a kiss on the cheek, and everyone left me alone in The Choice Room.

I took a deep breath and paced. I made up my mind, but I still considered the options.

Repeat. Remain. Unplug.

I put my hand on the middle button for the Remain option and pressed it with both palms before I became too tempted by the life-loop option again.

The other two buttons disappeared from the desk, and the door glowed white. I took that as my queue to walk through it.

I expected a big room with space scenery and skyscrapers ten times higher than twentieth-century New York City, but it was nothing like it.

My family was waiting on what looked like the deck of a cruise liner.

"Thank you," Cheryl said. "I'm glad you wish to join us outside of a life-loop this time."

"Of course," I said. "So... we're at sea. So, what does the world of 2429 look like?"

Cheryl held a flat tablet device, and the image of the open sea disappeared, revealing an incredible structure in the distance. I wasn't quite sure what it was, but it looked like a mountain range, except I could tell it was entirely level with the horizon and went on for many miles in either direction.

"We're in New Nippon," Cheryl said. "What was once Baja California in Mexico until the twenty-third century. The Mexican government needed money and wanted to be a bigger port of shipment between Asia and North America. In so many words, they auctioned the entire peninsula off, and Japan was almost ready to lose its bid to China, but the United States offered to match Japan's bid and it became the United State's fifty-seventh state. The initial name was going to be New Japan, but the Japanese wanted it in their native language, so New Nippon was born on the one hundred and fiftieth anniversary of Pearl Harbor in 2091."

"That whole... thing is Baja California?"

Cheryl nodded. "It used to be. And when it became a much bigger port for world commerce, the previously built cities all along the coast expanded. Then in 2276, the United States wanted to do something spectacular to celebrate its five-hundredth anniversary. They took some design inspirations from megacity designers and built an entire linear metropolis a thousand kilometers long, all within the view of the coast."

"That's impossible," I said.

"Hardly," Cheryl said. "Remember in the twenty-first century when we saw Dubai built literal islands? Or when the Saudis built their linear megacities? Don't forget about Nigeria's floating metropolises. New Nippon was inspired by such megastructures, and we did what America always does. We made it bigger."

I was speechless.

"With highly efficient holographic jobs and labor," Audrey continued. "Inhabitants rarely go more than a few miles to earn a living. What jobs require physical presence, the solar charged transit can get you from one side of the peninsula to the other within two hours."

"That'll save oil consumption," I said.

This time Tristan spoke up. "I'm surprised it's taken you this long. New Nippon isn't the only amazing sight. Check out the sky."

I did, and I saw the full moon, but I also saw several dozen smaller moons of varying colors.

"Those are the colonies," he continued. "All in precise geostationary orbit. All are built with raw materials mined from resources in the asteroid belt. Plenty of nickel and iron to smelt into shape and heaps of silicates for the strong panels of silica glass to give everyone in the colonies a great view. The biggest wonder is keeping such massive structures in place. That credit goes to the solar sails to counteract the gravity of the moon and even other planets in the solar system. Wouldn't want a sphere the size of Manhattan to crash into the ocean."

"Unreal," I said.

"The steam locomotive was unreal to those who only rode horses," Audrey said. "And I got to help figure out the planning of all of this."

"You did?"

"Well, I was the geology consultant," Audrey said. "The West Coast is known for its earthquakes, and the common fear of building a structure this big was the gigantic 'what if' surrounding the San Andreas Faultline. And many contemporary scientists tested the foundation of New Nippon's megacity to ensure that if an earthquake larger than the Richter scale could ever measure came, the city would be designed to be flexible and move with the earth, rather than break against it. Also, the city would be easy to evacuate within minutes, no matter where you were living. Japan and the United States had collective experiences and data on architecture and infrastructure to build on top of our geological data for maximum efficiency. America didn't want to build a seven-hundred-mile-long city for it to come crumbling down within a century."

"What a marvel," I said. "How tall is it?"

"It's a kilometer high," Audrey said. "It's groundbreaking marked the end of America using imperial system measurements. That's another story, but we no longer measure in miles in the western hemisphere."

"I wish I could see it develop over the years," I said.

Cheryl laughed. "That's a great place to start in the world of After. We could witness historical events like this from all over the world. As many times as you wish."

The cruise liner got closer to shore, and I saw a crowd of people waiting.

"They all showed up early," Trenton said. "I swear we always think we're late unless we're a good half hour early. Some things never change."

There had to be a thousand people there.

"Those... *those* are all our grandchildren, great-grandchildren, great-great-grandchildren, etc.?"

"Twelve generations of our progeny," Cheryl said. "And most of them have never met you. This is your day. Enjoy it before we go back to see all you've missed."

"Sure," I said as I raised my hand to wave at all the onlooking kin. "And then maybe you and I can do another life-loop. We have all the time in the world, right?"

Cheryl shook her head as she tilted her chin down in the cute way that made me fall in love with her that first afternoon in the diner. "You're hopeless, but yes, we can. As many times as you wish."

Our ship docked, and I took my first steps into the future. No more pain and no more strokes. Only an infinite number of wonders to observe, and memories to make in the hereafter.

I saw a large screen with old Super 8 camera footage of myself and Cheryl dancing in our living room. It was Christmas, and I forgot if it was Trenton or Tristian holding the shaking camera when it was taken.

When the footage cut to our three children, I realized it was 1989 when they tore open the wrapped present, revealing their Nintendo Entertainment System. Cheryl turned the camera to me when I had a giant grin on my face, knowing how happy I made them.

I saw a ramp lead onto shore, and I walked with Cheryl as the grand-kids embraced us, and I got to meet so many new faces of my descendants.

My family, I thought. My wonderful, loving family.

Always On My Mind by Elvis was playing over the footage, and the yearning to see everything again taunted me. But I knew whenever the nostalgia becomes unbearable, I can relive it all.

Life-loop after life-loop.

And if I become content with the past, I thought. I'll just be excited about the future again.

Until then, I thought. I'm going to go meet the rest of the family and celebrate my afterlife.

As many times as I wish.

ABOUT THE AUTHOR

Thomas Van Boening lives in Lincoln, Nebraska, with his wife, Sarah. When he is not wandering in the fantastic worlds of video games, movies, and streaming entertainment, he is creating fantastic worlds of his own. He has half a dozen short stories of horror, science fiction, and fantasy published. His debut novel, *Mead, Magic, and Madness,* is scheduled for publication in Summer 2022.

ON A DISTANT BATTLEFIELD

C.J. FERRELL

CHAPTER I
FROM THE CLASSROOM TO THE FRONT

J ames was sitting in his history lecture at the university just before Christmas break was getting started. They were studying one of his favorite periods of history, the American Revolution, or as he liked to call it, The American War of Independence. Everyone laughed at him for his love and knowledge of history. It often times got him called a geek or nerd throughout the campus, but it never bothered him. History was his passion as well as his hobby, which he thoroughly enjoyed.

The class seemed to drag on that day as they were learning about the hardships faced by the colonial army during the winter of 1776 and on the campaign to the battle of Trenton. This was a topic he always enjoyed debating because he loved writing alternate histories and what-if scenarios for his professor to read. On this particular day, his professor brought up the points that the continentals were undernourished, undersupplied, and morale was at its lowest point. They had lost New York earlier that year to General Clinton, and even though he had gone home due to his lack of action and the continental army faced a new threat in General Lord Cornwallis, they were able to take the small army they had and turn defeat into victory.

Now James always enjoyed being in the role of the underdog or the side that lost the war when he did his reenactments. He fought as a British Loyalist ranger or a Native American ally at each event he attended. With his time for Christmas break, he had decided to go to the Delaware Crossing and Battle of Trenton reenactment this year, one he had wanted to attend for a long time but couldn't for one reason or another. He checked the pamphlet in his book with the dates on it and the location of the site.

The clock hit two p.m. and class was dismissed. The professor waved to everyone and wished them happy holidays, but he stopped James on his way out of class. "You seem to know almost everything about the revolution. It's almost as if you were there fighting it yourself right along with the loyalists."

James smiled at the statement. "Well, I have great teachers, and my experiences going to the different battle reenactments and battlefields have helped me learn a great deal about the time period." James extended his hand and shook the professor's. "I'll be at the crossing and Trenton battlefield over break if you want to see me in action."

His professor nodded, then let him go on his way.

James left the building and headed for his dorm room to check his equipment and get ready for the event. He walked inside Tower Hall and hit the button for the elevator. Waiting for the elevator, he got one of his usual headaches that were getting more and more frequent. He reached up and touched the side of his head, and a vision came through to him of men on the banks of a river, watching and waiting for something to happen. He saw someone who he thought was George Washington riding back and forth on his horse, trying to keep their morale up, then all of a sudden, the elevator bell rang, and he snapped out of it.

"I've got to stop staying out so late and studying," he whispered to himself as he entered the elevator. He pressed the button for his floor and racked his head, thinking about the vision he saw. He remembered in one book he read about the crossing of the Delaware River that Washington had been trapped with his army against the river and had nowhere to go, but that one of his commanders, Colonel John Glover, went to find boats to ferry the army across the river before Clinton could destroy the Continental Army.

James got off the elevator and walked down the hall to his room. He took out his key and turned it, unlocking his door, and walked inside. He put his bag and books down on his bed and headed over to research some more on the Delaware crossing. He looked on his usual websites he did his research on and found what he was looking for. Washington's army was retreating across New Jersey into Pennsylvania and came upon the Delaware river. It was the largest obstacle between them and survival.

The British had chased Washington from his defeats in New York to where he split his army into three parts. One was led by Charles Lee, another by Horatio Gates and Washington led the final group in hopes that at least one of these armies would be able to escape the British. When Washington reached the Delaware River, he was trapped and sent Colonel Glover to find boats and ferry the army across the river. Glover was successful in his mission and Washington's army lived to fight another day.

Well, that was definitely interesting to read about. I had no idea that things were that dire for the continental army at that time. I knew that their enlistments were over with the new year, but that information makes me think I might like to experience that for myself instead of fighting for the British at this reenactment. James gave himself a minute or two to think about that, then stepped to his closet to look at his uniforms and equipment. He shuffled through his everyday clothing until he came to his reenacting gear. He took it out and started laying it out on his bed, trying to piece together a continental uniform.

The uniform that James usually wore was a green coat trimmed in crimson wool with cotton duck trousers. This regimental coat could pass for multiple units that fought in the war, but he needed a specific one on the continental side. He was awfully familiar with the British and loyalist units that wore this type of regimental but would have to do some research on the continentals. James started reading through his books on regiments and uniforms of the American Revolution until he found the perfect regiment to choose. The First New Hampshire regiment was clothed with a green regimental trimmed in crimson and they fought with Washington on the Trenton campaign.

He, of course, would have to go and pick up his musket and powder from his house and the rest of his equipment as well as send in his registration and fee to participate, but he was getting really excited about this event and being able to participate in it. He finished checking to make sure he had everything packed for the holiday, then walked out of his room, locked the door behind him, and headed down towards the parking garage, where he would get into his car and head home to pick out the rest of his equipment for the reenactment.

His drive took him about half a day to get home to Wheeling, West Virginia, from Huntington, West Virginia. He got out of the car and then walked into the house, saying hello to his mom and dad. His mother was always supportive of his adventures, and his dad loved talking history with him whenever the chance arose. On this occasion, he wouldn't be home long enough for that type of visit, but he enjoyed several days of spending time with them. He helped his mother set up their Christmas tree, and he set up his model railroad and village for the holiday. They had a wonderful family dinner where they caught up with his schooling and how he was doing in class, then the day came for him to load up and head to New Jersey.

He started by packing his tent, bed, and sleeping gear, then moved on to his equipment. He took his regimental shirt, trousers, and moccasins. After packing his clothing, he moved to his cartridge box and sword belt, followed by his powder charges and pre-made cartridges for the reenactment. On top of everything, he had to decide on what musket of his collection to take with him, his traditional Long Land pattern 1758 Brown Bess musket that was standard issue to the British and loyalist troops or his French Marine Musket model 1728 that was more common among the colonial militia and regulars. He decided since he was fighting on the side of the colonials, he would carry his French musket to blend in with everyone else. Now, with everything packed and ready to go, he went back inside, gave his mother a kiss, hugged his dad, then hopped in his car and headed for New Jersey.

CHAPTER 2

THE REENACTOR

James reached the spot where the colonials were going to be camped for the event, directly across the river from the Old Barracks in Trenton. He drove up to the gate and stopped. He rolled down his window as a security guard walked up beside him. "Hello there, sir. May I see your registration packet please?"

James reached over to the passenger side seat and handed the packet to the gentleman.

"Thank you, Mr. Nelson. You can take your car to the campsite to unload and set up. Reenactor parking is a quarter mile down the road there in the Union Bank parking lot. Here is your parking pass for the weekend. The parking lot is guarded 24 hours a day, and you'll have no reason to worry about damage or theft."

James nodded, then took his packet back, sitting it on the seat, and waved a thank you to the guard before heading off to find a good place to set up his camp.

James drove up the road through the camps and finally found a good spot to set up. He pulled up alongside a nice grove of trees and a downed log. He parked the car and got out. Reenactors were setting up already in other spots setting up company streets, sutler row, places for the artillery and supplies, and of course, Washington's headquarters.

James opened up the back of his car, pulled out the poles to set up his tent, and set them to the side. He then pulled out his equipment and clothing and hung them on the door while he figured out how best to set up his camp to look like he was part of the rest of the groups.

While he was looking and thinking, another reenactor walked up to him. "I noticed your regimental, first or second New Hampshire regiment?" he asked as James shook his hand.

"Well, I signed up as First, but if there are no others here reenacting as them, I would fall in with the closest group to that," James replied.

Then the man looked through all of James's equipment. "Well, we do the Second over there, and your gear matches ours, so you're welcome to join us on the battlefield."

James nodded his head and thanked the gentleman.

"I'm James Nelson thanks for the invitation to join you. I've reenacted now for almost ten years, started out as a powder monkey for the artillery, then moved up to a drummer until I was old enough to carry and fire a musket. Since then, I've been fighting on the other side actually as Butler's Rangers and British Indian Department and Kings Royal Regiment of New York."

The man smiled and nodded. "Well then, we've certainly fielded against each other a time or two, especially at Brandywine and Monmouth Court House, quite some enjoyable times."

James smiled. "Don't forget Germantown; that's always fun keeping you colonials from taking the building from us." They both laughed, then went back to getting James' camp set up.

"Well, whatever the reason, we're glad to have your help this year. There's always enough Hessian and British soldiers, but never enough colonials."

"I have noticed that before at other events, so I'm glad to be on the right side for once." James smiled then they went about setting up his camp.

It didn't take long for them to get James set up and him all ready and comfortable for the night. "Get yourself a good night's rest, for tomorrow we start our march from here for two miles to the ferry crossing and then our six-mile march into Trenton." James nodded and thanked the gentleman for his help again, then stepped inside his tent to unpack, get into his clothing for tomorrow and unpack his gear, so he was ready to do battle. James finished dressing in his uniform and clothing, then laid down on his bedding and fell asleep, getting some much needed rest before tomorrow.

Sometime during the night, James had another dream. It was a dream of a group of colonial officers gathered together as if for a council of war to plan a battle. He could see General Washington, General Sullivan, Colonel Glover, General Gates, and General Knox. Washington and Gates seemed to be arguing about something. "One thing is apparent, sir; you don't know when to quit. These boys you command are just that; they will run from the Hessian soldiers and not stand or fight. They are scared of the Hessians, and rightly so. The Hessians are the best trained military force in Europe, after our mother country, of course, so you will not defeat them. We will lose this battle, this army, and this war, sir. Admit it," General Gates said to Washington.

Washington sat in his chair for a moment, then stood up. He began to pace back and forth on his end of the table where they were all seated. "Well, sir, you are correct in saying that I command boys. They're just lads of fifteen, sixteen, even seventeen years old, and they have been in battle more times and defeated at every turn, but you know what, General Gates?" He paused for a moment. "These few men who are left, those who have stayed with me this far, they would go to hell with me if I ordered them to. They fear the Hessians because they've never been beaten. Well, gentlemen, with my plan, I guarantee you they will be."

Washington laid out a map showing the Delaware river and their current camp as well as Trenton and the Hessian garrison there. "Here is my plan, gentlemen. In three days' time, it will be Christmas Eve, and the Hessians will do a great deal of celebrating and drinking that night. While they're celebrating, we will march a short distance to the ferry and cross the river under cover of darkness and attack. We will then march towards Trenton from the ferry, and then at this point, where the roads split, we will split into two columns. General Sullivan and Colonel Glover will command the first group. Myself and General Knox shall command the second. General Gates, you sir, I am ordering back to Philadelphia; you want nothing to do with this army, then you may go and be Congress's problem."

Washington stared him down, then turned to Alexander Hamilton, his Aide. "Alex, go with him. See him out of my camp and far enough away that should he choose to say anything about this plan, no one near here can alert the Hessians to my strategy." The gentlemen stood up and walked out, and soon afterward, James woke up from his dream, or at least he thought it was a dream.

CHAPTER 3

THE PUBLIC DEMONSTRATIONS

James woke up in another cold sweat and sat up on the edge of his cot. *What's going on? Why am I having such realistic dreams?* He pondered for a few minutes trying to rationalize his thoughts, but there was no easy explanation for why he was having these dreams. He looked out the door of his tent. It was beginning to get light out, so he put his buckled shoes on, grabbed his accouterments, musket, and regimental, and headed out to heat up some coffee to help him wake up.

The man James had met the evening before was also sitting by the fire getting some coffee. "Need a bit of a warmup there, lad, before the spectators start arriving?" he asked while pouring another cup for James.

"Yes, it would be greatly appreciated, thank you." James took the mug of coffee and took a quick couple of sips. He looked over at the other gentleman thinking maybe he should say something, but he might get sent home instead as someone not fit to take the field and fire a musket in the reenactment.

"So what time are we mustering to march to the ferry and do the crossing?" James asked.

"Well, we're supposed to drum revile here at 8, then we'll be on parade for inspection and other such activities for the public, then we're supposed to march to the ferry somewhere around 6 o'clock pm and then board the boats and do our crossing."

James had a fairly good idea by now of how the events were going to play out, so he was ready for the event of a lifetime. He finished his coffee and then checked his equipment one more time. He tightened the jaw on his musket to keep the flint tightly in place, took a scrap piece of cloth and wiped down the pan part of the lock where the powder was placed to ignite the main charge, wiped his musket down with oil so it wouldn't rust, and almost as if on cue it started to snow.

James looked up as the snow started falling. "This'll really be an experience for sure. I'll know exactly what they went through during this trying time." He grabbed his musket as he heard the drummers start pounding away rhythmically, sounding the reveille for the reenactors to wake up and get ready to muster for parade. The public spectators started arriving as the camp opened up for people to walk through. Some folks loved asking the soldiers questions about their life in camp, how they made their uniforms, and of course, if they used real bullets. They lined up for inspection in their winter gear and clothing. The acting commander who played Washington walked along the ranks inspecting his soldiers, then they were dismissed to go about their daily duties.

James was assigned picket duty, which at that time was an important job because you were all that stood between the enemy and your camp. His day was spent walking along the tree line in front of the camp as if keeping an eye out for the enemy, even though the men who reenacted as the Hessians were camped at the barracks in Trenton. Several folks stopped to ask him what he was doing, and he would explain to them what picket duty was. There were occasionally reenactors who would walk past, and he would stop them and check for a pass out of camp or ask for their pass code. He continued his duty until the next reenactor was sent to relieve him of his duties, and he could return to camp.

James walked back to his tent, then sat down on his chair just outside the doors. He reached into his haversack and pulled out some jerky and an apple to eat for his lunch while watching the rest of the camp going about drills, practicing musketry and bayonet drills, and other such things for the spectators to see what the camp life was like. These little demonstrations continued throughout the rest of the day until the camp was closed to the public. It was time to march to the ferry crossing. James walked back to his tent then sat down on his chair just outside the doors. He reached into his haversack and pulled out some jerky and an apple to eat for his lunch while watching the rest of the camp going about drills, practicing musketry and bayonet drills, and other such things for the spectators to see what the camp life was like. These little demonstrations continued throughout the rest of the day until the camp was closed to the public. It was time to march to the ferry crossing.

CHAPTER 4

THE CROSSING

The muster was called, and the drums again beat out the assembly beat. The reenactors gathered in their groups and stood shoulder to shoulder in preparation for the five-mile march to the ferry. They went through one last inspection as they were told of their mission by the acting commander, then the immortal words of Washington were shouted out, "Liberty or Death," and the men went wild cheering. The officers of the respected groups then gathered the reenactors and readied to march them to the ferry.

It was a long march from the camp to McConkey's Ferry, where Washington made his crossing. They walked along in columns of two on a path that was believed to be the original path that had been taken in 1776. The sun had gone down, and it was still snowing. The men were growing colder, but the marching kept them focused and warm enough. "It must have been so hard for these men so long ago. Underfed, underequipped, little or no clothing or shoes on their feet, but they endured for the cause of liberty."

They finally reached the ferry in four hours. It was a long and hard march through the snow and cold, but they finally made it. The men were allowed to rest until the boats were brought across the river to the ferry, and they could begin boarding to start crossing. Now the crossing was to take place in a matter of several hours, but as the history books tell us, it took quite longer than was anticipated. The river was starting to freeze, so they had to carefully pole their way across and not run into ice drifts, or thick ice flows that could damage or sink the boat.

There were many difficulties. For instance, each trip across had to be repeated multiple times since only so many men fit in a boat. The cannon, which would be particularly important to any army on the field of battle, would have to be transported across lastly because each cannon transported had to be taken across on a platform built across two of the boats, which took that many boats out of the transporting of the troops which were also especially important, but they needed to be across first. You can attack without artillery, but if you don't have enough troops, you may lose your artillery during a battle if a superior number comes against you.

For this event, there were, of course, fewer soldiers to ferry across the river and fewer cannons also, so that wasn't something that needed to be worried about. However, the current of the river, especially at this time of year, was dangerous. Modern-day technology has helped with that problem to a certain degree, but even the Army Corps of Engineers and their lock and dam system can only hold nature for so long. Luckily for them, today, the river was quite calm.

The boarding of the boats at the ferry was going quite smoothly, and there were no incidents to be had. James stood in the line waiting for his turn to board the boat and help to row across the river. As could be expected with these things, it took a bit longer than anticipated. Even when the battle happened, Washington complained about how miserably slow it took, but he understood why. The men rowing the boats across the river time and again did that all night; the rest of them made only one trip across. Several more hours passed, James guessed it must have been about midnight, but his group was finally next in line to board and cross.

The group stood on the dock as the two boats came in. The boats were large enough to carry five men on the sides rowing and fending off the ice flows, as well as twenty others seated inside and waiting to disembark on the other side. It was easy to follow; one man walked in front of the other and then took turns getting into the boat and sitting down.

Once the groups were seated, the man at the back of the boat who guided the pathway across called out to the men, "Cast off your oars," and the men pushed the boat off the dock, placing their oars in the water and pulling towards the other bank.

You could see the strain of the men pulling on the oars on the way across. Each stroke warranted a low groan as they pulled and pulled their way across the river. The boat commander stood up and started singing an old whaling tune to help them as they pulled. Once he started to sing, the men all got in sync and began pulling rhythmically together, and the pace across the river quickened. The whole trip, just going one way, took them almost ninety minutes. James couldn't think about what the men endured at that time, although he was sure they were so tired and exhausted that they wanted to quit. But they kept up with it because their commander asked it of them. One thing Washington was certain of was that his men were loyal to him, and they certainly would follow him into hell if he asked them to.

The boats finally reached the other side of the river, and they were able to disembark. It didn't take long for the group to exit the boat and assemble on the shore. From now it was only a matter of a few more trips gathering the rest of the reenactors and bringing the cannon over from the other side. All the men and cannon were brought over in a little more than half an hour after James's group had landed. Once everyone was on the other bank, it was time to march on Trenton.

By then, it had stopped snowing but had grown much colder. They would have to march sluggishly through the mud and wet ground until they reached the edge of the town. This march took more than five hours for them to reach where they would attack from. The field was laid out in the normal fashion, although there would be a small battle through the streets of old town Trenton up to the meadow at which the Hessians surrendered. It was a few hours before dawn, so the men were allowed to stack their muskets and rest. Just after dawn broke, more spectators started arriving and taking their seats to watch the battle unfold.

It was finally time for the reenactment to begin. The narrator started by giving some background about events leading up to the battle and just how dire the situation was for the continentals at this crucial time in our history. The man playing Washington rode up the road in front of the reenactors, and they all stood up and saluted as he passed. Then, it was time to get into formations and begin the attack on Trenton.

James grabbed his musket from the stack of arms and readied for the next few commands. Orders were given to form up into regiments, and the individuals gathered together in their regiments and groups according to the order of battle. James and his group were located near the middle of the marching line. The groups with the cannons pulled them along to the front of the line and stood ready to enter the town after their first shots were fired. The order was given for everyone to fix their bayonets. James reached down to his belt, felt around for the edge of his bayonet, and pulled it from its sheath, attaching it to the end of his musket and then pulling it up to his shoulder.

The cannons fired their first shots, and then the order was given, "The army will advance!" The general yelled to them as they began their movement into the old town. This was where things got to be a bit hectic. Different groups of reenactors broke off and searched through different buildings bringing out Hessian prisoners and occasionally firing their muskets at lines of Hessians trying to form a defense of the town, but they were unsuccessful. Now history tells us that the battle of Trenton itself lasted almost seven hours, from nine in the morning to four in the evening, but for the public eye today, the demonstration was cut short just so the spectator could catch a glimpse of what it was like at that time.

The groups went on fighting for almost an hour until the major event of the battle happened, the death of Colonel Rall, the commander of the Hessian troops. The final scenario of the battle was where the Hessian troops were finally surrounded in the great meadow by Washington's army, and a rifleman shot Colonel Rall. Not long after that, the call was made to lay down their arms and surrender to the colonials. By now, it was getting late in the day, and time for the public to go home. James and his group, as well as quite a few others, went together to the barracks and joined a group of Hessian reenactors in a post-reenactment celebration.

Of course, what historic site would be complete without a tavern for men to let off steam? James joined the men headed there, leaving his musket and equipment at the barracks for the night. They sat around for a few hours talking with each other about their day jobs and families; eventually, someone started singing, and they all joined in. James drank his weight in whiskey that night for sure, but not quite enough to be blind drunk. He got up, thanked everyone for a great time, and said he hoped to see everyone at another event. They all waved, and James headed out the door to find his bunk for the night.

James was walking along the trail back to the barracks when he noticed something shining on the ground. He bent over, picked it up, and examined it closely. It appeared to be an antique compass from the revolutionary war era. Of course, it looked as though it was brand new, so James thought it could have possibly been a replica, but something about it was out of place. It was made out of a copper material around the outside with the marks on the floating wheel inside the instrument. James turned it around a few times to check and see if it would actually work, and of course, the needle stayed true to the north no matter how much James moved it. Looking around, James couldn't find anyone to whom it could belong, and knowing that the museum would have already had it in a display case, he naturally took it with him.

CHAPTER 5
WHERE AM I?

James managed to fall asleep rather quickly that night. For once, it seemed like he wasn't going to have those rather interesting dreams that he had been having. He found an empty bunk, unwrapped his blanket, climbed up onto the bed then fell fast asleep.

"Wake up, ye rebel!" James felt a sharp poke in his ribs as he rubbed his eyes, waking up. "Where'd you come from, laddy?" A bearded man wearing an officer's uniform stood at the edge of the bed where James had just woken up. "Come on lad, roust yerself. I don't want these Hessian lads to skewer you."

James looked around the room. There was a mix of blue-coated Hessian soldiers as well as red-coated British soldiers, of which James recognized the uniforms.

"Where am I? What's going on?" James asked the officer.

"Well lad, yer continental friends left ye behind. They've all gone back across the river and left you here with a few others, it seems, to get captured."

James thought to himself, *something isn't right here. I must be dreaming again.* "Where am I? What year is it?" James asked the officer as he stood up.

"Ye must be hurt, lad to be asking such questions." The officer began to look James over to see if he might have some sort of head wound. "Ye look to be fine. It's December 26th in the year of our lord 1776. Ye are in the town of Trenton, General Lord Cornwallis is in command, and we just arrived here last night after Washington ran back across the river."

James shook his head. There was no way it was 1776; it couldn't be. Time travel didn't exist, unless something had displaced it. James remembered getting drunk and stumbling across that compass he found, then falling asleep on the cot in the barracks. He looked around, and as far as he could tell, it was the same place. James followed the officer out of the barracks and out to where the prisoners were being held. About two dozen soldiers were wearing different mixed continental uniforms that James could recognize: the second Virginia, third New York, 8th Pennsylvania, and some militiamen from all over the area. He sat down with them as the officer took his soldiers and searched the other buildings for more stragglers.

"What regiment are ye with, lad?" One of the older continentals in the Virginia regiment leaned over and asked.

"Second New Hampshire, Ethan Allen's Green Mountain boys. What happened? I must have fallen asleep and collapsed in the barracks," James asked the gentleman.

The man looked around. A set of silver epaulets were on his shoulders, indicating that he was an officer. "Well lad, Washington is setting a trap for old Lord Corny there. He pulled the army back across the Delaware yesterday and left us few here to keep him confused and his attention in the wrong place while the rest of the army is marching around their rear to capture Princeton."

James smiled as he knew what happened during that battle. The British were utterly humiliated and reminded of their victories on Long Island. After hearing one of the regiments at that battle sound a fox horn, Washington himself was quoted to have told his men, "It's a fine day for a fox hunt, my boys!" Shortly after that, the British would be routed and running from the field of battle.

"Aye lad, are you in for an escape?" the officer leaned over and whispered to him. "They'll be sending us on up the road towards Princeton here soon, and they can't spare many guards, so we all were planning on escaping and rejoining the army at Princeton."

James thought about it, but he'd also read about the prison ships in New York harbor like the Jersey, and he didn't want to be stuck there in the event that it was true that he was in 1776 somehow. "I'm with you lads. Just tell me when and what to do." James sat down and waited for the redcoats to finish rounding up prisoners. By the time they were all rounded up, there were about fifty men in a group in the barracks square.

"Well lads, for you, the war is over. Yer all bound for the Jersey ship in New York harbor. Come on now, on yer feet, and get moving." The officer took about twelve guards with him as the prisoners stood up and got into a line. "Forward march!" he shouted, and the line of continental soldiers started out away from the barracks.

They were marched several miles down the road from Trenton and out of view of everyone before they took their first break from the long march back to New York. They had left several hours before dark, but now as they marched eastward, the sun was setting quickly over the horizon. The officer looked around and nodded to the men who were going to help in the escape. They would go just after dark when nobody was watching.

They got up from their break and, after fetching water to fill their canteens, were back on the road, marching towards New York. It wasn't long before they finally stopped for the night. James watched and checked on the guards to see how long they were taking to walk rounds and where they were posted to watch the prisoners.

"Looks like we'll have about a ten-minute time where they're not watching us get to the woods and scatter. That's our best chance to make it or split into groups of two or three and work our way to Princeton," James told the officer after they relaxed for a while.

Just then, James remembered the compass. He had placed it inside his haversack the night before. He pulled it out, and the needle was going around in circles now instead of pointing north. "Looks like ye broke yer compass there, lad. I'm sure there's a man who can fix it back in Washington's camp once we get there." The officer winked at James, then nodded to his plan.

All the men planning to escape gathered close together and waited for their opportunity to run. The guards made one final check to see that all the prisoners were asleep then they went back over to the fire to drink their rum ration for the night. James looked around to make sure there were no hidden guards anywhere, then grabbed his things and stood up.

"Now lads, let's go," the officer looked at James as they quickly got the rest of the men and headed towards the edge of the woods. It was a good twenty or thirty-yard dash to the tree line, but they all managed to make it. There looked to be about twenty of them altogether.

"Right lads, here we part ways. Each group is to meet back up in Princeton in Washington's camp. It's due east of here, so be sure to watch the skies and keep going till you reach safety. I look forward to serving with each of you again." The men all saluted, then went on their way into their groups and headed north.

CHAPTER 6

THE ESCAPE TO FIGHT AT PRINCETON

J ames and the officer headed off on their own, but it wasn't long before they heard a few shots from the guards in the British camp. "They're on to us now. We best get to running, sir," James said as they both got up and turned to run east toward a creek behind Trenton. "Aye lad, but they'll never be able to track us in the dark. We'll make it," the officer replied.

James smiled, and they were off on their way through to Princeton. The journey was difficult as it was almost pitch-black outside, but luckily enough the moon showed just enough light for them to find their way through the thick of the forest. "This way, lad, there's a stream over here that we can cross to slow them down a bit." James ran in the direction the officer showed him, and sure enough, there was a small creek that was frozen up.

"We'll cross here, the creek isn't frozen fully yet, and there's a fallen tree here for things to be easier across." The officer climbed the embankment and jumped across onto the tree, and though it was hard balancing his way across, he finally reached the other side and waited for James to cross.

Before they crossed the creek, James stopped for a minute and reached into his haversack, and pulled out the compass he had found

179

before. He held it in the light so he could see exactly what way they were traveling.

"Where did you get that lad?" the officer asked, looking at the compass that James held.

"I found it on the ground a few days ago, sir. I didn't think anyone would mind it, having been tossed on the road." The officer looked at James and then said, "Well lad, it's a beautiful instrument that is, so mind you take good care of it for sure."

James hopped up on the log and balanced himself as he made his way across. The log was wet and icy from the cold weather the last few days, but he didn't slow his pace to get across. It wasn't long before he had reached the other side, and they were off and running again. "You know I don't think I ever caught yer name, lad," the officer asked as they made their way through the forest.

James nodded, then answered, "It's James Nelson, sir."

The officer looked shocked; that name must have been familiar to him. "Does yer family hale from New Hampshire originally, lad?" the officer asked as they slowed their pace, sure that they had outrun the guards trying to find them.

"Well, no, we originally hale from a little place on the Virginia frontier called Wheeling. I don't suppose you've ever heard about it."

The officer nodded, "Aye, I've heard of it. I have family from up that way, Pittsburgh area of Pennsylvania."

James thought for a moment, then asked, "What's your name Sir?"

"Thomas Whyte, at yer service lad, Second lieutenant of the Virginia Continental Line." Once James heard that name, he thought back to a project he had done in high school, it was a genealogy project for a science class, and he and his mother had gone as far back as the first family members to settle in America, and they had the surname of Whyte. James still had no idea why he had been brought back to this exact time, maybe to meet his long-ago relatives, but in any case, he couldn't let him know that he was from centuries in the future and knew of his fate.

They continued on for several hours before reaching the road that led into Princeton. James was getting excited that he was going to witness history being made. The continental army hadn't made the attack on the town just yet, so all they had to do was stumble across the camp, and they would be home free.

As the two walked further down the road, they came upon a stream. Of course, they were thirsty from running away from the redcoats all night, so they stopped for a moment and dipped their heads into the stream to drink and refresh themselves. After drinking all he could, James got up and adjusted his uniform, but as his back was turned, he heard the familiar click of a musket being readied to fire.

"Who are ye, and what's the challenge phrase." A strong stout Virginia voice said from behind him as the barrel of a musket was pressed into his back. "Liberty," James said as the man lowered his musket.

"Or death," the man answered and held out his hand to greet them. "Sergeant Thomas Fraser of the Pennsylvania Line, good to see you found your way back to us, and that means the redcoats can't be far behind ye. Follow us, and we'll get you back to regiment proper and ready for the next battle."

They followed the sergeant and his group of pickets through the woods near the stream and to a clearing where the army had gathered to collect themselves and resupply before attacking Princeton. "Here we are, lads. The supply wagon, fresh with powder and shot from our victory at Trenton, and I'm sure we can find you a spare musket as well."

James walked up to the supply officer and grabbed a new Brown Bess musket and accouterments as well as a cartridge box filled with thirty rounds to fire should they need it. After receiving the gear, he and the officer parted ways. "Well, sir, thank you for helping me get back to the army." James reached into his haversack and took out the compass. "I want you to have this, sir. It is much more useful to an officer than a lowly private."

The officer took the compass in his hand and then placed it gently in his hunting pouch, "Thank you, lad. Good fortune to you tomorrow, and remember, keep your powder dry."

James nodded, then followed the sergeant to a group of men wearing the same uniform as him. "There's your regiment, I believe, lad. Get some sleep, for we'll be getting battle orders any time now."

James introduced himself around to the different lads of the regiment and heard tales of how they had whipped the Hessians just a few days ago and again the following days at Assinpunk Creek.

Most of the Hessians had surrendered after their commander, Colonel Rall, fell, and all their supplies of food, powder, muskets, and canons were captured as well. James was assigned a company to join for the coming battle and found their camping area. After finishing a few mugs of rum, they all turned in for the night.

Revile came early for the men, and the sergeants all went around from group to group waking the men up and having them fall in for battle. The sun hadn't risen in the sky yet, but it was time to fool the British army once again. It wouldn't be a huge battle today. After all, they were only going after the rear guard of Cornwallis's army, but it would still be a victory that the continentals needed.

It didn't take long before the army was on the move toward Princeton. Under cover of darkness, with the British behind them across the creek in Trenton, Washington's army was moving toward Princeton in what would become known as one of the greatest flanking maneuvers of history.

CHAPTER 7

THE AFTERMATH OF BATTLE

James stood by the officer's side for a while, contemplating what he was going to do. Death was a serious thing, and he had absolutely no desire to be killed in the wrong time. He needed to get home. He picked up his musket and gear and started back to catch up with the army. It didn't take him long to find where everyone was fighting again; he just followed the sound of the cannons and muskets firing.

He found a group of mixed continental soldiers firing against a group of grenadiers slowly retreating back toward Trenton. James reached into his cartridge box and began loading and firing his musket as fast as he could. He had made himself a promise that once he was home, he would find the grave of that officer and pay his respects.

The continentals were firing so fast at the retreating grenadiers that they finally broke off and ran away. The continentals cheered, watching as they ran away, but artillery shells suddenly went off throughout the line of men. The redcoats had managed to bring up two small six-pounder cannons to fire on the advancing continentals. An officer walked up from the rear and spoke to them, "Come on, lads, this battle is far from over. We need to silence those guns and, if possible, capture them for our use."

By now, the men were starting to tire from exhaustion. "Form on the line here, men, check your muskets and make ready to advance. Shoulder your firelocks!" James joined the line of men and checked his musket to make sure it was ready for the attack.

The order finally came, "Forward into line!" and the continentals moved forward in unison towards the canon.

James knew that as they got closer to the cannon, they would load with grapeshot, a cannon charge of smaller balls packed into a wooden block that, when fired, would spread out over the field, killing or wounding as many as possible. This was the moment of truth for James. Would he face his fear of death in this time, or would he turn and run away? James was no coward, though. He marched forward in line with the other continentals following in the footsteps of his ancestors.

The line of continentals finally came within musket shot of the canon. James looked and could see the gunners on the canon loading the grapeshot as quickly as they could. "Make Ready!" the officer shouted to the continentals.

James drew his musket up tight to his shoulder and aimed down the barrel at one of the redcoats pushing the charge down the barrel of the canon.

"Take aim!" The entire line lowered their muskets at the redcoats, who were just about ready to fire the canon.

"Fire!"

The line erupted in a wall of smoke, fire, and lead as the continentals fired at the redcoats standing around the canons. "Charge men, Forward!" The order came, and men erupted up the small rise towards the canons. James ran up the hill, yelling and screaming with the others through the smoke, only to see the toll of their shots when they reached the canons.

Red-coated men lay everywhere around the canons. The gunners were lying on the ground, one holding his leg, another grabbing his shoulder. The cannon barrels and carriages had been riddled with musket balls, and at least twelve men were either wounded or dead on the ground.

"Good job, lads, more artillery for the cause of liberty." The officer rode up behind the group of men who were now sitting down and drinking from their canteens. "Not bad for a day's work. You deserve a rest. I'm sure we'll receive new orders here soon, lads."

James found a tree to lean himself up against, then sat down. He sat his musket up against the tree and pulled out his canteen to take a drink. He looked around at the other soldiers, ragged, dirty from combat, and fatigued. This was the price of liberty, and James now knew exactly what that cost was.

James watched the soldiers talk about their experiences, exchange plunder taken from the enemy, fall asleep from exhaustion, and some were ready to fight on. James was glad for the break in the battle, but he hadn't noticed that he was bleeding. Apparently, the highlander had gotten in a blow that he didn't notice, and the adrenaline had just been keeping him on his feet.

"Hey there, lad, let me look at that." One of the soldiers had come over to sit beside James and noticed the blood. He took hold of James's arm, lifting it up so he could see the gash in James's side. "Doesn't look serious, lad, but you best be getting to the surgeon and have it fixed up. You've fought enough for today."

James nodded and gathered his things, then headed for the rear of the battle to find the surgeon to get fixed up.

James walked along for a while before stopping to take a drink. His equipment was beginning to feel very heavy, and he wanted to lie down, but he knew if he did that, he might never make it up again. He wandered along, pushing himself to stay on his feet, but every time he looked down, he saw the blood and wanted to stop and rest again. The journey back to the hospital was a long one, almost a good five miles distance. James stumbled into the hospital and sat down on a stump to wait his turn with the surgeon.

"You look exhausted, lad. Let me take a look at you." The voice came from somewhere in front of James, but he was too exhausted to care. The man wasn't much older than James and wore a surgeon's clothes. "Ah, it's nothing there, lad, just a deep cut. We'll have you fixed up in no time," he told James, then motioned for one of his assistants to come over and help him.

The surgeon wiped the blood away from the wound to see how bad it was. "Well lad, looks like you got into a fight with a highland laddy. This is a deep cut, looks like a butcher's blade made it."

James nodded his head. "Yeah, I crossed bayonets with a highlander a while ago, he seemed more like he wanted to split me in half, but I had other ideas, sir."

"Well, we'll have you fixed up here in no time and back to the fight should you want." The surgeon gathered his tools and instruments and began his work on James's wound. He scraped away the matted blood and then fixed up some cordage to sew the wound up. The surgeon gave James a bottle of wine to drink while he sewed up the wound. "Now this might hurt a bit, so drink away, and it'll be over with in no time at all."

James took a few good gulps from the bottle as the surgeon began stitching him up. He was right. It didn't take long at all for him to sew it up, but with each stitch, James felt a small jolt of pain go through him, so he would drink more wine until the bottle had disappeared. "Almost done lad, just a few more stitches and you'll be good as new." The surgeon said as he finished the stitches.

James looked down at the wound now that it had been stitched up. "Thank you, sir. I'm in your debt."

The surgeon nodded, then turned to walk away. "Just make sure next time, lad, that you're not taken aback by a highlander's blade. They're not so easily mended as this one was." James shook his head, reassuring the man, then got up and gathered his things to head back to the army.

It wasn't long before night fell, and the army had assembled together once more to decide whether to chase the redcoats and further humiliate them and Lord Cornwallis or retreat back across the Delaware river and set up winter camp somewhere. Washington had been arguing to make their victory complete by defeating Cornwallis in the morning, but his officers all knew the true disposition of the army.

They had fought four battles in as many days, they hadn't been to sleep longer than a few hours, and most were dropping with exhaustion instead of wounds from battle. With much reluctance, Washington agreed with his commanders that it was wiser to save the army and retreat rather than press their luck, and so at about midnight, the men were woken up and put back on the march away from the redcoats.

James knew where they were headed when he had studied the battles of Trenton and Princeton. He knew that afterward, the continentals retreated to Morristown, New Jersey, and set up winter camp there to refit and train recruits for the coming spring and the inevitable campaign that would be launched against the redcoats.

James began thinking about how he might be able to get home. He still had no idea exactly what happened for him to get here, but he had somewhat of an idea that it dealt with that compass he found. Not wanting to be shot for desertion, he followed along on the line of retreat as long as he could until he just fell to the ground from exhaustion. After a while and watching the continentals pass by, the sergeant who met him after he escaped happened by.

"Well, lad, you look like you've been through quite the experience. How was the battle for you?" he asked as he stopped for a moment to talk with James.

"It was quite the experience for me, sir. I had a run-in with a high-lander that I almost lost, the officer I was with when we got here was killed, and I was at his side when he passed, so yes, I've been through quite a lot this day."

The sergeant stood there for a moment before he started talking.

"Aye lad, we lost many a good lad over this year. I was with Washington in Brooklyn when we retreated, I lost three of my sons there, captured at Fort Washington when it surrendered, but I haven't lost my faith in the cause of liberty. Stay the course, and things will get better for us." He reached into his bag and pulled out something to give to James. "Here, lad, this belonged to my eldest. Maybe it will bring you some luck."

James held his hand out and took the trinket that the sergeant handed him. It was a small pewter cross on a length of sinew. On the back of the cross were the initials JLM. "What was your son's name, sir?" James asked.

"James, James Lawrence Nelson," he replied as he started off to catch up with his men.

"I'll cherish it always, sir, thank you, and may God bless you and keep you through the rest of this war." The sergeant turned to James, bowed his head, then turned and marched off.

CHAPTER 8

THE LONG JOURNEY HOME

James thought long and hard about the name that the soldier's son had been given. They shared that name; it was a common bond between them. Perhaps this was the connection he was looking for to get him back home. James reached into his haversack, pulled out the compass, sat it on the ground next to him, and examined the cross. James held the trinket in his hand, but while he was looking at it and thinking, the cross began to burn hot.

James dropped the cross on the ground next to the compass, which began to glow a bright yellow that seemed to emanate from the inside of the compass. James stared at the two items. There must have been some magical element built into the metals or something supernatural that connected them that had brought him here, and he hoped it would now take him home.

Still exhausted from the events of the day and the march towards Morristown, James managed to pick himself up and start walking back away from the column of soldiers towards a stream. As he stumbled towards the stream, he could hear some kind of a humming pulse. He had no idea what it was or where it was coming from. He had picked up the compass and cross and put them into his pocket as he steadily walked towards the stream.

It was only a few more yards to the edge of the stream, and James fell down to his knees and crawled the rest of the way. He reached the edge of the stream and dunked his head into the water to cool off and refresh himself. After pulling his head out of the water, he sat up, took off his canteen, and dipped it into the water to refill it. "Today was a great day, I got to witness history firsthand, and I'm still alive to talk about my experience."

After filling his canteen, James looked around for a spot to rest for the evening and possibly the night. James looked across the stream and saw a small clump of trees that would hide him from any passing redcoats until he was rested. He got himself up and fixed his equipment, then found a shallow spot to cross. Once he was across, he walked towards the grove of trees and walked into the thickest part and then dropped his equipment and sat himself down to rest.

James didn't know how long he had been asleep, but he was awoken by the sounds of approaching horses. He jumped up quickly and gathered his equipment before moving to the edge of the tree line to see what was going on. The moon wasn't out, so it was hard to make out uniforms of the dragoons who now watered their horses in the stream.

James didn't want to get caught and sent to the Jersey ship, so he lay down on his belly so that his silhouette wasn't visible to the men on the opposite bank. He wasn't sure how long they had been there, nor how long they would be staying there. Perhaps they were just watering their horses for a continued journey later that night, or perhaps they were hunting continental stragglers like himself. Whatever the reason, James would just have to wait them out.

James heard a noise behind him and turned to see what it was. Behind him stood a young woman who couldn't have been much older than he was. She was carrying a yoke across her back with water buckets hanging from either side. James stared at her for a minute, not sure whether she was a friend or foe.

She stared back at James, who had now put his hand on his musket. "Don't worry, I'm a loyal American. You're safe," she said in a low whisper to James. She looked across the creek seeing the dragoons camped on the opposite side. "Come on, follow me, and I'll get you out of here. My house isn't far. You can hide there until morning."

James jumped up quickly and followed the girl up the bank behind the trees and into a nearby farm.

The girl brought James to her barn and ushered him up to a loft filled with straw and alfalfa. "It's not much, but it'll keep you safe until the redcoats are gone." She offered to turn down a bed that was crudely made out of a spot in the straw, but James shook his head.

"Thank you, you've done enough to help me. I'm very grateful to you for sheltering me, miss." She bowed her head, then blew out the lantern as James settled in for the night.

James wasn't long to stay awake as he was still exhausted from all his experiences. He lay in the straw staring up at the barn roof, thinking about his family back in his own time, wondering if he would ever see them again. He thought of everyone he missed, his mother and her wonderful home cooking, his father and all the war stories he used to tell about his time in the service, and especially his younger brother. Even though they often times butted heads, he still loved and missed them all.

James finally drifted off to sleep after an hour of lying there and thinking about home. He almost didn't notice the sound of horses outside the barn just before he drifted off. He carefully got up from his bed and wandered over to the edge of the barn to take a look out between several loose boards. He saw lit torches and men on horseback, but they weren't wearing redcoats like the men at the stream were. *They must have been loyalists,* James thought, seeing that they were mostly wearing civilian clothing.

"In the name of the King, we order you to open your home to be searched for rebel traitors and deserters." James watched in horror as the men dismounted and walked up to the door of the small cabin. James looked around to find his musket as the girl opened the door and answered the man who was standing in front of her.

"What rebels do you harbor here?" he asked her, placing a hand on the hilt of his sword.

"There's no one here but me. My husband died last year of pneumonia, and I've been tending our farm ever since."

The man in charge didn't seem incredibly pleased with her answer. "Go inside, men, search the place, leave nothing untouched." He forced his way into the house and past the girl, and his men followed him through. James could hear china dishes being broken and glass shattered, but he was helpless to do anything, for if he intervened, he would most certainly be killed, and so he stayed silent, watching the destruction happen.

The men began to filter out of the house, each of them carrying some form of loot, like a chicken and some bottles of Madeira. The woman stood by as they took what they wanted and then loaded their plunder onto their horses. The man who was in charge was last to emerge from the house. He had a very sinister smile forming on his face. He took hold of the woman and then slapped her, knocking her to the ground.

"Burn it, leave it to serve as an example to others who would harbor traitors to the crown."

One of the men handed him a torch, and he threw it through a window shattering the glass and catching the curtains on fire.

James, by now, had seen enough. Even his conscience wouldn't let him stand by and watch this happen. He picked up his musket and put it through the hole in the barn siding. The men were getting ready to leave, with the man giving orders riding in the front of the group. James watched and took careful aim as they began riding in his direction. He gently pulled back the lock on his musket into the firing position, and when the man was just five yards away from James, he pulled the trigger.

Fire burst from the end of the barrel of the musket as the ball sailed straight and true for the man's chest. The ball hit its mark, and the man screamed in pain as he fell from his horse. The rest of the men who didn't see where the shot came from were looking at each other, trying to figure out what to do next.

James was quick to reload. He had the cartridge in his mouth and powder down the barrel before the men had started dismounting their horses. James took the musket ball, rammed it down the barrel, and took aim at another of them, which he could see very clearly because he was carrying a torch. James took aim for the man's chest and pulled the trigger. The musket belched fire again, and the ball carried towards the man but missed his chest and hit his shoulder, making him drop the torch.

There was some loose straw on the ground, and when the torch hit it, it started a chain reaction. The flames caught one pile of straw after another on fire and spread towards the barn where James was hiding. James saw the flames beginning to climb towards him, but his adrenaline had already begun to keep the thrill of the battle inside him. He grabbed his things and climbed down from the loft of the barn just as the flames reached the doors.

James had a quick decision to make: stand and fight from where he was in the loft and surely perish, or jump down and fight them one on one. The possibilities ran through his mind as he looked around. Below him was a pile of straw that hadn't started to burn yet. James backed up against the barn wall, got a running leap, jumped out of the loft, and landed in the pile of straw.

James was stunned after the fall and stumbled a bit, getting up. By now, the men outside had dispersed around the front of the barn where they knew the shots had come from. James looked around and couldn't find his musket. It must have fallen someplace else, so he grabbed his bayonet from the sheath and a knife he had at his side and then pushed his way through the barn doors.

The men all lowered their muskets at James, who stood there looking like a caged animal ready to fight to the death. "Surrender yourself, lad. You're outnumbered and surrounded," one of the men yelled at James as the muskets all clicked, ready to fire. "This is your last chance lad. Give up now or perish."

James stood there looking into each of the other men's eyes. The fire had engulfed the barn behind him, giving him a more menacing look and highlighting the other men. Some looked frightened, and others had the look of death on them, but James stood his ground. A warming sensation began to heat up around James's neck, and a glow started coming from inside his haversack. James didn't notice what was going on until there was a loud clap of thunder, and the sky lit up white, almost blinding everyone.

The men looked around after gaining their sense, there was a burnt spot on the ground around where James had been standing, but he himself wasn't there. "What in the bloody hell just happened? Where did he bloody go?"

· · ·

CHAPTER 9

THE RETURN TO NORMAL LIFE

J ames had no idea what happened to him. He saw the flash of lightning and then woke up lying back in the bunk he had laid down in just before he left. James jumped from his bunk and ran outside. The sun was just beginning to rise over the horizon of the city, and he was relieved to see that he was back, but everything had seemed so real to him. Was it all just a dream, or did he really get taken back into history to experience it firsthand?

He reached down to where the wound was from the cut of the highlander's sword and felt a small scar. Frantically he reached into his bag and felt for the compass, but it was no longer there. Only the pewter cross remained around his neck, with the initials JLN now gone. "It must have been a dream; the compass is gone, and this cross had the initials of JLN on it. I wonder, though, is it possible that I was given the opportunity to experience history alongside my ancestors?"

He just couldn't wrap his mind around the experience, but he dismissed the entire thing as a figment of his imagination brought on by too much to drink the night before. Everyone was gathering their things to go home after the weekend of the reenactment and James began packing up his tent and equipment after returning to the campsite from the day before.

There, the men he had fought alongside were just beginning to tear down their own camps, and the man from the day before was just getting ready to leave. "You gave us quite the scare there, James. Yesterday, we thought you'd gone crazy with the cold from the crossing. You kept spouting off about the attack and how it would fail. Gave me quite the fright but looks like you're back to normal now."

James nodded his head, then turned to talk with the man, "I'm sorry, sir, I don't know what came over me, must just have been the excitement for the event and having never participated in it before. I thank you for your concern and for keeping an eye on me for sure. How can I repay you?"

The man shook his head. "You already have, lad." He showed James the compass. "You gave me peace and saw me die so I can join my comrades finally." He tossed the compass to James. "Here, lad, remember, it is better in your hands now. Take good care of it." The man smiled, then slowly faded away into the morning mist.

James almost ran away from what had just happened to him, but he understood what had happened now. The compass he found connected to that particular person and that moment in time. James smiled, knowing that he had helped in some small way. Afterward, he finished packing his things and readied himself for the long drive back home.

James took a detour on his way home; he had a few days before he had to be headed back to college from Christmas break, and he headed to Washington, DC, to look into the records and see if he could trace his family back to that man. He went straight to the books he knew had his family's earliest recorded member from the early 1800s. He found the marriage records for a Robert Whyte, the son of Elizabeth and Thomas Whyte.

James looked through the records a little bit further and found the record he was looking for. A pension to the widow of Thomas Whyte, who was killed at Princeton in the service of the 2nd Virginia Regiment of the Continental line. This was the man whom James had encountered. James looked at the entry and found where he had been buried. This would be James's next stop to fulfill the promise he made to the man.

It wasn't a long drive from Washington to Frederick, Maryland, where Thomas was buried in the military cemetery of Fort Frederick. James walked through the rows of white headstones for what seemed like hours until he came to the section on soldiers of the American Revolution. He walked in about five rows until he found the stone he was looking for.

The stone commemorated the service of a Captain Thomas Whyte of the Second Virginia Regiment. James kneeled beside the stone and said a small prayer thanking Thomas for his service and sacrifice in the cause of liberty, but then stopped and thanked him for the help he gave James that day to escape the redcoats and serve at Princeton.

"Thank you for looking after me, Thomas. I wish I had known you were my ancestor. I had so many questions I wanted to ask you, but now I am headed in the right direction and know where to start looking."

There was a faint tap on James's shoulder. He got up, startled, and turned around. There behind him stood the ghostly white figure of his ancestor. The ghost smiled at him, then stood back and saluted James. He had been put to rest and finally at peace with his deeds. James would now know the history of where his family had come from and where they were going from his small experience of being transported through history. James shed a tear, and as the tear hit the ground, it was as if all the spirits in the cemetery woke up and stood facing him at attention.

James returned home, not knowing if he could ever tell anyone else about his experience or if they would even believe him, so he kept quiet about it. When he got home and parked in his parent's driveway, they emerged from the house ready to greet him and talk all about the reenactment and how his trip was. James smiled, then wrapped them both in a huge hug and followed them inside to return back to his normal college life.

ABOUT THE AUTHOR

C.J. Ferrell was born in Wheeling WV and moved to Sundance Wyoming in 2017 where he developed his love for history and Indigenous culture. Currently studying at Black Hills State University majoring in History and minoring in Indigenous Studies and Creative Writing, his first major work was the Untouched Captain as part of the Untouched Heroes Anthology this will be his second published work. He currently writes in the genres of Historical fiction and paranormal romance.

NEVER A NO

LINDA MARIE PANKOW

CHAPTER
ONE

I have finally reached my nineteenth birthday and I'm so over the regular grind. I know, it's gotta be done, but you do know that everyone gets bored working the job they were assigned from a young age on.

I get the pleasure of doing the farming, watching the crops, and making sure we have enough food to survive the winter. What bothers me is that I could have been born into a different time. I'm not exaggerating. One of my moms, Elaina, is actually from the year 2019. I am now living in the year 820.

I know you think I'm crazy, but I've been told the story since I was a little boy. You see, my dad is a Viking, a man of Norse descent, from our time. He met my mom in 796. My mom is an Irish woman from the year 2019.

Both she and her cousin tell me how they traveled through time. They saw a rainbow on the way to their Catholic church one day and they jumped into it. It was a rainbow, minus the bow; it was shaped like a ball. I have always explored the area, hoping to find another ball of multiple colors to travel in. I have no idea where I would wind up, but all I can think about is meeting my cousins.

As I plant the last grain of wheat from our stock that is meant to grow into the next year for us, I look off to my left. I see a sudden glow. I don't bother to say anything to my parents. They know I've been looking for the mysterious ball of light my whole life. If I disappear, they will assume that I am safely with my aunt.

I approach the ball of many colors, looking into it to see if it has answers. I take one last look back at my homestead, my parents' house and all my siblings that I'm leaving behind. I smile, knowing that I will have fun, no matter where I wind up.

As I step into the ball of light, I feel it surrounding me. I feel the warmth of the many colors as I let go and hope that I wind up at my aunt's time and am welcomed in. I don't know if they even know about us, but I do know that my mom is writing a book about how she and Eveytte went through the sphere of many colors.

I smile as I let go and think of the cousins I may have in the future. I know that wherever I wind up, I will be happy and look forward to it. Suddenly, I feel a thud, as though I've just landed on the ground. I open my eyes and look around. I see two young men standing against a tree.

I have no idea who they are, but this field looks a lot like the one my mom, Elaina, described. I hope it's the right field and I've been brought to my family again. I start the trek up the hill to where there should be a road. I smile as I see a car.

I ignore the two young men making out as I look at the car. It's not exactly like the kind we have back home. This one looks so nice. Ours are raggedy and don't get very far without needing more corn fuel. I take the chance and sit on the hood of the car, grinning as I touch its blue paint. I smile when I hear footsteps coming from the direction of the young men I saw making out.

"What are you doing?"

I turn around so I can see the source of the voice. "I am trying to figure out where I am, or rather, when I am."

The two men smile at me. I can tell that they understand exactly what I'm saying. The tall blonde one reaches his hand out for me to shake as he smiles wide. "I'm Corbin! Come down from my car and we can talk."

I look at the two men, nodding as I get off the hood of the car. "Okay." I take Corbin's hand, shaking it as I jump deftly off of the car's hood. "I'm Asher. My mom is Astrid. She is married to Jorge. Jorge is also married to..."

The two interrupt me, each of them saying words at the same time.

Corbin says, "My aunt Elaina!"

While the other man, much chunkier and with darker hair and skin, says, "His aunt Elaina!"

We all laugh as we realize this is more than just an accident. Corbin looks at me, smiling. "My aunt Elaina described a rainbow sphere, just like the one you came out of. We saw you when we were making out, by the way. She wrote a book and it's been in our family for centuries."

The other man smiles. "I'm Eli, by the way." He taps his chin. "So, what are you, like, cousins with Corbin?"

I look into the man's dark brown eyes, shrugging. Corbin answers him, "I guess if his mom is married to my aunt's husband, then yeah. Welcome home, Cousin Asher. Mom is gonna shit when we get home."

Corbin opens the back driver's side door, letting me in as he smiles. I just enjoy the smooth ride. Cars were not as easy to ride in back in my time. I smile the whole way to Corbin's house. When we get there, I can't help but smile. My dream of meeting my family is about to come true.

When I see my aunt, it's like looking at my mom. She is identical to her. I can't look away as I say, "Caroline?"

She looks at me confused as she looks between Corbin and me. "Yeah, that's me. Who are you, son?"

My smile grows as I rush into her arms for a hug. "I'm Asher, Elaina's son, well, stepson, I guess you'd call me."

She immediately pulls me back, looking into each of my eyes as though she's searching for something. "You are from the 800's?" I just nod as she continues talking, "You are my nephew through marriage?"

I nod, looking into her eyes that look so much like my mother's. "Yes."

She pulls me in for an even tighter hug as she grins. "Oh my god! I never thought I'd meet one of her kids. I miss my twin so much. Do you have any updates for me on how my sister is doing? I've read the book she wrote, but I need to know..." She trails off for a moment, shaking her head slightly. "Is she well? Is she happy where she is?"

I meet my aunt's eyes, grinning. "Yes, she is doing amazing. She told us kids all about you and how she had to leave. She knows you must be worried about her and expected me to run off. I've always been out there looking for the rainbow ball, and I found it just today, well, June of 820 is when I found it."

She looks at me as though I hold all the answers. I know I don't, but she asks, "Do you know what year it is? What day is it now?"

Corbin smacks his knee. "Nope, I forgot to tell him, momma."

She looks into his eyes, then back at me. "It's the year 2038. It's been exactly nineteen years since she and our cousin disappeared."

I smile when I look up at her. "That's so cool and weird all at once." I smirk. "So, what does a nineteen-year-old man do around this time? Do I need to work? I've gotten great at growing a garden for food."

My aunt looks into my eyes. "Well, these boys are about to head off to college as soon as the summer is over."

I look at her. "My mom mentioned something about that a few times. I always wanted to see what it was like."

My aunt smiles. "You know what, we are gonna get you an ID and get you enrolled in school with them since you are all around the same age."

I look at my cousin and his boyfriend, smiling. "I get to go to college! This is gonna be a fun ride."

They both pull me into a hug and smile as we hug each other, Corbin saying, "Yeah, it will be a blast."

CHAPTER

TWO

The next few months we spend together, they help me learn how to fit in and teach me some of the ropes of basic education that my mom missed out on, being in the past. It doesn't take long, and I fit right in with the crowd.

When college starts, I find myself making a lot of friends. So many people who are my age, but act so immature compared to me. I fit myself in with an in-crowd, going to drinking parties and having a blast. Of course, being a Viking I can handle my liquor better than any of these kids.

I find myself at a party one night, handing out an ass load of liquor to all these party people. When I hear a voice asking me something I look up. It's Corbin.

"Asher! How has it been?"

I look at Corbin, drinks in my hand. "Corbin, Eli! It's been great. I didn't even think I'd make it to college." I lean in towards them, whispering, "Or make it this far into the future."

I get a hug from Eli, then from Corbin. As I hug them, I remember when I stepped into the rainbow ball of light. Corbin looks at me, smirking. "So, meet any ladies that interest you yet, Asher?"

I look around, spotting a redhead, her eyes are green, and she looks so Irish. I just love the way she looks at me through this whole crowd. She starts walking towards us and I can't keep my smile at bay. "Yeah, she is amazing! You guys need to meet her."

As she makes her way to us, she curls up under my arm. My cousin and his boyfriend smile as she holds her hand out to them. "I'm Jackie."

I watch as my cousin and his boyfriend take turns shaking her hand, Corbin first, saying, "I'm Corbin, this one's cousin," as he looks at me.

Eli grins, the biggest smile I've ever seen. "And I'm Eli, Corbin's boyfriend."

Jackie smiles as she shakes both of their hands, saying, "Well then, you came to the right party! This frat has a no-judgment policy. To each their own."

I don't miss the look that Corbin gives Eli as they take in her kind words. I pour them each some beers and smile as they make their way to the dance floor. I smile as I see the love between them. I dance for a bit with Jackie, grinding into her as she looks over at the two of them.

She leans back as I grind against her backside, whispering, "we should go check on your cousin, Asher."

I, not caring about anything right now except pleasing my woman, grin. "Sure, let's go over there. Even though they seem to be having as much fun as we are, babe."

She nods. "I know that that's why we should go over there. They need to know about the party rooms..."

I smirk. "Oh, do we get a party room too?"

She leans back against me. "Yes, we do, Asher."

We go up to a giggling Eli and Corbin, looking like he's ready to go. Jackie smiles as she says, "There are bedrooms, if you're getting horny."

I watch as my cousin and his boyfriend smirk. Corbin says, "Point the way."

Jackie points to the stairs. "First room on the left looks open."

I smile as I watch them walk up the stairs. They are a cute couple, and they have had such a great life. Their parents have supported them in their choice to be together. Which is more than some of the gay people in Ireland get.

When the two of them are out of sight I look at Jackie, my eyes telling her all she needs to know. She smirks as she takes my hand, dragging me up the stairs after my cousin closes the door she pointed at. She pulls me into a room a few doors down the hall.

"I am gonna take you so hard, Asher. I know you love it when I take over."

After only a few weeks of knowing her, she already knows just how I like my sex. The woman is great in the sack, and she knows it.

"Yes, yes I do love it when you take over."

She strips off all of my clothes, grinning as she does. "You know, I want all of you tonight, Asher." She looks up into my eyes, pleading. "Are you gonna deny me?"

I look up at her, my own eyes reflecting her anxiousness to get me out of my clothes and on the bed, or floor, wherever she takes me this time. "I would never tell you no, Jackie."

Her grin reaches her eyes as she looks into my own eyes. I know it's not a good idea to give anyone so much control over your own body, but I can't resist as I let go and let her do as she pleases with me.

I look into her eyes as she lays me on the bed. My clothes are all off. I smile, knowing she is not hesitating to take what she wants. I just watch her as her eyes meet mine. She holds eye contact. As long as her eyes are on mine, I'm not allowed to reach my peak.

Without her eyes leaving mine she gets up and straddles my face, looking hot and sweaty. "I want you to lick me until I can't hold back, Asher."

Ever the good boy, I do as I'm told, licking, sucking, and tasting her. I smile as I look up into her eyes. She slides down my body, not bothering with a condom; we never do.

Her eyes light up as she lets me fill her completely as she lays over me, kissing my neck and my lips. She looks away from my eyes, biting my neck. She is definitely drawing blood from me this time. I can tell by how hard she is sucking.

I just let her; like I said, I would never tell her no. This woman is too perfect for me. All the other women I've met since coming to this time seem weak compared to what I've been used to at home. I was no virgin when I came to this time. I may even have some kids in the past.

Her body just makes me want everything she has to give me. I smile when she rolls over, pulling me with her as she groans. "I'm ready for bed, Asher."

I smirk as I am too exhausted. All this partying is catching up to me. The next morning, I wake up to Jackie kissing my lips. "Good morning, sleepy head."

I grin as she looks wide awake. She climbs on top of me. Her eyes meet mine and she smirks. "I want you, Asher."

I nod as she gets up off me, letting her have me how she wants me.

I love nothing more than waking up next to this woman. She is perfect for me. When I reach my peak, she looks back at me, smirking. "You do know I'm not on birth control, right, Asher?"

I nod. "So? If you get pregnant, I will help you raise it. You know that, Jackie."

She grins as she stands up, leading me to the bathroom that's in this room. She has me take her two more times in the shower. When I come out of it, she smirks. "You're still hard, Asher. How much do you need?"

I laugh. "When I'm around you, the answer is all of it."

She claps her hands together. "We should head down and help with clean up."

I nod. "Yeah, we should."

THREE

The weeks fly by as I enjoy partying and living it up. I know my cousin is having fun with his boyfriend, but I don't know why I saw another guy come out with them that morning. When we go to the next party, I find that he lets Eli go upstairs with the other guy, Dan, willingly. He seems to need a distraction. So, I head downstairs and start cleaning with Jackie. There is a lot of mess here and we have to clean it as a part of getting into the party. As I'm cleaning, I hear my cousin.

"Why did I let him go up there with him, alone?"

I pat his back as I approach him. "Because you love him, man. He asked for something, and you let him have it," I pause, gathering my thoughts, "you know that you should probably talk to him about how you feel. You shouldn't let it bottle up. Speaking of, do you wanna help us finish cleaning up these bottles? Who knew that a college party could get so messy?"

I watch as Corbin nods, helping me clean up. After a couple of hours of cleaning, Corbin comes up to me, smirking. "Well, that only took two hours."

I burst out laughing. "Yeah, but it distracted you. How are you feeling, Corbin? Are you okay?" I see my cousin look around at the clean dining room, and the whole frat house. I see his eyes finding Dan's door as disappointment spreads over his face. I can't stop myself from saying, "Hey, he loves you, Corbin, only you. You know he's just getting some experience. He's going to come back downstairs, and everything will be okay."

I watch as my cousin lets a tear fall from his eye. "Okay."

I hold him in a hug as I look into his eyes. "How long does it take to make that lasagna that Eli loves so much?"

At my question, Corbin works his way through the cupboards, smiling when he finds all the ingredients he needs. "About an hour and a half, Let's surprise him."

I help my cousin get his lasagna started and head back to the room where I know Jackie is. I smile when I find her lying in bed, waiting for me. "Miss me?"

She spreads her legs as she answers, "Maybe a little. Why don't you come find out just how much I've missed you, Asher."

I smirk as I quickly lose all my clothes and rush to her. I feel so excited to get her whenever I want. I just love this century. I smile as we get up and get showered, having more time in the shower. We have school tomorrow and I am all caught up on my assignments too. Jackie invites me back to her dorm for the night. I accept and love every minute of it.

CHAPTER

FOUR

O ne day, after a party, I find out from Jackie that there may be more to this third party than meets the eye. Julie's phone confirms it too. They are really setting these guys up. I just can't let this happen. I find out through the grapevine that the asshole, Dan has been drugging them, so I make sure to find out where he's doing all of this and call the cops. They meet me at the dorm, and I lead them to the door where the man himself is already having his fun with them, all drugged up.

Eli turns towards me, confused. "What the hell?"

I yell, "I couldn't let it happen. I'm too late though. Eli, Corbin didn't want this. He wanted only you. He was holding it together because these assholes are professional fucking rapists and mind fuckers. They made up some bullshit so he would cooperate. Eli, while you were having fun, Corbin was being tortured."

Eli crawls over to Corbin, crying as the cops listen in on what's being said. "I'm so fucking sorry, Corbin! How could I not tell? Will you ever forgive me?"

Everything goes by so quickly, the cops taking Dan and his crew away and the friends from the frat look down on him. Not understanding what possessed him to do this. I stay and give my report on what happened. After nearly three hours of interviews and waiting for my cousin to get out of the hospital, I see Corbin.

I run up to him. "I thought he was genuinely a confused not-out gay guy, Corbin. I am so sorry for sending you to that room. The second I heard Julie talking to the other guys, I went and got the cops."

Corbin pulls me in for a hug as he tells me, "it is okay, Asher. I should have been able to tell. I should have told Eli how uncomfortable he made me right away. I didn't, you told me I should, but I let it slide until it was too late."

I push Corbin back as I look into his eyes. "This is not your fault."

Eli comes up to us, sulking. "No, it's mine. I thought having another guy, a buff, hot football player, would make you happy. I decided to try it. Although the sex was good, I was not into the whole sharing thing either." Eli pauses, letting his thoughts gather. "Dan told me that you had told him you wanted it. That if I didn't want it, I'd lose you."

I cut in, looking between the two of them. "See he had you both fooled, wound up your emotions until you couldn't see your way up."

Corbin nods. "Can we go home and sleep for the next twelve hours now?"

I hug both my cousin and his boyfriend as I help them to their dorm room. We all sleep in his dorm room; I know they both need my comfort too. The problem is, now it's Monday morning. How are they ever going to be able to focus on school after all of this?

Corbin bolts out of bed, sitting up. "Oh shit! I have to get the papers to Mr. Clink!"

I sit up with him. "Nope, you stay here and cuddle your man. I will take your work to Mr. Clink. I've already called in for your classes for the whole week."

I get up and grab the papers from Corbin's desk. I smile as I head out of their room, locking the door and delivering the papers to his teacher. I can't believe that this whole mess happened. I mean, haven't we as a society evolved to stop this kind of stuff? I know my mom really worked hard to make sure there was no judgment in our village. It wasn't an easy task with all those Vikings around.

I keep working on improving this whole thing as I attend school. I make good grades and I help my cousin out. They keep getting roped into things that are beyond their control. All because they are gay.

I make my way over to my cousin's dorm room. He answers, and he's in the buff, while Eli is still asleep. I look Corbin up and down, asking, "are you gonna wear pants today, Cuz?"

Corbin smacks his head as he closes the dorm door and goes to the dresser to grab some boxers. "Yes, I will be. I just didn't expect to be woken up at four am. What are you doing here, this early anyway, Asher?"

I smile. "Well, the guys still don't know I'm leaving the frat. Thing is I got nowhere to go. Can we get a spare bed here for me?"

Corbin smiles as he nods. "I'm sure that can be arranged. Did you overhear something at the frat house of importance?"

I nod, having heard a lot that they didn't want me to hear. "For one thing," I take a bite of my breakfast bar as I continue talking and chew, "Butch is pledging..."

My cousin is watching my mouth as I chew and talk. "So, he was connected this whole time?"

I nod, taking another bite. "And it sounds like he won't even be getting hazed. He's just in. Meaning he did something."

Corbin's face is filled with worry. "Like what?"

I shrug. "I know I was hazed, but some of the others in my class weren't. So, yesterday I asked them what they did to get in." I stop to swallow my food. "Man, they did some dirty stuff."

Corbin's look turns serious. "Like what?"

I sigh, taking a deep breath. "One of the guys was told to find Hailey alone and rape her. Haley is a lesbian, Corbin."

I can see the wheels turning in Corbin's head as he processes this information. "So, he raped a lesbian to get in, in exchange for actual hazing?"

I nod, confirming his thoughts. "They apparently hate all things LGBT. So, I don't know how Butch plays into this, but he is still an outed gay. So, he must have something else in his bag of tricks to get in."

Corbin nods. His mind must be processing this all. "Well, he is made of money. Speaking of money, I'll send mom a message. I'm sure she will get a bed here for you tonight, yet."

I nod. "So, after classes, I'm grabbing my stuff and moving in here."

Corbin agrees, nodding, as he looks at his bare upper body. "I guess we'll have to wear clothes more."

I bust out laughing. "Back home, with papa Jorge, no one was embarrassed about their bodies. I don't care, honestly."

Corbin joins me in laughing. "Yeah, well, you're from back before all our junk shrunk. I'm surprised you're not surrounded by women, Cuz."

I laugh some more, forgetting that Eli is asleep. "A lot of them have run from me. Like I get them back to my room, and we start getting hot and heavy. Then the second they see me, I am left hard and cold."

Corbin's laughter is louder than mine was. He wakes up Eli. It's been an hour already since I got here. Wiping his eyes of sleep, and smiling, Eli asks, "What's so funny?"

He gets up, not realizing that I'm here yet. He comes out and wraps his arms around Corbin's waist, still naked. Corbin kisses him, then says, "We were just laughing at Asher's sexscapedes. Did you know that most women run away from him cause he's so damn big? Also, he's moving in here tonight. Mom's gonna send a bed."

Eli looks down. Realizing he's naked, he rushes to the dresser, saying, "Didn't see you there, Asher."

I just shrug. "It's really not an issue."

Corbin gets up, starting breakfast. He makes some eggs in a nest as we all continue chatting. When we've finished eating, we get dressed and ready for the day. We manage to make it so that all of Corbin and Eli's classes, but one is together. We all head out of the dorm room.

Corbin says, "Well, this is us, Eli, first class without any creepers. See you later, Asher."

I wave as Jackie comes up behind me. "Hey boo! I missed my daily dose of you this morning, Asher."

She unabashedly reaches down, rubbing my bulge, which is obvious to anyone even when I'm completely flaccid. "Yeah, we had some cousin stuff to discuss."

Corbin looks at me, waving again. "See you later, Cuz."

I wave again too. "See ya."

Corbin watches as Jackie escorts me into the janitor's closet, looking at him and winking. I know this woman can't get enough of me. I also know that neither of us has classes. I push her up against the wall when we get inside the closet. She moans as she pushes me back, making my back hit the wall.

"I'm in charge, remember?"

I swallow hard, letting her do as she pleases with me. "Yes, I remember."

Her smirk widens as she gets on her knees. I love it every time she does this. I take after my dad, a full two feet of manhood when I'm ready for my woman. She loves it so much she begs me to feed it to her sometimes.

By the time Corbin and Eli are out of class I have banged Jackie so hard on every surface in this closet that I just know the class next to us heard every bit of it. I smirk when we get up to leave the closet, knowing that I am definitely knocking her up soon.

CHAPTER

FIVE

L ater that day I make my way to the dorm with Corbin and Eli. When we get there, the bed has already been delivered, and I have to thank my aunt for it. It's already past eight PM when I come strolling in with Jackie. "Well, that took forever to pack up. Thanks, Jackie."

Jackie leans in, kissing my lips as she moans, "You can always thank me with more of this."

She kneels down in front of me still in the kitchen. Corbin clears his throat, loudly exaggerating it. "Ehh Hem!" Jackie looks up like she only now sees him. "Take it to his bed, woman. We put up dividers and curtains."

Jackie gets cocky, nodding. She grabs my bulge, dragging me to my bed. "Sounds great to me!"

I smile when I see the divider that separates our beds. Even though it's not a full room it will work. Jackie throws me down on the bed, riding me before I even have a chance to ask her what she wants to do tonight. It's obvious that she always wants to do me. So, I let her whenever she wants, as long as my grades don't start to slip.

I know Jackie is much louder than me, but my cousin and his man sure put up a good contest for who is louder. The next thing I know,

Jackie is lying on her belly on the bed, naked as can be. She looks back at me, smirking. "I want you to take me back there, Asher."

I swallow hard. I know she will only ask for what she really wants. If she wants me there, then that's what she will get. When I look into her satisfied eyes, I grin. "You liked that, didn't you?"

I decide that I'm hungry after all that. I can't wait until I get her alone again, though. She grins as she leans against me, her tummy grumbling. "I want to eat, Asher."

I smirk at her. "What, my rod didn't feed you enough?"

She slaps me as she looks back at the kitchen area. "Let's go grab some food."

As we leave the room, I hear my cousin and his boyfriend going at it. Just as we make it to the kitchen, they come out of the bathroom in just their boxers. I look between them getting ready to stuff my face with the food we planned to eat.

"Damn, you guys outlasted us."

Corbin looks at me with a wink. "Yeah, we like taking our time, Asher."

Jackie butts in, "I just love his rod!"

We all laugh. I pull Jackie close to me as we sit at the kitchen counter eating. Eli and Corbin go to bed, hiding under their sheets. When we finish eating, I look towards my bed, smiling as I lead Jackie to it again. We lie down and fall asleep quickly.

I wake up early the next morning, and Jackie is already busy under the covers. I give her what she wants, taking her over and over again. I heard her in the middle of the night. I only got bits and pieces of the conversation, but I do know that she was talking so quietly so she could hide it. I was worried when she went on the other side of the divider. I hope she's not a bad person. I really do love this woman. I would never tell her no... Unless she was hurting my cousin.

As I get up to cook breakfast, Jackie kisses me hard, grabbing my bulge. "I love you, Asher, but I've gotta head out. I've got some business to handle."

I smile as I look her in the eyes. "I love you too, Jackie. I mean it."

She pulls me close, grinning as she does. "I will see you and your crotch later."

I shake my head as she leaves the dorm. Just as I get started on the cooking, Corbin comes into the kitchen. "So, where's Jackie?"

I smirk. "She got what she wanted out of me, then she went to change at her dorm. Why?"

Corbin takes a cautionary glance at Eli. "Can you explain the technology part, Eli?"

Eli nods, doing just that. He explains to me how Jackie got up in the middle of the night and put a tracker on Corbin's phone. He tells me how he also put a backtrace on Butch's phone. I am baffled at the fact that she would do that.

I sigh, looking down at the food I've made. "Well, I guess that relationship is over."

Corbin shakes his head. "No, not yet, Asher. You gotta keep her believing we are all clueless."

I smirk, asking my cousin, "so I can keep, what do you call it, dicking her down? At least until this is all over."

Both Eli and Corbin bust out laughing. "Yes, you can. Keep her busy while Elie does his technology deal."

I put on a brave face, making it seem like I'm taking a hardship for the team. "If it must be done! I'll sacrifice my giant cock for the greater good."

CHAPTER

SIX

The whole day I go about my business, meeting Jackie like I do every morning. We have a great time together in the closet again, and she goes on her way. I smile on my way to check into everything with Mr. Clink, who I know is keeping track of the whole situation.

Mr. Clink tells me all about the events of the day. Apparently, when I was out getting with Jackie, Butch was sneaking into my cousin's dorm and trying to rape him and his boyfriend. I nod my head giving Mr. Clink a serious look. "That's it, I'm breaking it off with her. Jackie doesn't deserve me if she is encouraging this bull."

Mr. Clink nods. "Yeah, good idea. Your cousin has been through a lot this year, Asher."

I nod as I head out of the room. "I know, this bull needs to stop, here and now."

I make my way to the hallway as I call Jackie. She sounds seductive and ready for me. I smirk as I hang up, having told her to meet me in the closet again. When I get there, I hear her giggling in the closet waiting for me.

I open the door and slide in. There is no way I'm going to miss out on one more good time with her. "Hey, Jackie."

I smirk as I pull her up on top of me, kissing her lips as I take what I know she is willingly giving to me. I moan as we both reach our climax. I then toss her off of me, looking her in the eyes.

When her eyes meet mine, I know she knows. "What's wrong, Asher?"

I look her in the eyes. "You know damn well what's wrong, Jackie."

She swallows hard as she looks me in the eyes. "So, you've found me out." She looks down at her hands, asking, "how long have you known?"

I meet her eyes as I see true regret in them. "I've known since you spent the night at my cousin's dorm. You think we didn't hear you sneaking around and doing something with my cousin's phone? We did. Now that we've caught Butch, I don't need you around anymore, Jackie." I look down at my feet. "I really meant it when I said I loved you, Jackie, but this shit you're doing." I wave my arm out indicating that she's done a lot of bad things to my cousin. "It's a deal breaker for me. Family comes first, Jackie."

She looks at her feet, laughing, then up into my eyes. "As much as I love you, I have to agree, family comes first. I did all this for my sister. And I would again. I finally got my sister back after years of no contact with her. This was the only way she would talk to me again. So, you go be with your family. I'll stick with mine."

I look her in the eyes before we leave the closet. "I wish you would stop hanging out with bad people. You do know rape and hurting people is bad, right? I'm a damn Viking and I know it's bad!"

She looks me dead in the eyes. "You know, I never believed your time travel crap anyway, Asher. But that," she looks down at my bulge, "was too good to resist."

I smirk. "Well, you don't get it anymore unless you change your ways drastically. Stop being an evil person. Oh, and if you're pregnant, I plan to use all the charges of involvement with hurting my cousin to get my baby from you, Jackie."

This sends her out of the closet, tears streaming down her face. I feel bad for her while still hating her for what she did to Corbin. I make my way up to the dorm, disappointed with how the day has gone. I really did love, hell, I still do, love her. I just can't date someone who would willingly be involved in this stuff.

By the time I get to the dorm, Eli and Corbin are there. I walk in, explaining to them what happened throughout the day. "Well, after Mr. Clink updated me, I called it off with Jackie. She was super disappointed but laughed in my face when I told her that family comes first." I go to my cousin and his boyfriend, wrapping them both up in a hug. "At least it was fun while it lasted. Are you both okay?"

I go with my cousin, sitting on his bed, looking between the two of them. They have been through so much. I wonder where they would have been if I hadn't come through time to be here with them and help them. I know there is a reason for the time and place I came to. I feel like this is it.

As I'm lost in thought, Corbin looks over at me with a half-smile on his face. "We definitely are. We need to stop ruminating on those jerks. Do you wanna watch a bit of TV? I hear they are playing re-runs of My Norse Lover."

I bust out laughing. "I still can't believe auntie turned it into a script for a TV show."

Corbin and Eli both start laughing with me. Corbin says, "I know, right!"

Eli looks between us both. "I mean, they have to be using prosthetics to make those bulges look so big. You know men are definitely not that big nowadays."

Both Eli and Corbin look at me, laughing. "Well, except you."

I grab my bulge, jiggling it. "And this isn't even hard."

We all sit up watching My Norse Lover until we fall asleep. We are all huddled together on Corbin and Eli's bed. I dream of Jackie being pregnant. I wish so hard that this dream could come true, but she is such a horrible person to do what she did, what she helped do. I just can't do that to my cousin and his boyfriend.

CHAPTER

SEVEN

I wake up way before my cousin and his boyfriend. I get busy making some breakfast for us all. I can tell the moment they wake up. Their whispers are heard through the dorm. I know they are going to be going at it, so I leave them be and just focus on my cooking.

When they finally come out of their bed, I get a text from Jackie. I read it as they come to the kitchen to grab some of the breakfast I made.

Jackie: Well, Asher, you really did it. I got knocked up by you, and you just broke up with me yesterday.

I, never wanting to lose contact with any of my kids, look at this text for a long time. How can this be? She has done some horrible things. I look over at my cousin.

"Hey man, Jackie just texted me."

Corbin looks at the phone as I hold it facing him. "Well, congratulations are in order then."

I look at him. "But how can I raise a kid without its mom?" I start to tear up. "I don't understand how she could be so evil and help Butch with all he did to you two."

Corbin holds my eye contact as he clears his throat, saying, "If she can be bad, she can also be good. You need to go to her and try to talk some sense into her."

I nod, knowing my cousin wouldn't say this if he didn't believe it. I quickly text her back, wanting to know what the hell she expects me to do.

Me: What is it you want me to do about it, Jackie? You fucking helped someone take my cousin and his boyfriend against their will. How could you expect me to care about you after all that?

The bubbles come and go a good ten times before I see Jackie's message on my screen.

Jackie: I'm sorry I did that, Asher. I really am, but my sister meant the world to me. I just realized now, looking at this positive pregnancy test, that I really do love you, Asher. I love you more than I loved my sister.

I'm confused by this. As I read the message, I think about what to type back to her.

Me: Jackie, you say that now, but how am I supposed to believe you, when this whole time you were using me to get to my cousin? I need something to be sure that you aren't the kind of person who does that to people. I need to know that if I let you back in, my family will be safe.

Jackie: I am willing to cut all ties with my sister just to be with you. I want to be with you, while we raise this baby together. Besides, my sister tossed me out of the frat house. She doesn't let pregnant people live there, even if they are her sister.

Against my better judgment I find myself laughing at this. She did all this for her sister only to find out that she was a backstabber. I look at my phone, ready now to actually talk to Jackie.

She picks up on first ring, like she was waiting for my call. "Hey, Asher."

I sigh as I start to talk. "Hey, Jackie."

She just starts bawling as I pace around my side of the dorm. "I didn't know that what I was doing was wrong. I really thought there was a good reason for them to track your cousin's phone. I thought that maybe he had done something to her, something to deserve all this."

I listen to her talk, not wanting to interrupt her, but she seems to need a bit of prompting. "But..."

She takes in a tearful breath as she continues, "but I learned rather quickly, as Julie spelled it out for me, that the frat truly hates gay people, that they are a horrible place."

I nod as I look down at the floor. I can hear the sincerity in her voice. "I know you really seem to sound regretful, but how do I know you will stay on my side of this, Jackie?"

She huffs. "My sister kicked me out, Asher. I don't mean figuratively, I mean literally. She kicked me in the stomach. I'm sitting in the hospital right now."

That gets me moving my feet, rushing out the door without even giving my cousin a glance. I can update him later. I find my way to the campus hospital. When I get there, she tells me what room she is in. I find myself by her side holding her hand and forgetting to hang up my phone as it falls into her lap.

We sit like this, me holding her as she cries, and I start to cry too. Just as we start to calm down, and lose our tears, I hear the doctor clearing his throat. "I'm sorry, Jackie. Can he hear the update?"

She wipes her eyes as she looks up at the doctor. "Yes, it's his baby."

The doctor looks sullen as he looks into each of our eyes. "Was." He takes a deep breath in as he continues, "You're losing the baby. The blow to your stomach has displaced the baby and it is no longer attached to your uterine walls."

My heart fills with rage, rage at her sister, rage at this crazy situation. I push down the rage to hold Jackie as she cries, mourning the baby that we would have had. The doctor stands there, watching us cry as though he has no idea what to do.

Finally, after a good ten minutes of crying, the doctor looks between us. "If you let it miscarry naturally, Jackie, you will be able to try for more. The D&C comes with the risk of complicated pregnancies down the line. You can stay here until you've lost the baby completely, Jackie, or you can go home and spend as much time together as you can while you miscarry."

She looks up at him. "Can Asher stay here with me?"

The doctor nods. "Yes."

I look at him, my eyes still filled with tears. "Good, because I wasn't planning on leaving her side, doc."

We spend the next few days in the hospital as she miscarries our baby. I text my cousin off and on, making sure that they take the cops and go grab all of Jackie's things. She is staying with me from now on. When we finally get back to the dorm room, Corbin and Eli greet us with hugs. They would have loved to have met the baby too.

EIGHT

The rest of the year finishes up uneventfully. Well, except for one happy event that happens a little bit after we start packing up for home for the summer. Jackie got pregnant again, and this time that baby is staying on board. In true Viking fashion, I knock her up every year, and I will, until we physically can't have any more babies. This woman is up for the challenge too.

We finish up college and both get amazing degrees, all while my aunt helps us raise our growing brood. By the time we celebrate Eli and Corbin's tenth wedding anniversary, we have eight kids. Our youngest at the time is just over nine months old.

I smile as our little one poops while being held by Cousin Corbin. He hands her back to me, saying, "Okay, little one, time to go back to your daddy!"

I smile as my four younger kids climb all over me. The three older ones are off playing with some of their cousins. I hold my little one close as I look into her eyes. "Again? That's the third poop in the last five hours. What is in your boobs, Jackie?"

Jackie comes up to me, taking our daughter from my arms, saying, "what's the matter, babe? You can make 'em, but you can't change 'em?"

I laugh as I look at my wife. "Well, it would be easier if you weren't feeding our daughter stool softeners in your breast milk, love. Also, how should I change a diaper with all the kids piled on top of me?"

Jackie smirks at me as she pats her belly. "Well, you better get used to it. I think you've done it again."

I watch as Jackie walks away from me to change our youngest daughter. She looks angry, but I follow her, nonetheless. I shrug off some of the kids as I make my way to her, wrapping my arms around her waist as she changes our baby.

"Do you mean it, Jackie? We are having another baby?"

I feel her laughter as she answers, "Of course we are. You and your Viking genes won't stop impregnating me. And we all know I'll never tell you no, not since our second year of college anyway."

I smile as I look down at her, kissing her neck, remembering what happened in our second year of college.

We are just about home to check on our first kid, when Jackie looks at me, a bit of guilt written on her face. "I think that my sister wants to come back into my life."

I look over at her sternly. "Do you remember how she treated you? Do you remember what she did to you?"

She looks at me, her eyes filled with tears. "How could I forget?"

I pull over the car, getting safely to the curb. Wrapping her up in my arms, I whisper, "I love you, Jackie, but you can't see your sister. She only uses you. She is bad news, and you know it."

That was the conversation we had right before she went to see her sister again. Well, all her sister wanted to do was hurt her again, and in doing so she hurt us both again. Another miscarriage. The woman known as Julie is a horrible sister. There is something wrong with her brain. She was put in jail for the second offense. Jackie never went to see her sister ever again. It took two lost babies for her to realize that her sister is no good to anyone.

I start to think about the past, the real past, where I was born. I wonder if my siblings have as many kids as I do right now. I wonder if they are happy. I know that I could read the book and know some of the things that had happened to my siblings, but I can't help that they are in the past. I want to leave them there. My home is right here, right now, with Jackie, and at least nine of our babies.

I look Jackie in the eyes as I kiss her lips. "You are perfect for me, Jackie."

ABOUT THE AUTHOR

Hello, it's me again, your friendly erotic romance author. I really enjoyed writing for this anthology... And I have many more coming. Please do check out my Amazon author page, and follow me on Instagram (lindamariepankowauthor). I hope you enjoyed reading my part in this anthology, and will continue to read the rest of the stories on here.

LET ME GROW YOU A GARDEN

A GARDEN

AMANDA FAYE

In a world where true love is indicated by flowers blooming on your skin, Mia Naerie's body is a garden.

Song inspiration
A Safe Place to Land
https://youtu.be/Ht2NCrlghS4

This story is set in the Submit for Salvation Universe. In a world where Humans and Fae live together, Dragon shifters have to file a flight plan. It's a common complaint about how wrong Game of Thrones got the portrayal of dragons.

Well, it's a common complaint in the royal household, at any rate.

Consort Drake, The Golden Dragon, Duke of Dragonborn, right hand of the Queen, a devotee to his Tree Lord's branch, is personally affronted. Dragons can't hover, as he's made it a point to whine about it every time he can. Which is often because he's married to the King and has an incredibly loud mouth.

Let Me Grow You A Garden takes place approximately twenty-five years past the end of The Vanquishing Prince.

It has nothing to do with Consort Drake, but he thinks *everything* has to do with him, and as he is technically a king, (and please don't get him started on *that* headache!) he demanded to be mentioned in the blurb.

IT'S SUPPOSED to be a raid, just like any other. Something simple, something the three of us have been doing together since almost the first day we met, sneaking onto the castle grounds rather than sneaking into terrorist compounds.

And it is.

Until it isn't.

~

OWEN BREAKS MY CONCENTRATION.

"What do you think, Mia, The Golden Dragon for dinner?"

We're lounging, and I use that word *very* loosely, outside the property lines of the house we're about to raid.

My eyes flick to my best friends in the entire world.

Owen, big as a bear, with hair as red as the fire that spews from his fingertips. He's a fascinating juxtaposition. Fire elements are all about their emotions. They're always brimming with dramatics and, well, fire. But Owen is as calm as a dandelion. He's the most level-headed person I've ever met.

With a stomach that never stops grumbling.

It's comforting in a way to know that no matter how much has changed between tonight and the day we met, Owen's hunger can always be depended upon.

I barely hear when Emeran replies to the rumbling of Owen's belly.

"I have a roast in the oven," he says with a smile in his voice. "You asked for it last night."

"Oh yeah," Owen grunts dumbly. "Well, then maybe we can grab a snack after we finish here. They have great onion rings. I'm starving."

Emeran snorts, and I know without looking that he's rolling his eyes.

Some things truly will always remain the same.

Like Owen's obsession with the Consort's namesake pub and Emeran's desire to keep Owen well-fed and happy.

Emeran, The Prince Who Wasn't, with blue hair and a frame as sleek and trim as his adopted father, King Liam of Argulthion. Emeran, the only man in the country—in the world probably, besides his favourite father, Drake—who didn't want to wear the crown.

Adopted by the then Vanquishing Prince and his Human Weaver wife during the first war with Rahma, he was raised as the oldest child and heir-apparent of the Argulthion kingdom.

My prince passed up his right to inheritance and bequeathed his crown to his half-fae sister, then fought a war for the right to do so. Like his birth-mother, who died fighting for equality against purist Rahma invaders. Like his adopted parents—The Royals Four, The Quattro Bond, who scooped him from the battlefield little older than a babe then fought for the right to love each other.

The minute they were defeated, the purists chose Emeran to build their future rallies around. A pureblooded Fae in line for the crown. I'm still convinced that *that*, if for no other reason, is why he surrendered his right to rule to his half-fae siblings.

Emeran, and us with him, fought for what was right, as a true Argulthion always should.

Another thing that will never change.

Emeran is the first through the door, putting his body and strength between us and danger. Owen is the comedic relief. Don't get me wrong; he's grown into a capable weaver in his own right. But if Emeran weren't an Enforcer, Owen wouldn't be, either. He's only here to keep Emeran sane. His role in the grand scheme of things is to ensure that Emeran doesn't get lost in the darkness of his own head.

My job, as always, is to ensure they get to go home every night in one piece. Well, relatively in one piece. We've had a few close calls over the years. We three each have a lot more scars than we did at the end of the second war with Rahma.

Still, some things never change.

I'm the planner. The nit-picker.

I, too, am only here because where Emeran goes, I have always followed. I'm here to ensure my boys stay alive. The entire country knows that they would be dead ten times over without me. What can I say? I'm good at what I do.

I'm not even technically an Enforcer. My job title reads Analyst. But Emeran is no typical Policeman, and the types of missions he's sent on require my expertise.

Besides, we made a vow—to *always* be together. Forever. We might not be oathsworn in the usual sense, but the vines that trail up my spine and over my hips make that promise as everlasting as the sun. I'm sure the day will come when they'll each take wives and build their own families.

For me, though, I will always belong to them.

The boys chatter amongst themselves while I look over the floorplan of the house we're raiding tonight. Leo Sandragon fancies himself a Dark Lord. Claiming to be a direct descendant of Maul himself, he's been wreaking havoc across the continent for months. But he's no budding Hitler.

He's not even a contender.

Emeran thinks he's simply read too much Harry Potter.

The buzz of excitement is nowhere to be found this afternoon. The old adrenaline of fear mixed with anticipation that used to accompany our forays into danger, has long since been replaced with...boredom.

I—am bored.

There. I said it. The thrill of the chase is gone.

The only thing I'm nervous about now is whether they'll get home in time to eat that roast at a decent hour or if Emeran's Fairy, Moonbeam, will have to pull it from the oven and keep it fresh with a preservation spell. We stand concealed, each in our own invisibility cloaks for extra precaution, using a spell I created myself so that we can see each other. It's tied to our magical signatures.

It'll only work for us.

We're waiting for the go-ahead to breach the Manor House, where this latest cult has taken up residence. It used to belong to a member of the aristocracy until Sandragon magick'd it away from the old fellow.

No matter. That will all be set to rights after tonight.

Still, even though this is an old routine, I double-check my spare blade. I confirm our backup is in place, our communication coms are open and clear, and my utility pockets are filled with any gadgets we might need. I make sure the bracelet on my wrist is tight enough that it'll never lose contact with my skin.

I'd rather lose my life than lose my glamour.

I share everything with the men at my side. Everything but the secret that the glamour hides.

"You're clear to go, Team One."

Emeran grins at me over his shoulder and twirls his fingers in a complicated formation before clasping his hands together and pulling them into his chest, bringing down the outer wards. He's gotten so cocky. I shake my head in exasperation, then give him my hardest glare.

Owen sniggers, Emeran shrugs, then, like a second skin falling into place, their expressions change to one that means business.

Owen seems to swell into his impressive size while Emeran melds into the night.

"Team One is advancing," Owen growls into his com.

We don't make it farther than the front door.

"Emeran! DON'T!" I scream, but it's too late.

I don't know what alerts me that something isn't right. Intuition, maybe. Long years of walking into booby traps? But even with magick pouring from my fingertips, the millisecond warning is *far* too late.

It happens in slow motion but faster than the blink of an eye.

We forgot, as all powerful beings eventually do—sometimes basic is better. We're the best FORCE team there is (Fae Observational Retribution Corrections Enforcement Agency).

The best that's ever been.

Our techniques are on the cutting edge of magick—which is how none of us sees the magickal residue of the crude, inelegant bomb until it's already begun its detonation. For all I know, downing the wards is what activated it. We were looking for the worst that magick had to offer. We aren't prepared for...whatever this is.

Emeran's trademark smirk is still on his face when the room explodes into a thousand broken pieces. My arms are raised to stop him, my shield bubble blooming between my boys and the blast when my body is thrown into the air like a rag doll. The final thought in my head is how the ruby coloured blood clashes horribly with the firey red of his hair.

Then blackness claims me.

You know when you accidentally sit on the remote, and the telly starts flipping through channels so fast it makes your head spin? The volume sounds like fuzz, flicking in staticky pops as images fill the screen too quickly for you to catch more than a burst of colour before it's on to the next image.

I feel hands roughly tugging on my body; the next moment,

they're a gentle caress, then they are gone altogether. One minute I'm in the rubble, the next, the sterilised scent of a hospital assaults my senses.

I hear the ringing of my ears, the sound of my screams echoing without end in my imagination. I hear Emeran and Owen talking as if from a distance, but the pressure on my hands tells me they are at my side.

The soothing, deep timbre of their voices fades in and out around me.

"We should have told her when we had the chance."

"Don't talk like that, Emeran. This isn't the end. We've been through worse than this."

"It's my fault."

"No, it's not."

"We can't lose her, Owen."

"We won't."

"I never knew flowers could be so beautiful."

Then everything fades into blessed blackness once again.

My eyes fly open when the shock of electricity, or maybe magic, explodes against my body.

It feels like I've been struck by lightning.

Flicker. Flicker. Flick.

Am I dead?

I can't feel my limbs, but... maybe I can because they dangle uselessly at my sides while a half-dozen Fae Healers and Human Doctors in pale green scrubs break my body in an attempt to put it back together again.

Someone wipes tears from their face with the back of their hand, and I retain my senses just enough to contemplate the sanitation of crying while tending to a patient.

I must be breathing, but it doesn't feel like it. My chest feels cleaved in two and doesn't respond to my commands to expand and contract. The room spins, an alarm screaming somewhere in the distance that splits my head into a million pieces. If I'm not dead, this must be what dying feels like.

King Liam lied then, because this doesn't feel like falling asleep. It feels like I'm being ripped apart from the inside.

I open my mouth to scream, but nothing comes out. With every blink, the scene changes, but somehow, it seems to stay the same. Maybe I'm the one who's changing? Before, I was whole, and now I'm scattered across the pavement. My head falls to the side. My muscles can no longer carry the weight of my neck, and I see two men crying together. The smaller of the two is trying to hold back the larger, his sinewy arms wrapped tightly about the chest of the bleeding, red-headed man.

I think they're crying my name.

But I can't be sure because I can't remember who I am.

~

THEY SAY your life flashes before your eyes when you die. For me, it was like travelling through time.

King Liam has talked extensively about the day he died and his queen brought him back with True Love's Kiss. He claimed his life didn't flash, but then he didn't really die, did he? His soul left his body, yes, but it didn't pass on. I *must* be dying then because as screams rend the air and pain wracks my soul, I see the flowers blooming on my body and the stories of how they got there.

~

I GET my first bud when I am thirteen. It was pure luck that I was there when Rahma tried to take the princess. A by-product of being best friends with a prince. Queen Adeline used to tell me all the time the chaos *her* prince brought into *her* life.

The princess got away without a scratch. As for me—

I entered the coma with skin as unblemished as only a babe can be, and I wake with two unfurled flowers over my heart. They stand out stark and bright against my shimmery bronze skin. Their stems are entwined. The flowers will be separate but forever connected.

They almost look...proud.

I've never been more thankful for the suffocating stiffness of the High Fae clothing than I am when I see them for the first time. My clothing becomes my armour, and I use it to protect myself from prying eyes. I share everything with Emeran and Owen, but I'm not willing to share this.

Not yet.

My buds are mine and mine alone.

I can't stop touching them. I take to rubbing over the spot with my thumb through my shirt as if caressing them will make them bloom faster.

My mother gives me curious glances, and several times I tense, positive she's about to ask questions I'm unsure how to answer. But in every instance, she smiles instead, a small, private smile just for me, and we turn our attention back to other things.

But she knows, and I know, that her daughter is in the beginning blooms of first love. Of *true* love. Because flowers won't grow if you're in the throes of a crush—to grow a garden, your heart must be pure.

Only—behind the excitement and the flowing feelings of wonder is a burning curiosity that grows brighter by the day. It consumes my waking thoughts and flitters in and out of my dreams.

Without seeing the match on their skin, how can I tell with whom I am in love?

Emeran? Or Owen?

It's not unheard of for school-aged younglings to present with flowers, but it's not a common occurrence either. I spend most of the summer looking for instances where buds appear on someone so young. The anecdotal evidence is few and far between. Unlike Owen and Emeran who live at Bettenbough full time, I go back and forth between my mother's house and the castle.

As the child of a human woman and a Fae man, my magick more resembles Queen Adi's than your average elemental. In theory, I no longer need the training the castle provides those in need of assistance with the magic. I return year after year because that is where my heart lies.

"Can we go shopping, Mum? Before I go back to Bettenbough? I've outgrown a lot of my clothes."

My mum gives me that secret smile again but nods her head in fast agreement. If she thinks anything particular about my new high-necked shirts and cardigan sweaters, she keeps her comments to herself.

Fourteen is...hard. Harder than anything I've ever faced before. Once again, I find myself alone. *It's for the best*, I try to tell myself. Emeran is lost to the horrors being committed in his name, and Owen is lost in his attempt to comfort Emeran. Who can blame them for pulling away.

Every day another story reaches our ears about Rahma allies rallying under banners plastered with Emeran's name. An elementary school filled with mixed-species children in a country a half-world away was set ablaze with terrorists taking credit in Emeran's name.

Those are burdens I can't understand. I'm not the daughter of a king nor the daughter of a Priestess. They don't mean to leave me behind, but they do, and it's the hardest time of my life.

It's for the best, I tell myself. Our friendship could not have lasted forever. They were born for a life that I can't follow. Better to go our separate ways now then make the break when it's twice as hard later.

The buds on my chest prove, however, that those words are only lies. I don't mean them in my heart. I take to studying my buds in the mirror at night. I rub my fingers over their closed edges and attempt to will them away. By the end of the year, when I'm holding onto Emeran's waist while the wind whips through my hair sitting on the back of a dragon, my buds have doubled to four.

Owen is right behind me.

The question still stands.

Do one of them love me too?

~

THERE'S a reason why flower names are so popular for little girls. Sometimes you're named for the flowers that bloom on your parents. Sometimes, they choose the flower they hope to see on you one day.

I'M fifteen when the buds that cover my skin finally bloom. Emeran vanishes from the castle, and my heart...it...stops. Owen holds my hand in a death grip; then, when that is no longer good enough, he pulls me bodily into his arms. He tips my head tight under his chin and tries to shield me from the terror, but Emeran...he's ours. What hurts him hurts us. When he's finally recovered, on death's door, but alive, my knees give out.

Only Owen's arms keep me from hitting the floor.

Owen holds me as we scream and cry, and listen to our best friend re-tell the worst night of his life since the night his birth-parents were murdered before his eyes.

When I finally crawl into bed, exhausted in every sense of the word, I barely notice the tell-tale bursts of white and purple across my chest.

It's when I drag myself out of yet another nightmare where they die and I'm unable to save them that I realise I'm in love with them both.

Two flowers for the men that will be the loves of my life.

EVENTUALLY, I stop keeping track of when a new flower appears. There's really no point when every time I get a glance at myself in the mirror, another bundle has arisen. I become an expert in botany, or at least in things that bloom.

A ring of purple mallow rings the breast that covers my heart. Mallow has several meanings. I know, without ever seeing their twins on flesh reflecting mine, that the Mallow blooms for Emeran. It symbolizes surviving harsh conditions and surrendering to love.

I couldn't have picked a more perfect representation of my love for Emeran if I tried.

Emeran's flower bloomed first.

Entwined down my spine are Daffodils. Rebirth. Hardy. Everlasting. My mother planted daffodils one spring, and they bloomed, then died in the circle of life. I forgot all about them. But, year after year, without any tending, they bloom again under my bedroom window. It doesn't matter what mother nature throws at them through the winter; they burst forth from the dirt every spring without fail.

I love Owen almost against my wishes. I didn't have any choice. Year after year, no matter what sort of chaos he creates, my love for him regrows.

As the boys begin to date other people, I spend hours by myself. I sit in the bath and run my fingers over the daffodils that have begun to creep over my hips. I smile alone behind the curtains of my four-poster and admire the way the purples entwine with the white.

From the beginning, my flowers were different. I've never heard of a person who blooms for two. Our rulers share a Quattro Bond. They share the deepest love most of us have ever known, and even they didn't bloom for each other.

Mallows and Daffodils are certainly not something you'd find together in real life. But the way they cross and entwine over my flesh is nothing short of magical. They share stems and leaves and vines, like veins circulating under my skin. They burst into being almost on top of one another.

It makes sense. To me, at least. Walking the halls of Bettenbough, you won't find one without the other. Emeran and Owen? They're like two sides of an unbroken being.

I love them each separately, but together?

Together they make *me* whole.

After I leave my mother, I make a trip to Leachlainn's chambers. She doesn't look surprised to see me. I suspect that *she's* suspected this day would come for longer than either of us care to admit. Without saying a word, I remove my cloak and, for the first time in my life, show another person my markings.

I wear a thin-strapped camisole so she can feel the depth of my terror.

They reach my elbows and crawl up the back of my neck. The closer we get to the final confrontation with Rahma, the faster and thicker my flowers grow. I read once that only one in ten thousand people have flowers, not just on their torsos.

My love for them feels rarer than that.

Her smile is sad and knowing.

"Oh dearest," she says in a voice brimming with emotions. "You never do things halfway, do you?"

I am a garden. A secret garden for two.

My flowers cover me from neck to knee.

I never have done anything halfway. Loving my boys is no different. I've given them my all. I'm sure before all is said and done, I'll give them my life, too.

"Have you thought about telling them?" she asks gently.

I scoff. I can't help it. I wipe the tears from my face but it doesn't stop their flow. Have I thought about telling them? Only every moment of every day since the day I turned sixteen. But I can't.

I won't.

I won't ruin what we have.

I know they love me. I do. Just not how I love them. I long ago made my peace with the matter. What I need now is a way to keep us alive without letting them know.

"There isn't time for all that," I whisper. "I need to concentrate on keeping them alive. If we make it through this..."

I shrug helplessly and wipe the fresh set of tears from my eyes.

That's good enough for her.

My favourite priestess, my mentor, my friend, leaves me silently crying in her sitting room only to appear with a plain wooden box in her palm.

"I don't need it anymore," she tells me with a soft smile.

She opens the lid to show a plain silver band. It's nothing. It's less than nothing. A trinket you could pick up at any discount store at any shopping centre.

But I recognize the metal.

Fae-wrought has a gleam all its own.

I suspect what it'll do before she snaps it on.

"So long as the inner rune touches your skin, the bracelet will keep your secret."

It's snug against my forearm, as it's supposed to be. As soon as the clasp closes against my arm, my garden disappears.

I feel like I've lost a limb. Like I've lost a part of my soul.

Leanchlainn holds me while I cry for my loss.

EMERAN KISSES me in the silence of our tent one night when the day had been filled with killing. I kiss Owen during the Battle For The Crown. Those are the first, last, and possibly only kisses of my life.

THE BOYS still live together in a house inside the capital, but I have an apartment of my own across town. My bracelet comes off only during the witching hour. When I'm alone in my bedroom, the pain of being apart from them only equal to the pain of always being so close.

"I love you," I whisper into the nothingness of darkness. "My love has grown you a garden."

MY BED IS...LUXURIOUS. Maybe even...ostentatious. But I love it. My flat is plain, covered in books. My dishes and furniture were purchased from estate sales. Most of my clothing is purchased at consignment shops to curb expenses and to do my part for the world's unimaginable waste.

But my bed is like sleeping in the arms of a lover. Or at least what I imagine it would feel like.

The lumpy, uncomfortable thing underneath me is *not* that.

Then the smell hits me.

I'm prone to scented candles in my private space. Using them when I soak in the bathtub or light my bedside reading in the middle of the night. The smell that creeps into my nostrils is bland. Sterile. Like antiseptic.

Then there's the silence.

It's oppressive without the comforting hum of my ceiling fan and the traffic outside.

The first thing I see when I open my eyes is the acid green nails of one Lilly Naekrana and the cover of Argulthion Elle Magazine. If you'd have told me the first day I went to study at Bettenbough that Lilly Naekrana would become my best friend outside of my boys, I'd have laughed in your face. A month as dormmates, however, proved we were more alike than different.

She might be a snake shifter, but her hiss is worse than her bite.

Mostly.

I open my mouth to get her attention, but all that comes out is a gravelly groan. The magazine claps closed and is flung almost over her shoulder, and Lilly's perfectly coiffed green razored bob jerks as she jumps to her feet and reaches for me.

There must have been water on the bedside table because without saying a word, she lifts a pink cup to my face and wiggles the red straw.

The furthest colour from healing and soothing that I could ever imagine. Fairgaurd needs to change their colour scheme. Hospitals shouldn't be covered in baby tones.

My brain– it's...not functioning right!

"Baby sips," she admonishes, using a softer, kinder tone than I've ever heard leave her mouth before.

I drink the water down gratefully, pausing to clear my throat before starting again.

She takes it from me before I'd like her to, but I don't have the strength to complain right now.

"Wh-what happened?" I mumble, still trying to get my bearings.

"You don't remember?" she snaps with wide eyes, her voice back to the sharp, slightly sarcastic timbre I've come to know and love.

"N-n," it shouldn't be this hard to form words. My eyes blink in rapid succession, and I give my head a little shake, trying desperately to form coherent thoughts. "No," I finally push out.

"Well," she sighs, leaning back in her chair and admiring her nails before she looks me in the eye. What I see there makes my heart speed up and my stomach clench in anxiety.

Underneath her unflappable facade, fear brims behind her expression. She clenches her fists and tucks her hands into her lap when I see them shaking.

"You blew yourself up, Mia," she tries to say flippantly but instead states with a tremble in her voice. "It was quite inconvenient. I was in the middle of showing Tomas what a snake can do with their tongue when we got the call. The next time you plan on dying, I do wish you'd give me more warning. Chanel is utterly wasted in the Fairgaurd waiting room."

Dying?

Blown up?

Owen and Emeran!

"The—the boys?" I gasp, bringing my hands to my head and heart, respectively. Why can't I remember?!?! Some unseen alarm begins to alert as my pulse skyrockets, and my breathing comes in sharp, stabby pants. I try to sit up, but Lilly leaps from her seat to push me back down. Despite her prickly exterior, her hands are soft when she pries them from my chest and presses them into my sides.

"Calm down," she admonishes gently. Or as gentle as Lilly is capable of. "The Red-headed Wonder and the Drama-Prince are fine. They barely had a scratch on them. Apparently the mission went wrong, and instead of saving yourself like any normal person would, you erected a shield between them and the blast, which left you to take the brunt of it. Half the house landed on top of you. They haven't left your side for a week. Daekas told them if they didn't come in this morning and meet with some overseeing board..."

Daekas is the second highest ranking FORCE member outside of the crown.

"The oversight committee?" I interrupt.

It must have been bad, then.

Real bad.

We...had a mission? The Maul wannabe, maybe?

She sneers, and it's *such* a Lilly expression; perfectly sculpted eyebrow lifted in a way I can only dream of being able to accomplish. Lip turned up. Eyes rolled into the back of her head. But still, for all the disdain pouring from her person, she looks like a movie star. "I don't know. I don't want to know. Anyway, Daekas told them he'd fire them. When Emeran told him to go blow a Dragon, Old Daek changed tactics. He told the dimwitted duo that he'd tattle on them to *you* when you finally graced us with your presence again if they didn't come in for a few hours. That did the trick."

I can't help it. I laugh. It makes my stomach tighten and then makes me cough, but then Lilly is snorting through her nose, bent half over my body where she still grips my forearms, and even if I can't remember what happened, I can completely see the scene play out in my head.

My laughing/hacking breaks into a sob.

They're okay.

Whatever happened to me, at least they're okay.

Lilly pushes my hair behind my ears and runs her fingers down the side of my face. The unexpected tenderness startles me, and I freeze with wide eyes and a pounding heart when she blinks away wet eyes so her tears don't fall.

"Please don't ever scare us like that again, Mia."

I don't know what to say to the thickness in her throat, and so say nothing at all. I reach up and grasp her wrist where her hand still cups my cheek and squeeze her as hard as my paltry strength will allow.

She sucks in a sharp breath and snaps her chin down in a semblance of a nod, then pulls away and turns her back to me. When she faces me again, everything is back in place. Her hair is perfect, her green silk blouse tucked into a charcoal pencil skirt, and her face is pale and lovely, not a splotch of red on it.

She drops back into the chair at my bedside and crosses her legs like she doesn't have a care in the world.

I must look a mess. She said I've been out for a week? I'm sure that means no one has touched my hair in that amount of time. I'm lying on my back, which, no wonder it hurts. When you have an ass and breasts like mine, flat on your back is the last position you want to spend any time on.

Oh, Mother. So Emeran and Owen have been at my bedside for a week with me looking like an Oompa Loompa. Fabulous.

"Help me sit up, will you?" I ask, and Lilly presses a button on the side of the bed to raise the headboard.

Already I'm starting to feel more myself. My brain is firing on a faster level. My chest doesn't feel as tight when I breathe. From that feeling alone, I should have known I hadn't been taking any deep breaths recently. My stomach lets out an undignified rumble, and Lilly snorts again.

I look down the line of my body and try to get a sense of my condition. I don't feel any I.V.s in my arms anymore, so that's good. Means I'm not on any medications or brews.

I'm in a hospital gown and...

I suck in a shuddering gasp when I see my skin.

My flowers.

I throw back the blanket and take in the broken, blemished shimmer of my skin. It doesn't have the sickly pallor I'd expect from being in a hospital bed for as long as I have.

I'm...glowing. My flowers seem to stretch and preen, proud to *finally* be seen.

Purple and white blooms crest over my kneecaps and end halfway down my forearms. My hand lifts to my left ear unconsciously, where I know a vine twirls over the arch like a tattoo.

Like a brand.

I heave in air through my lungs, suddenly tighter than even when I crawled my way back to consciousness. My hands claw at my throat, but this time the woman beside me makes no effort to calm my panic.

Lilly barks at the nurse to scram when they burst into my room and turns off the alarm with a flick of her finger.

I think I've lost the feeling in my feet.

"Yeah," Lilly says, and there's so much—*everything* in her voice. She sits back in her seat and crosses her arms over her chest. "Have I ever complimented you on your ability to keep a secret? I mean—" that lifted brow again. "I knew you had it in you; our school days laid the foundations for that. But honestly, Mia, I didn't *quite* understand the strength of your convictions. Wow." She claps her hands in a slow drawl. "Well done."

"Where's my bracelet?" I demand, looking around the room like a wild person.

I've been in enough hospital rooms to know where the controls on the bed are and reach out blindly, fumbling for the buttons that'll lower the sides. They fall in a clank, and I swing my legs over the side of the mattress.

I take in things I hadn't noticed yet. The piles and piles of bouquets and flora. The blanket my mother quilted me that usually rests on the back of my couch. Sweaters and cloaks that obviously belong to Emeran and Owen are draped haphazardly across chairs and the back of a pull-out sleeper.

Lilly doesn't answer, just watches me with a half-amused, half-exasperated smirk on her face.

"Did they see?" I ask, almost begging for an answer I know I won't hear.

"You mean the garden you've been growing under your clothes?" She grins ear to ear, pearly white teeth gleaming sharply. Her eyes glow in mischief. "Oh yeah."

I...collapse in on myself. My hands come around, grabbing the backs of the opposite arm in a feeble attempt to contain all that I feel.

It's pointless.

Suddenly, I'm thankful for my empty stomach. It's the only thing that's keeping me from sicking up all over my lap when I heave at the sensation of my armour being ripped away without warning.

It's over.

Everything I've lived my life for, all the hiding and planning and ensuring that I always, *always*, protected them from the burden I carry... it's gone.

I'm bare, in a way I've never been before.

"Why?" Lilly says quietly, pulling me from my own head and back into reality. The reality where I'm naked under a hospital gown and half of Argulthion has traipsed in and out of my room with my flowers exposed for anyone to see.

It's not simply that Emeran and Owen know. By this point in time, *everybody* does...

"Why would you hide this from us? From *them*?" Lilly asks, and if I didn't know any better, I'd swear there's accusation and reproach in her voice. "*How* could you do it? I don't understand."

With shaking hands, I wipe the tears from my eyes, sliding from the bed and attempting to stand on quaking legs. I let go of the sheets, and though I feel wobbly and weak, I can stand on my own.

"What the hell, Mia?" Lilly snaps, jerking to her feet and holding out her hands to my sides as if to catch me if I fall. "Get your arse back in bed! I knew you had a death wish, but even for you, this is obscene."

I ignore her and instead waddle on legs as fresh as a newborn baby over to the corner where a gym bag I recognize as my emergency go-bag sits in the corner. With shaky fingers, I rip the zipper back, and there; on top of clothes and toiletries and emergency supplies, any good FORCE member and war survivor should have, is the three-inch-wide silver band Leachlainn gave me five years prior.

"This is how," I say, proud that my voice is strong, despite its rather soft declaration. Without further explanation, I snap the band on my arm and watch as the flowers flow away like water, leaving my skin clear and burnished gold once more.

Lilly takes in a deep breath, then closes the distance between us.

She grabs my arm and tries to dig her fingers under the silver, scratching my skin in her attempt to peel it off my flesh. She shakes me like a wild woman, and all I can do is hold on. For maybe the hundredth time in the short space, since I woke up, I'm caught unawares and can do nothing but watch with shock when she stomps her foot and throws my arm away from her with a frustrated growl.

I stumble on my feet but right myself before falling.

"Take it off," she demands, voice harsh, movements jerky. "Take it off, right now! What you have, Mia..." Her eyes go fuzzy, and her fingers find the buttons on her shirt before she unclasps the top three and yanks the silk aside. A small bushel of yellow, black, and white pansies cover her left breast.

That's as far as they go.

Despite myself, I smile, and hiccup a watery laugh. She's in love with Tomas.

I saw his flowers a year ago.

I'd never seen hers.

"I can't imagine, Mia. I really can't. I've never seen anything like it. Never even heard of flowers like yours" She laughs self-deprecatingly. "But I'm not surprised. I should be, but I'm not." She runs her pointer fingers under her eyes, wiping away the moisture. "Of course you're in love with them. Look what you've done for them. What you've sacrificed. Mother, Mia!" She stomps her foot again, fists clenched at her sides. "Your heart stopped five times before they got you stabilized after the explosion!"

I close my eyes to keep my composure, still wearing nothing but the hospital gown while Lilly gathers her resolve.

"I don't understand how you could hide—" She stumbles to a halt, seeming unable to articulate the magnitude of her feelings. "Tell me when, Mia. When did it start? How old were you when you got your first flower?"

I can't do this. Not here. Not now. She might be the person I'm closest to outside of Owen and Emeran, but I don't owe her anything. I turn my back and flex my hands, desperate to get the feeling back in my fingertips. I sway on my feet, trying to reconcile the ways in which my life has imploded.

It's gone. Nothing will ever be the same again.

I'm weeping, and I can't make it stop.

I can't...I have to focus on something else. I'm not equipped to handle this...

"Mia!" she snarls. "Tell me!"

When I open my eyes and jerk back around, the men I would happily die for, the people I love more than anything else in the universe —stand just inside the door.

They're wearing their Fae cloaks over regular clothing. Haggard is the only way I can describe their appearance. Owen is so pale he looks like a ghost swaying in the wind. Emeran's face is flushed pink. His hair is even worse than usual, his neatly trimmed beard no longer tidy. Their clothes are wrinkled, shirts untucked.

Owen hasn't shaved in days.

"Tell her, Mia," Owen pleads.

I reach for the band on my forearms and let a stream of raw magic flow around it. The click of the clasp is audible. The clacking of it hitting the cheap linoleum flooring is thunderous.

My garden blooms back to life, and Owen's groan is the loudest sound yet.

"Thirteen," I whisper. Lilly grins like she just won a prize. Owen closes his eyes and shudders. Emeran steps forward before Owen grabs him by the wrist and holds him back. I look over Lilly's shoulders and meet Emeran's eyes. "I got my first bud when I was thirteen. Two of them entwined over my heart. They appeared while I was in the coma, after they tried to take princess Annie. I was thirteen when I fell in love with them and I didn't even have to be awake to do it."

I grab my pack, open my hand and throw out my arm. My phone snaps sharply into my palm. This time it's Emeran yelling my name. Owen throwing out his arms.

Lilly cackles gleefully, bent in half with her amusement when I portal from the room.

I KNEW IT WAS POINTLESS. This is a battle I can't outrun. I can't help thinking about how un-Fae it is to flee from a fight when I portal into my bedroom, but sometimes you have to retreat to gather your defences.

By the time I leave my room, showered and dressed, and having ate a granola bar, they're both sitting in my living room.

Or, well, Owen is sitting. Elbows on his knees, leaning forward over his legs with his hands clasped. I've lost track of how many times I've seen him take that pose.

Emeran is pacing the living room.

I almost smile.

Almost.

It's like any other day. Only...

I don't know what to say. I've spent the last hour taking as long as I dare to braid back my black hair and getting ready for the upcoming confrontation. I hold myself as tight as I can, praying I can keep my emotions in check while I lose my best friends.

I don't put my bracelet back on.

The time for hiding is done.

~

IN THE END—IT doesn't matter.

I don't get the chance to talk.

I've barely come to a stop before Emeran is on me. His grip is rough, just this side of painful, when he digs his hand into the hair at the nape of my neck and wraps the other around my neck.

He kisses me, and kisses me, and—

His kisses are harsh and broken, a whimper slipping from his mouth to mine. I open my mouth to gasp, to breathe, to ask what the fuck is going on, and he slips his tongue between my lips and tangles it with mine.

I don't know how to act. I can't think. I can't...

I kiss him back.

I moan, or sigh, or melt into his jagged embrace. One of us is crying, and I couldn't tell you who if you put a blade to my rhroat and told me to choose. He backs me up until I slam against the closest wall and, with a hand on my bum, hitches my legs up around his waist.

"Gods, Mia," he moans when he jerks his mouth from mine.

I'm lightheaded, gasping. I can't feel my own body, but whether the weightlessness is from shock or because Emeran is holding all my weight—

This doesn't make any sense...

My eyes focus enough to see Owen standing mere feet from us.

His jacket is gone. His shirt.

He stands in nothing, but his jeans, and his stomach is...

I choke on a sob and try to blink back my tears, but it's pointless. Utterly and completely inconsequential. Daffodils cover his skin, twined and twisted with Tulips a shocking yellow.

Hope.

Emeran is still kissing down my collarbone. I bury my hands in his hair, if only so I have something to hold onto.

"Why didn't you tell us, Mia?" he demands. All I can do is cry.

I can't see bare skin on Owen's torso. They cover his shoulders, his stomach, his pecs. Flowers flow over his muscles and seem to shimmer over his biceps when he runs his hands roughly over his hair.

Owen's flowers don't match mine...

"Let her breathe, babe," Owen says with a soft smile. His hand reaches out and touches the back of Emeran's shoulder. "Show her."

"Emeran?" I ask.

My voice is quaking.

He steps away, lowering me softly to the ground. With a final caress of his fingers on my face, he gives himself enough space to move and reaches over his head, pulling his shirt off and allowing it to drop to the floor.

His skin is empty.

Until it isn't.

I double and triple take, my hands rising to cover my face before he reaches out and pulls my fingers from my eyes.

"My father taught me how, during that final year with them. How to conceal my heart. He knew, in a way I didn't yet understand, that love would be my salvation but that I couldn't let it get it my way. Once cast, the concealment charm stays in place, even if I fall unconscious. I couldn't—" he swallows thickly. "I couldn't take the risk."

Risk.

The risk that I wouldn't feel the same. The risk that it would make things harder. The risk that I wouldn't let him fight the battle that needed to be fought. Not for himself, but for the priniclple of what was right verses what was wrong.

Risk.

What a scary word.

Emeran's skin is...Owen steps forward until Emeran rests against his chest and reaches his arms to hold the smaller man to him. Emeran sighs into his touch and lets Owen take his weight. One step. Two. One of my hands is on my lips, the other stretched to touch what would be Emeran's skin if he wasn't covered in flowers.

Steam rises from where their flesh touches.

It's what happens when heat caresses water.

They're stacked on top of one another. Purple Mallows mating with Yellow Tulips. There isn't an inch, a millimetre of his flesh that's bare. They tumble over his shoulders and down his arms. I trail my hands over his fingers and see the vines that go all the way to the tips. Owen jerks at Emeran's zipper, and his jeans fall to the floor.

I tumble to my knees when my legs give out and run my hands over his garden.

They're everywhere. I help him step out of his trousers, and vines crawl around his ankle. Without conscious thought, I lean forward and kiss a Tulip on his thigh. They disappear into the band of his tight boxers and reappear against the sinewy muscles of his legs.

"Since when?" I ask, still crying.

At this point, I'm wondering if I'll ever stop. Emeran's eyes are closed when I gaze at them from where I sit weeping on my ankles, and Owen is holding him like his touch is the only thing keeping them whole.

Owen's smile is soppy and soft.

"Fourteen," he tells me, his voice deep and rough.

"A month before I turned twelve," Emeran admits with his gaze locked on mine. I feel like he's seeing through me.

"We've known about each other since our time at Bettenbough," Owen tells me. "Since before they tried to force Emeran to take the crown." He grimaces. "Mother, Mia. That year. I didn't think we'd make it without telling you. To be that close, but unable to touch..."

Like Emeran's parents shared a tent during their war, we refused to be seperated, even in the middle of a war. I slept at their sides for thirteen months. The longest year of my life.

His face falls, crumbles, before he rebuilds it before my eyes. Almost as if he's using magic, he locks away the distress he must be feeling and gives me a tiny smile. When did Owen become the strongest of us?

Suddenly, things become so clear. I've laughed at the rumours that bled like fire about them, just like I scoff at the rumours of the three of us. Hogwash. People pulling inferences that simply weren't there.

Now, though—they live together. I make it a point not to go into their bedrooms in the house they share.

But...bedrooms? Or bedroom?

Their flowers...Tulips, for each other.

"You've been—" I'm suddenly dizzy, my stomach clenching and my fingers tingling. I have to swallow twice to get the words out. "You've been...*together*—?"

I can't finish the sentence. Owen knows what I'm trying to ask.

The answer is bare before me anyway. The way they touch each other. Years of practice and ease between them. The obvious love, and not simply the love of brothers who have fought side by side.

"We've been living half a life without you, Mia," he says with his cheek pressed into the side of Emeran's face. Emeran reaches up behind his head and digs his fingers into Owen's hair. An anchor in the ocean of revelations. His other hand reaches out for me.

"You have so many," I croak through tears.

"We love you that much," Owen says with shining eyes.

"Why didn't you tell us, Mia?"

It's Emeran who speaks this time. He's trembling with his arms linked with Owen's. Owen shakes his head. He steps out from behind piercing blue eyes, and Emeran changes their positions, holding the larger man from behind now. Owen drags me to my feet.

"It doesn't matter," he says. His eyes have about a dozen shades of fire swirling around his blown pupils. He smiles, and it lights up his face in a way I've never seen before. Fifteen years at his side, and I've never seen him smile at me like he is now.

"It doesn't matter," he says again. "We're here now." He pushes the hair that's escaped my braid behind my ears and runs his nose against mine. "Do you have any idea how much we love you?"

He's covered in Daffodils.

Owen's kiss is completely different from Emeran's. Slow and deep, it makes my toes curl and my back bow. His breath catches, and our combined tears drip down my throat, but I can't bring myself to care because Owen is kissing me as I'd always dreamed it could be.

Except I'd never dreamed I could have *This*.

A second pair of hands slide around me from behind, and I tense and gasp before sinking into their combined touch.

"Let us see you," Emeran begs, his lips so close to my ear that I feel his mouth form the words. "Let us see how beautiful you are. How perfect you look wearing our flowers."

I nod, still trying to kiss Owen, my hands clinging to his broad shoulders.

Emeran's hands slip into my shirt and start rucking it up my stomach. Owen pulls away reluctantly, keeping our lips connected even as he gives Emeran the space needed to pull the shirt higher. My arms go into the air, and Owen and I only break apart when the taut line of fabric forces us to separate.

I open my eyes and lean forward to capture his lips again, but he's not there. He's on his knees before me, and when his hands join Emeran's against my body, tracing their brands reverently on my skin, I close my eyes and place a hand on either side of their heads.

"We thought we lost you," Owen says. It comes out jumbled with his lips against my belly as they are. "We thought we lost you. They removed your ruined and blood soaked clothes, and you were so still, and so small, lying on that table—"

He wraps his arms around my middle and hides his face in my stomach.

Emeran picks up the story.

"Word traveled fast. They thought—" his voice hitches, and teeth drag across my bare hip. I hiss and try to turn into the burn, but together they hold me still.

"They thought you were going to die, so I went and fetched Leach-lainn. We wanted to make sure she could say goodbye, before..."

How can one person cry so much? Shouldn't I be out of tears by now?

"She arrived as they were still fighting to get the bracelet off. It was in the healer's way. She—she took it off you. She bared your flowers to the room, apoligzed, and fled."

"It was hers, first," I tell them with my head tipped back. My knees are shaking, my fingers numb. Owen has fled the safety of my skin and is on his knees, touching my sides reverently. "She gave it to me before I left the castle, *before...*"

"Can I?" Owen asks, looking at me through thick red lashes with his hands on the button of my jeans.

I nod, my voice still un-trustworthy.

He spreads the zipper while Emeran rises back to his feet and unclasps my bra without asking.

I step out of my jeans as Owen and Emeran both groan in appreciation and awe. I'm wearing a thong, and my arse, covered in Daffodils and Mallows, is bared to the world. Owen can see the ring of Mallows that circle my breasts as Emeran admires the bursts of Daffodils that trail down my spine like vines on a trellis.

"I've never seen anything so beautiful," Emeran whispers before dropping kisses over my shoulder blades.

It goes quickly from there—without words.

Emeran shakes out my braid while Owen pulls down my panties. They rise to their feet and shed the remainder of their clothing.

I knew they were fit. They work hard, and work harder still to ensure that they are at the top of their physical and mental conditioning. After all, it's not their own lives on the line, but each others. All three of us could handle our own deaths but wouldn't survive the loss of one of the others.

But I've made it a point never to see them with their shirts off. Not if I can help it. I didn't want to see the proof that their skin didn't mirror mine.

What a waste of time.

Now, not only do I see their flowers, but I see the thick, stacked muscles of Owen's body. The way his broad chest narrows down into a tapered waist and wide thighs. The red fur that covers his skin. The flowers cover him like a t-shirt. They don't go as far as mine but are thick and overlaying. One on top of the other, they sweep down over his hips and end halfway down his thighs. I don't have any experience with dicks, but even if I did, I don't think I could have been prepared for this.

Emeran is as lean as he's always been. But his strength is obvious in the sinewy lines of muscles that define his arms and the definition of his abs and the trail of hair that leads to a thick cock standing proud between his legs.

Owen and Emeran kiss, and the sight of it steals my breath away.

Even here, with this, their personalities shine through. Emeran is all emotion, all neediness, and desire. Owen holds him close, one hand around his back, the other still linked tight in mine. He offers Emeran his steadiness. His strength. He calms Emeran's ardour until Emeran seems to settle back into his skin.

They turn to me as one, pulling me between them.

"I haven't–" I say brokenly. Ashamed. They've had each other, while I've... "I've never—" I can feel the flush burning my cheeks pink. I hold out my arms in a show of resignation. "Who would want me like this?" I say in explanation.

I don't bother to mention I could have always had lovers while wearing the bracelet. But even though my boys weren't mine, I always belonged to them.

"Us."

It's so simple when they say it like that.

This time when they cloak themselves around me, I don't have any reservations.

I don't really know how we end up on the floor. All I know is one minute, hands are trailing up and down my body, one palming my arse while another tweaks my nipple and yet another still pulls my hair, and the next minute, Owen is flat on his back with me on my hands and knees above him.

We're still in my living room.

My hair falls around us like a curtain.

"You're so beautiful," Emeran says.

"Do you have any idea how often we dreamed about this?" Owen asks between wonton kisses. As one, they grind my weeping cunt down on Owen's cock pinned between our bodies, and my eyes roll in the back of my head at the unaccustomed sensation.

It's too much, the two of them together.

But at the same time, it feels like we were almost meant to be like this. I can't imagine having my first time with one and not the other.

I don't believe in fate, but if I did, I'd believe in this.

"How often we'd talk about it?" Emeran adds, trailing his tongue over my bum. "We used to fuck and talk about what we'd do if you were there between us."

The image he paints should upset me. The brutal knowledge that they've had each other while I've been alone. It doesn't. I feel a wave of relief and excitement knowing that they've been together. They, at least, know what comes next.

My mother always told me I should lose my virginity to someone I love. Barring that, lose it to a man who knew what he was doing.

I feel like I've never heeded her advice quite as I am today.

When a tongue slips between my legs, I squeal in surprise and supplication.

"Oh, Mother, Owen," Emeran moans with his lips against my pussy. "She tastes so good."

His tongue spears me, then sucks me, and then I buck against the fingers that slide inside my body.

I don't know if it's the fact that his digits are longer and thicker than my own or if it's just the experience in its entirety. But I shatter against them with trembling legs and sublime surrender.

Emeran digs his teeth into my shoulder while Owen swallows back my howls with his kisses.

It takes me longer than it should to come back to my body.

"Can I?" Owen asks. I blink dumbly, trying to focus on his face. They lift me slightly, and I attempt to take some of my weight onto my hands on either side of Owen's face. "I want to—Can we...?" he asks again, and—oh!

His cock slips between my folds, pressing at my entrance.

Anything. Everything.

I sink onto him slowly. Reverently. Emeran's hands are everywhere. His mouth sucks spots into my flesh and outlines my flowers with his tongue.

But Owen...Owen slides himself inside me with his eyes closed and a sigh of relief and benediction on his face.

I lift my hips and fall back down, and he hits something inside me that's never been touched before. His grunt of pleasure shoots through me like lightning. It's intoxicating. Addicting. A sound I want to hear every day for the rest of my life.

"Sit up," Emeran commands.

I must look as confused as I feel because Emeran reaches around my waist and pulls from the middle and—

and—My eyes widen then snap closed as I groan at the full-bodied deepness of Owen shifting inside me. Owen takes my hands and places them on his chest, and I'd be worried about squishing him if it weren't for the fact that...well, he's massive underneath me. It's obvious that this is something the two of them have done before. Lots and lots.

I can't wait to watch.

"Rock," Emeran orders, then grabs my hips and *shows* me what he means.

I rock back and forth on Owen's body, his cock so deep I feel it in my gut. It radiates through my pelvis and turns into heat at the back of my spine.

With a hand on my hip, still roughly rocking me to and fro, Emeran forces my face around and kisses me like he's trying to meet Owen in the middle.

When I orgasm the second time, Owen stills beneath me, Emeran bending low to kiss the man we're both in love with. It's filthy, pure, and beautiful to see.

"Don't come yet," he orders with a final kiss between them. "Wait for me."

I expect to see him wrap his hand around his cock.

He crawls behind me instead, pushing on my shoulders as Owen pulls with his hands against the small of my back until I'm flat against him.

Is he gonna?

Oh!

I expect him to enter my backside. How else could they take me together?

He doesn't.

A pulse of magic slips over my body and...

I groan when I feel him press himself in against Owen. His cock inches in next to Owen's, filling me beyond any stretch of my imagination.

"Shhhh," Owen whispers, rubbing his hand up and down my back, the other still reaching around to help spread my arse. "You're the most amazing woman, Mia. You can do anything. You can take us."

Yes. I can.

My entire being gives up, and my head falls onto Owen's shoulder, but without thought or consideration, my hips press back into what Emeran's doing. The burn is...and the stretch...but Emeran...

"Oh, MOTHER!" I cry out when Emeran starts to move.

He doesn't move much. There's not a lot of room. There's no need. With the three of us here together? The two of them *inside* me together? Sparks shoot off behind my eyes, and my stomach clenches, my walls spasming against the push and pull going on between my legs. They both groan when the crest of my orgasm overwhelms me.

It's devastating what they're doing to me, like the world's sweetest torture. I know it's not a dream because I could never dream this. Owen's hand covers half of my face when he cups my cheek and drags my mouth to meld with his.

We can't really kiss. There's not enough air for that. I don't have that sort of coordination. But he licks into my mouth and sucks on my lip, and tells me how much he loves us.

Us.

Together.

I'm pressed against Owen so tight there's not an ounce of space between us. Every slap of Emeran between our legs causes my clit to rub against Owen, sparking the inferno exploding inside me.

They're touching...everything. Everywhere.

I've been so alone, so empty all this time, and now they are here, around me, inside me. They are all I can see and smell and taste and hear.

"Gods, Mia!" Emeran grunts, losing himself to the rhythm of our bodies.

He has one hand on my hip and another on my shoulder, and my skin burns and tingles at every point of contact between the three of us.

I've never been a multiple-orgasm girl. When I got myself off, alone, in the darkness of my bedroom, I was always one and done. I did it because it was a biological urge, and it helped me sleep. I could close my eyes and pretend the fingers on my clit were Emeran's and the rubber cock in my cunt was Owen's and tried to forget for just a minute that I was utterly alone in my bed.

Now though—I've lost track of how many times I've come. I couldn't tell you if we'd been here on the floor for five minutes or five hours.

What I do know is Owen shouts Emeran's name, Emeran drops his head between my shoulder blades, and a blinding, dangerous, incandescent wave washes over my body. It bursts from my spine, ripping through to my fingers and toes.

I arch and cry out, and the last thing I hear is Owen moaning my name before I hear nothing at all.

≈

They say only one in ten thousand has flowers that go past their torso. Well, we've always defied the odds.

Together, we grew a garden.

A blue-eyed little boy with untidy brown hair who loves to fly. A black-haired son who always gets into trouble and our red-headed emerald-eyed daughter.

Rose.

ABOUT THE AUTHOR

Amanda Faye lives in Phoenix with her high school sweetheart, married eighteen-years, and four monsters. (They claim to be children. She has her doubts.)

When she's not writing, she's reading. Or writing fan fiction. Or talking about fan fiction...

If all else fails, she's probably sleeping and dreaming about books.

Her monsters learned long ago never to bother momma when she has a book in her hands.

Links

facebook.com/amandafayebooks
   amandafayebooks.com
   https://www.facebook.com/groups/wickedwhispers/

ALSO BY AMANDA FAYE

Doctor Drama Series

Just A Dream

Beautiful Trauma

S.O.S.

Forbidden Fruit Shorts Series

Good Boys Talk Dirty

One Night Only

His

Tall, Dark, and Brooding

Beat of His Heart

Grounded

Partners with Benefits

The Doctor and the Detective Series

Bulletproof

Stand Alone with Boom Publishing, Until Series

Until I Met You

Submit

For Salvation Series

The Cursed

The Lord of the Keyes

The Golden Dragon (coming soon)

The Vanquishing Prince (coming soon)